I am
Ned Pine

a novel

For Ron!

I am
Ned Pine

a novel

~~George Byron Wright~~

C3 Publications
Portland, Oregon
www.c3publications.com

I Am Ned Pine: a novel
Copyright © 2018 by George Byron Wright.

C3 Publications
3495 NW Thurman Street
Portland, OR 97210-1283
www.c3publications.com

First Edition

Library of Congress Control Number 2018908518

Wright, George Byron
I Am Ned Pine: a novel
ISBN13: 978-0-9632655-7-9

Cataloging References: I Am Ned Pine
1. Home invasion-Fiction 2. Traumatic brain injury-fiction 3. 4.
Coma-Fiction 5. Conspiracy-Fiction 6. Marital relations-Fiction
7. Idaho/Oregon-Fiction 8. St Johns Oregon-Fiction I. Title

Book and cover designs by Dennis Stovall.
Cover photo © 2015 courtesy of Marshall Snyder Photography,
    Portland Oregon.

Author photo by Sergio Ortiz: www.sergiophotography.net.

I Am Ned Pine is a work of fiction. Names, characters, places, and
incidents are the product of the author's imagination or are used
fictitiously. Any resemblance to actual persons, living or dead,
events, or locales, is entirely coincidental.

Printed in the United States of America.

Novels by George Byron Wright

Baker City 1948
Tillamook 1952
Roseburg 1959
Driving to Vernonia
Newport Blues, A Salesman's Lament
In the Wake of Our Misdeed

They intruded into our lives and destroyed
all we were or ever would be.

———————

Edward Longren Pine

For Betsy.

-1-

First, let me tell you how it all began.

They crashed in while Ashley was at the sink rinsing dinner plates and I was gathering empty wine glasses and what had been a bottle of middling Merlot with a short swallow left in it. We had spoken perhaps six words over our dinner of the chicken pot-pies I'd picked up from Ringer's Deli; that, along with mixed greens out of a cellophane bag tossed in a too-tangy vinaigrette, was a meal fit for the distracted. It had been close to nine thirty by the time we sat down; I'd gotten home late due to it being tax season. The meal felt routine and unsatisfying, tasty enough but not appealing. I doubt that our eyes met once while we ate. It was just one of those dispassionate, uninspiring occasions that happen between couples who've been through most everything together—thrice over. And it had been just the two of us as usual. Both of our offspring were gone by then, had been for some time. Only their time-warp rooms, those once-pulsating accordion boxes of raging hormones, reminded us that they had lived there at one time. Their absence accounted for most of the loss of energy between us. Who knows when it happened? It just did. One day you look across the table and see a stranger sitting where the one-time love of your life used to be. The realization that you and your mate had graduated from the years of marriage into strangers was chilling and corrosive. It left me feeling desperate—about what I wasn't sure, just desperate. What could I do about it really?

I doubt that fact was directly on our minds that night; it had become something we managed to chronically ignore, even as it stared us in the face every day. Just then, we were functioning with rote domesticity when the backdoor off the kitchen imploded, splintered on the sole of a black lugged boot.

There were three of them. They were dressed like ninjas: shrouded in black, eyes glaring at us through ski mask eyeholes. I almost laughed out loud at the triteness of their assailants' habits, but I didn't. Ashley dropped a plate that broke into three equal triangles on the floor. I remember thinking: *How odd.* Then the wine glasses collided at my feet, popping into bits and pieces, and the bottle hit my foot and caromed off, spinning on the floor. It seemed that we were caught in a surrealistic video game scene.

When Ashley shrieked, I made the mistake of yelling, "What the fuck!"

The first man through the door took exception and came at me with a metal baseball bat gripped in skin-tight vinyl gloves; they all had bats. I raised my arms but only managed to delay the inevitable. My left arm broke with the first blow—after that my head exploded. The only sound I remember before I lost consciousness was Ashley screaming something, just screaming, I knew not what. It didn't matter. Well, maybe it did, but I was forced from the scene.

It was March. March 17, 2010. St. Patrick's Day. Everything had just changed. But it took me longer than it should have to get a grip on just how much that one act of violence would reshape things, or more to the point, how it would expose what a small life I'd been living under the guise of success, even normality. From that traumatic moment the road ahead would expose that my pretense of a credible existence was not true, and I would watch all of my self-assurances begin to unravel.

Who attacked us? That was in my head before I lost consciousness. I didn't know then or later, at least not right away. Anyway, whoever it was, they made a mess of our lives, and this is how it rolled out. By the way, I am Ned Pine, and this is a recounting of the most abominable six months of my life. Here we go: blackout.

-2-

I didn't dream; at least I don't think I did. Nor measure time. There was no great void. One cannot describe nothingness.

Sound. My returning senses first took in undecipherable voices followed by an antiseptic tang. Olfaction was making a comeback. My eyelids resisted. I flexed my brow until they rose. There was movement, and words spoken in precise cadence.

"Hello there." Once my cerebral cortex was back on task, I focused on her. Her blurry image seemed Eurasian. Very white teeth flashed as she smiled down on me. Brown eyes were studying me carefully. "Can you tell me your name?"

I did.

"And how are you feeling, Mr. Pine? Headache?"

Hell yes. I licked my lips and moved my head affirmatively. That hurt. Damn that hurt. I squeezed my eyes shut.

"Okay." She rested a hand on my shoulder. "We'll see about upping your dosage."

I raised my left hand to scratch my nose it was heavy, wrapped, a splint. The bat, I remembered the bat—that aluminum bat and the metallic thud. My right arm was connected to an IV line. An electrode was taped to my chest. I wasn't going anywhere, and my head hurt.

Before I drifted away again, I blinked my eyes clear and made note of the name badge on her blue scrubs: Molina, RN.

I don't know how much time passed before I came around once more. Must not have been long; I was still where I'd been, in the

ER no doubt. With the halo of indirect lighting, the background of voices, rubber-soled shoes on vinyl flooring, along with the lights from the monitors that were tracking my vital signs, I felt like lab specimen. Hell I *was* a lab specimen. My head throbbed when I moved it even slightly. I reached up with my good arm and touched the bandage on my skull; it was a big patch bandage, and my head had been shaved around it.

Then it came to me. Why I hurt. Why I was in that place. The flashback was like an electric charge. Ashley. Ashley! I tried to rise up, couldn't. To speak, I only rasped. I closed my eyes; I couldn't get my breath.

"Mr. Pine." It was a male voice this time. "Mr. Pine," he said again. "Can you hear me?"

I opened my eyes. Nodded. "Ashley," I managed to say on a coarse breath.

"Ashley? Oh, your wife." I saw a skinny white guy wearing green. His teeth weren't as bright as the woman's had been, maybe because he wasn't smiling.

"How is she? Is she all right?" My throat constricted just before I asked, "Is she alive?"

He stared down at me and hesitated for a moment. "Yes. She is," he said and distractedly took hold of my left wrist before looking at the monitors. "How's your pain level? One being low, ten high."

I thought about it. "Eight, I guess. My wife," I said. "I need to know how she is. How bad is it?"

"You just take it easy," the skinny guy said. His name badge only had a last name on it, Simmons, MD. "Right now we have to take care of some things. We'll be moving you to get a CT scan, see about your head injury. Then get your arm set and in a cast."

"But my wife, I have to know."

He hesitated, glanced at the monitor again. "The neurologist will see you soon. He'll answer all of your questions. Okay?" And with that he walked away.

––––––––––

When they rolled me back from having the CT scan, there was a presence in the ER bay, a solemn presence. He stood aside while the nurse with the white teeth positioned my bed; his big hands bulged in the pockets of his Levi's. He stared at me from beneath the bushy white eyebrows I was so familiar with. Our eyes met; we locked on. Nothing was said for a long moment. It was my father-in-law, Isaac Tucker, a big-shouldered man who once stood six four and filled every room he entered. He had been vastly disappointed when his Ashley and only child married a man who was too short to look him straight in the eye, had never shot a deer, and merely added up numbers for a living. We'd learned to dislike one another early and often. Isaac was a man's man who'd made his money in the construction business and had wished for a son to work beside him, or at the very least hoped that his Ashley would marry a man of like characteristics. His ardent desires, it turned out, were not fulfilled. He resented me for not, in his opinion, having any of the traits by which he judged a man to be worthy.

There he stood, shoulders down, eyes red-rimmed, face un-shaven, and stared at me in a manner registering hurt and disdain. I inhaled, held it, then asked, "How is she?"

I could see his jaw muscles flex. He didn't want to tell me, but he did. "Not good." He pulled out a big blue handkerchief and blew his nose. I waited. "It's bad," he added.

The room began to swim. I took in several breaths and gagged out a sob. "I...I need to see her. Can I see her?"

"She's not here."

"Not here? What have you done with her?"

He snorted his derision. "Me? I haven't done anything with her, you dumb ass. They had to move her."

"What?" I blurted. "Move her? Where?"

"To Pocatello." He glared at me. "To the trauma center." He inhaled, let out a ragged breath, and added, "Like I said, it's bad. Won't know for a long while how it's gonna pan out. They say she's in a coma."

I felt a keening rumble in my chest. I couldn't stop it. It went on, and when I looked at Isaac, he was shaking his head. "Those bastards," I choked out. "Who the hell were they? What'd they want?"

Isaac bit on his lip but didn't respond at first. "Nobody knows who they were," he said after glancing at my monitor, probably disappointed that I still had a heartbeat. "Guess stuff is missing, but won't know what 'til Ashley, and you I guess, can look the place over. Police have no leads. They'll be wanting to talk to you, by the way. I told them to wait."

I studied his familiar unpleasantness. "Who found us?"

He sniffed, pulled out the big handkerchief and blew into it once more. "Neighbor. Name of Stewart. Sound right?"

"Guy Stewart?"

"Guess so, you'd know. Was out walking his morsel of a dog. Was nearby when whoever those assholes were came out of your place and drove off like they had lightning up their butts. In a big pickup. Fella went in and found you...in the kitchen, I guess."

"This isn't happening," I whispered.

"Yeah it is," he answered. "Gonna have to live with it. It's bad, but she'll pull through. Made of tough stuff. And I'll be right there with her."

I felt a thread of anger at his possessive tone. "Me too," I said. "I'll be with her."

Isaac pulled on his nose and drew his shoulders back. "Maybe so. I'm only here to tell you a few things, mainly about the way things are for Ashley and her being moved and all. Secondly, I've talked with the grandkids, gave them the story, and told them it's best for them to wait before rushing home."

"What?" Mike and Roz—that old fart talked to them and told them to stay put? "Who the hell gave you the right to do that?"

"Don't be stupid," Isaac pulled up on his pants. "The both of you were out of it, little use in them kids rushing hell bent for election to get here. Best they wait."

"Damn your hide."

"Made a decision, best for all concerned. Get over it. Guess some of your kinfolk have been notified about your condition. Someone may be coming to see you. Not sure about that."

"Thanks." Kinfolk. They may have been notified; I couldn't think of which of them would bother to show.

After a pause, Isaac said, "You shoulda protected her. My little girl. Stood ground and kept her from harm."

"You son-of-a-bitch," I said through my teeth, but he'd already gone. So that's what I woke up to: big-time headache, my wife in another town with her brain shut down, and no idea who beat the hell out of us. The road ahead had no map.

I was dozing when the neurologist came. Dr. Caruthers was with him. Dr. Richard Caruthers. Latham's a small town, even by Idaho standards, and Dick Caruthers had been our primary care doctor for ages and one of our firm's clients. My mind rambled. Who was doing his taxes? Jack. Caruthers was one of Jack's clients. Dr. Caruthers and another doctor entered almost immediately after Isaac Tucker had gone, like they'd been waiting until the old man had done his duty, probably the case. Isaac usually got his way, and he didn't want any witnesses while he made sure I knew he was in charge of his daughter's oversight, not me. We'd see about that.

Caruthers had to say my name twice to pull me out of the field of anger I was in.

"Ned?"

Caruthers leaned over me. I blinked and stared into his black-brown eyes ensconced in his lean golf-tanned face. He was peering at me over his glasses, the kind with half lenses; a made-to-order smile hung on his lips. I gave him a tolerant patient's smile in return. "Hello, Dick."

"How do you feel?" he offered while maintaining the smarmy smile.

I coughed a dry cough. "Like hell."

"I understand," he purred.

"Forget that." I reached out and took hold of his forearm. "How is she?"

He took his arm back and studied me for a bit. "This is Dr. Sneed," he said and looked across the bed at a youngish balding man wearing a white lab coat over a blue shirt and red tie. "He's the neurologist managing your cases. I'm just along for the ride." Caruthers tried to laugh at his tinny joke.

Voices filtered into the quiet from people passing by the curtained bay. Dr. Sneed nodded to the nurse and waited until she'd left, pulling the curtain closed—as if that would give us privacy, I thought. The neurologist looked down into my face, sober, no nonsense. "Okay, Mr. Pine. Where do you want to start?"

"Ashley, of course. It's bad. I know that much." I inhaled. "My father-in-law said as much."

Sneed nodded. "It is that." He pursed his lips and nodded. "Very serious."

I raised my head. It throbbed, but I lifted it up from the pillow. "Damn it, just tell me."

The bald man nodded and pushed on my shoulder until I lowered my head. "The blow to the head, to Ashley's head, was severe." Dick Caruthers looked like he might cry. "Caused traumatic brain injury. You have a concussion, but her injury is much more severe. Our ER doctor examined her and immediately conferred with me, and I agreed that we order her air-lifted to Pocatello. To the trauma center." He inhaled. "Right now, she's in a coma."

I could feel my heart. My eyes watered. "Now what?"

Dr. Sneed watched as Dick Caruthers massaged his hands, then said, "With these cases they look for the best response in the first twenty-four hours. There's a coma scale they use and..."

His mouth was forming words, and his eyes were filled with professional concern, but my senses had suspended while my brain attempted to process the unimaginable. In my head I heard the dishes hit the floor again and the wine glasses shatter at my feet at the sound of the intruders. Most of all, I recalled her scream, Ashley's peal of alarm. Isaac was right. I should have thrown myself at them; I should have welcomed whatever punishment it would have taken to save her from all of this, even my own death if that's what would have prevented the mayhem. But if I'd had time to make such a choice, would I have sacrificed myself? Really?

Right then I was looking into the face of the man who annually ran his finger up my rectum in search of prostate irregularities while listening to another guy in a white coat speak of something called the Glasgow Coma Scale and the first twenty-four hours. He'd stopped and was looking at me quizzically.

"What?" I mumbled.

The doctor looked a bit peevish. "I was saying that a neurosurgeon in Pocatello is scheduled to confer with me by tomorrow morning about your wife's condition. As you are her most immediate next of kin, he'll want us to discuss her status, options, and her advance medical directives with you. It would best to have that conversation on site in Pocatello."

I said okay. After that, Sneed ran through my injuries and prognosis: a broken arm that would need a cast, a concussion, a laceration to my head that had been stitched up, and some minor cuts to my left hand; defensive wounds he called them. I hadn't even noticed the bandage across the knuckles of my writing hand.

"Let's keep you overnight," Dr. Sneed said. "Give you more recovery time. See if your headache subsides and make sure your cognitive status improves."

"Dick," I said, turning to his familiar face. "I have to get out of here so I can go to Ashley."

He nodded and looked to his colleague, who nodded in return. "Of course." He drew his mouth in and looked at me sadly. "But you're in no shape to leave here yet, let alone drive yourself. Plus, we need more time to make sure you're out of the woods. These concussions can hide symptoms that can come back on you. It's called post-concussion syndrome."

"Fuck that," I blurted. "Ashley. I have to see her."

Caruthers folded his arms and studied me. "And you will," he said finally and looked to the neurologist, yielding the floor.

"Not yet," Sneed said. "You need one more night's rest, and then we'll see. For now you must be patient." He glanced at the monitor. "I'll have them move you into the ICU."

"Tell me, just what is going on? I'm here, Ashley is the way to hell and gone. What?"

Sneed looked up as the nurse started to come back into the bay and waved her out again. "Like your father-in-law said, like Isaac said, Ashley's injuries are—"

"What...are what? Is she going to die? Is that it?" I dropped back onto my pillow. "That's it. Ashley is dying." I felt myself panting.

Dr. Caruthers placed the palm of his hand on my shoulder and pressed down gently. "Ned," he said, keeping his voice low. "You mustn't do this. Ashley's in serious condition, yes, but she is not dying. Her outcome is in the hands of those who know what they're doing."

I gave him my best Clint Eastwood stare, but he just gave me a palliative smile and whispered, "Please."

After a moment of quiet acquiescence between the men, they were gone. I was alone. My mind was in a tumbler, which kept mixing the same demonic scene—over and over. I was swallowing, choking on those images when they came to move me. The ceiling flowed by.

-3-

Ashley. I was just short of stewed when I met her for the first time. And back then when under the influence I tended to be a fun guy—back then being when I was twenty-five. She was three years my junior and observed my inebriated high jinks with amusement, as I recall. That first meeting between us happened at a New Year's Eve party on the cusp of 1986. The revelers were spawned from the accounting firm I was working for in Boise, Idaho, at the time, an outfit called Laxell & Crowne. It was my first CPA job after becoming accredited; I'd been on the job all of nine months when I proceeded to make an ass of myself. The partners hosted the year-end thank you party in the ballroom of the historic Owyhee Plaza Hotel. The place was humming with bean counters from the firm's offices in Boise, Nampa, and Pocatello, along with wives, husbands, and assorted significants and hangers-on. I attended with two guys new to the firm; we shared the same social beta-blockers—among us we had attracted zero party partners. After hitting the buffet line, we picked out a table somewhere in the middle of the gaily decorated ballroom, took our seats with aplomb, and impersonated cool guys having the time of their lives.

That was when Ashley first entered the scene. I was hunched over my dinner plate, and one of my colleagues was laughing like a soprano stuck with a hatpin. Ashley and her date, a tallish, slender guy, who I found out later was a junior partner from the Pocatello office, approached our table along with another couple. The fellow asked if they might join us. Our over-eager acceptance, complete with hand gestures from each of us, drew patronizing smiles. Ashley was seated on my left. I offered a polite smile, but she was inspecting the food on her plate. She wasn't ravishing, but interesting. I sipped from my glass of tepid water and considered whom she reminded me of. Then it struck me: Barbara Streisand. Her nose. It belonged to Streisand. The rest of her face was different, but the nose was prominent, and her forehead sloped back, a fact she tried to remedy with styled bangs.

She finally reacted to my staring by lowering her fork and studying me.

My grin was forced. "That's one of my favorites," I said above the din. There was a DJ churning out an ongoing play list of recognizable music by the likes of Glen Frey, Billy Joel, Whitney Huston, and Bruce Springsteen.

She stared at me without a trace of interest.

"Billy Joel," I said. "'An Innocent Man.' One of my favorites."

She sort of cocked her head then nodded. "Oh. Are there any?"

"Any what?"

"Innocent men." She flicked me a smile.

I raised a forefinger and pointed it at her. "Not nice. But funny."

Her smile twitched again and she lifted a forkful of pasta.

"I am Ned Pine."

She pondered my extended hand hesitantly, but put her fork down and slid a cool hand into mine. "Ashley Tucker." The clasp was brief and lacked sincerity. "He's Mike Stanton," she said, turning her head toward the tall guy I assumed was her date. "Pocatello, I think."

"How's that?"

"He comes from your firm's office in Pocatello." She gave a little shrug. "At least I think so."

"You're close then?" I teased.

Her smile was mischievous. "Right." She elbowed the Stanton fellow. He paused in his ongoing conversation with the other man who'd come with them and turned his head. "This is Ned Pine," she said to him. He wrinkled his brow curiously, gripped my hand across the table, mumbled some boilerplate pleasantry, and returned to his discourse.

"I'm usually found to be fascinating," I said.

That got a laugh out of her, and I could see how her plainness receded when her face displayed a smile: her brown eyes took on a glow of amusement, her cheekbones seemed to rise, and her lips seemed fuller. And I liked her ash-blonde hair, cut moderately short and swept back.

She caught me looking at her coiffure. "I have a bug in my hair?"

"Just admiring it."

"Thank you."

I shoved my chair back. "Say, I'm ready for some wine. How about you?"

And that's how it all began. With a hosted bar I could afford to be the gracious table companion—and I was. By the time there were maybe six empty wine bottles on our table, I was feeling witty, loquacious, and was sure I had captivated everyone with my erudite humor and sage observations. Little did I note that Ashley's table companions were unimpressed nor that my colleagues had abandoned me well before midnight.

The thing was, for some reason, Ashley was with me. She remained interested, laughed at my jokes, and actually had fun. Not so her date; he was not similarly amused. When the ballroom erupted at midnight, Ashley and I jumped up to shout *Happy New Year!* She leaned over to give me an innocent kiss on the cheek. Her date, mister smooth operator Stanton, was not amused by such celebratory antics. They had low words. Eventually she nodded and turned back to me; they had to go. I smiled and shook her hand, into which I slipped one of my Laxell & Crowne business cards. She paused, tilted her head, and gave me a slight nod.

———

My happy-drunk performance with Ashley had been worth it though I doubted I'd ever see her again. But she did have my card and had laughed at my lame humor. Regardless, I was surprised when near the tail end of January in the midst of ramping up for tax season she called me at work. It was on Friday—I remember the date to this day: January 10, 1986. It would turn out to be a memorable date many times over. She was in town and wondered if there was any chance we could catch a late lunch. My desk was awash with associate-level client work, and the pressure was on to produce billable hours. I admitted as much to Ashley, and in a controlled voice she said she understood and maybe we could do it another time. But before she hung up, I caved and agreed to meet her for a quick bite at Nellie's Deli near our offices in the Empire Building.

Being sober and reduced to my stolid self again made for a flip-side second meeting; I was no longer lubricated to an atypical fun self. Ashley Tucker was pleasant. I was pleasant. Beneath a long wool coat she was dressed in beige slacks and a dark blue blouse. I had rushed out into the January elements without an overcoat in my number one work-a-day gray suit off the rack at Sears; number two was blue serge. Along with a white shirt and a red-and-blue rep tie, I actually looked no different than I did at the New Year's Eve party.

"How long do you have?" she asked while studying the menu.

"I'm okay," I fudged. When she looked up doubtfully, I came clean. "Okay, forty-five minutes. Busy time. Plus I'm new on the job, low on the totem pole. Have to make my mark."

"What do you recommend?" She ignored my plight.

I suggested my favorite, the gobbler, turkey and cranberry, so she chose the pastrami on rye, of course. I would learn soon enough the lesson of her strong will countermanding whatever I preferred to her own obvious choice, no matter the subject.

I waited until she had taken a bite of the sandwich then asked, "So why are you here?" When her eyes widened, I added, "I mean why did you get in touch?"

"You gave me your card, remember?"

"Yes. I'm surprised is all."

"And why is that?"

"I wasn't at my best that night."

"Oh?"

"Too much to drink, as I'm sure you noticed. Not my finest hour."

"I had fun," she said and smiled. "You weren't the only one who imbibed."

I rolled my napkin into a tight ball. "What about your date? What was his name, something Stewart?"

"Stanton. Mike."

"Okay. He wasn't pleased."

"So what?"

"You and he..."

She grinned, which accentuated her Streisand nose in a nice way. "We are...seeing each other occasionally. In fact I was supposed to meet him here today, but he begged off. Guess there's a partners' meeting or something."

"Yeah. All the stiff suits are attending an annual tax confab at the Grove Hotel. Out of my pay grade."

I was pushing up against my forty-five-minute lunch break time limit when Mike Stanton materialized at our table. Surprised us both. He loomed over us, impeccably dressed, black hair slicked back, and stared at Ashley beneath a ledge of furry eyebrows. He did not offer her a smile or me a greeting.

"You were to meet me in the lobby of the Grove," he said.

Ashley pushed her chair back a bit and looked up at Stanton. "No, the last thing you said was you doubted that we'd be able to have lunch because your meeting would run too long."

"As you can tell, that was not the case."

"How was I to know that? By the way, this is Ned Pine. Maybe you remember that we sat with him at the New Year's party."

Stanton did not look at me. "Ashley, we have little enough time together. I expected you to—"

"What, wait for your beck and call? As far as I was concerned, there was no chance of us having lunch, so I called Ned to see if he could join me for a quick bite."

"Regardless, I don't expect this standing-me-up scenario to happen again. Understand?"

Color rose in Ashley's cheeks. "Mike, how dare you." She shoved back farther and stood. "You do not control my life."

Stanton stepped up closer to her. "You will do as I say."

I remember Ashley's shocked look; then she laughed. "How ridiculous. Who do you think you're talking to?"

"You will do as I say." Stanton repeated and took hold of her left arm.

It was then that I felt a rush of indignation and quickly rose from my chair. "I think that's enough," I said as my face reddened and I felt a surge of nervous anger.

Stanton didn't look at me but said, "Stay out of this."

Others in the deli were staring at us now. I swallowed and looked about at the shocked faces. "No." My voice was uneven. "I think it best if you leave."

Finally Stanton turned his head toward me. "Listen...whatever your name is..."

"Ned Pine. I also work for L&C."

"Oh yes, I recall now. Well, Pine, best you stay out of things that don't concern you."

It is a distant memory now, but I vaguely remember asking him to take his hand off Ashley, to which he replied, and I'll never forget, "Listen newbie, you're just a grunt and should be back at your desk making grunting sounds and creating revenue. Capiche?"

All in the deli were frozen in time, eyes wide, breathing shallow breaths. I traded eye contact with Stanton and in a rash moment reached out and took hold of his arm. "That's enough," I said. "Let go."

I felt his arm stiffen as if to resist. Then he suddenly released her arm and stormed out of the deli. And that's how things got underway between Ashley and me.

-4-

They docked me in a room in the ICU and left me there. Nurses would drift in, check my vitals, and drift out again. I slept and roused with a chalky dry mouth, sucked iced water through a plastic flex straw, then dozed again. Food came on a schedule. For lunch I sipped chicken noodle soup—that was all I wanted—and lay back with my eyes closed and ruminated over the horror show that ran continually in my head on a loop: the crash, the daunting figures in black, the metal bats, the pain, but mostly Ashley's scream. When, after another rerun, my eyes popped open and I gasped, heart pounding, a nurse in the room at the time came to me and asked if I was all right. I assured her that I was, that I'd had a dream. She looked concerned but eventually just checked the monitors to her satisfaction and left me alone again. My head was pulsating, but my breathing had stabilized.

After a couple more swallows of soup, I laid back, closed my eyes, and entered a calm state of slumber; the disaster loop did not return right then. But Ashley did. It was so torturous to know that she was somewhere else, that she was severely damaged and I was not with her. Our marriage wasn't perfect, but this wrenching disconnect was beyond my emotional capacity to absorb. She tumbled through my memory bank as if I was flipping through photographs of our life together.

We would always credit our eventual union to the day Mike Stanton was cleaved from Ashley's life in one boorish act of chauvinism. Like I said, the image of Stanton disappearing from Nellie's

Deli while Ashley and I stood like manikins has stayed etched in my memory. Two very important outcomes emanated from that moment: Ashley and I connected, and Mike Stanton began an orchestration for my eventual severance from Laxell & Crowne. He would become a senior partner long after I had carried a banker's box of my personal belongings from the L&C office under the scrutiny of a sober security guard on a warm sunny Friday afternoon, April 18, 1986. They'd kept me on until the crush of tax season had passed. One of my few friends at the firm, Ralph Simms, a six-month newbie, took me out for a beer, and we celebrated my tax-season-to-tax-season tenure at the firm. I warned him about Mike Stanton and wished him well. Never saw him again.

When I called Ashley to give her the news of my ouster, she was her usual cool, collected self. "Saw that coming, didn't you?" she said.

So like her: focused and pragmatic, never one to emote needlessly or spontaneously. From the moment that Mike Stanton had disappeared from the deli, she and I had worked on what was left—that being an attempt to find something pivotal between us. Not *Were we meant for each other?* Rather *Could we find common ground for some kind of relationship?* She lived in Latham, a four-hour-thirty-three minute drive northeast from my apartment. I took the I-84 swoop down from Boise and up to Latham many times in pursuit of an *alliance* linking us. That was her choice of word to describe what we were up to. It wasn't one wrapped in torrid romance, which should have more suitably been in the air—in my opinion anyway. It was more of a negotiated partnership than a falling-in-love plot line. We did have sex, of course. My ex post facto rendition is clearly lodged in my memories of those early days. That initial act was enjoyable, but then again, Ashley made it seem more like a lab experiment.

I was still on the payroll at Laxell & Crowne. It was the middle of tax season, another Friday, when at close of day I hit the elevator like a homing pigeon, jumped into my old college ride, a 1975 red Jeep Cherokee, its red paint oxidized to a soft coral with black trim and over 110,00 miles on it—we were pals. I arrived in Latham around nine thirty and drove right to Rick's Roadhouse Grill, the only place Ashley liked when eating out there. Not many dining choices in the town, which was about fifteen thousand back then with an economy mainly driven by two industries: a pet food factory and a sugar beet refinery. Toss in a couple of local cattle ranches, a small food processing company, some potato farms, and you had Latham's local payrolls.

Ashley worked as the office manager for her father's company, Tucker Construction, a position she reluctantly assumed when her mother had passed away. Isaac Tucker always got what he wanted, and he wanted his only child filling in for his beloved Isobel, regardless of Ashley's enrollment at Lewis-Clark College, where she'd been pursuing a degree in elementary education. Isaac had not been moved by the implication of Ashley following in her mother's footsteps as an elementary teacher.

Even for a Friday, the parking lot of Rick's Grill had thinned out considerably by nine thirty. I stripped off my tie, tossed my suit coat on the back seat, and rolled up the sleeves on my dress shirt in attempt to mitigate appearing as a stuffed shirt before entering the restaurant. It was still warm out when I exited the Jeep. I made sure my collar was spread, ran a hand through my hair, and sauntered in. Canned music was thumping in the adjacent bar, mooing voices could be heard over the din, and smoke was drifting in the air. Ashley was in a booth. She saw me come in and raised a hand; it was not an excited-to-see-you wave, merely a signal of location. It was always different for me back then. I did wave a bit excitedly, I did feel a rush of pleasure at just seeing her, and I did really want to be with her.

She already had a glass of white wine in front of her. I leaned over and kissed her on the cheek, a tender greeting that she accepted but offered no reciprocation; that always bothered me.

Guess I should have been more aware of her stunted tenderness side. I wasn't mindful enough, or probably I rationalized away my wish for even a trace more of fondness from her back then.

That night, she looked at me as I slid into the booth across from her and gave me one of her cynical little smiles. "Trying to fit in, are you?"

I felt color come onto my face and glanced around. "Clock struck five, I dove into the Cherokee and drove like mad to get here. No chance to get into my Levi's. Besides, couldn't wait to see you, change of wardrobe or not."

"How sweet," she said and sipped from her wine glass. "Let's order."

We both had the house specialty, medium rare T-bone steaks with baked potato and fresh green beans. It was then and there that we inaugurated what was to become a pattern of behavior between us from then on: little or no talking when eating. Ashley was a focused eater. The food before her always earned her full attention— no distractions allowed, even by the person who would potentially spend the rest of his life with her. I know, should have weighed that trait more carefully. By the time I had consumed about half my steak, I looked across at Ashley's face, noting the nose I loved, her brown eyes focused not on me but at the moment on spooning sour cream on her baked potato with her determined eater expression.

"You know," I interrupted her concentration, "it's been almost three months since we met."

She looked up and squinted as if I'd just intruded inappropriately on a private moment.

"Two days shy," I added.

"Is that right?" she said.

"The New Year's Eve party, remember?"

"Of course." When I thought that was the end of it, she looked down at her plate and went on. "I do remember. That night, after the party, my date, Mr. Stanton, and I, we had a heated disagreement in the lobby of the hotel." She shook pepper over her potato and continued. "In a snit, he stormed off and left me there. Since I had met him in Pocatello, left my car there, then ridden with him to Boise, I was stranded."

She looked up into my startled face and smiled. "So I had to rent a room. The hotel was totally booked, but they finally put me in a small room they hold open for just such occasions. Could practically touch the walls, side to side, when you held your arms out. It was that tiny. But a bed was a bed."

"Then what?" I asked.

"I went to bed. The next day, New Year's Day. My father drove over from Latham and picked me up. End of story."

"Ashley, you should have called me." I brandished my fork. "You had my card."

"That didn't make us chums, now did it? Besides it was just your business number."

"Well, yeah but…"

"Besides, we hadn't even been to Nellie's Deli together, you and I." Her laugh was gently mocking.

"Tell me," I said, "after that atrocious behavior, why did you see Mike Stanton again?"

She shrugged. "I don't know. To see if there was anything to it, I suppose. He had certain traits that intrigued me."

I hesitated then asked, "Why'd you call me that day for lunch? Was I just a fallback option because Stanton was unavailable?"

"Exactly."

"Boy, do I feel special."

"And you should. Look who I'm having dinner with. And how many times have we seen each other since then?"

A waitress had begun clearing our plates while asking if we wanted dessert. Ashley ordered apple pie à la mode. I just asked for coffee. "Let me ask you this," I said when we were alone again. "Is there anything to this? Between us, is there anything there?"

She looked straight at me, unblinking for a moment. "I think so."

"You *think* so?"

"Yes, I do."

"Okay, what?"

"Something. Indescribable, but yes."

"Indescribable? Is that good?"

She folded her hands on the table. "Yes. To me it is."

Her pie arrived, and my coffee. I added some sugar. "How do we verify this something between us? Do we just keep testing it around the edges?"

She eyed the apple pie and said, "There are ways."

I followed her for the first time to her house, a small craftsman cottage in a nice neighborhood in the older part of town. She hadn't invited me to her place since we'd begun seeing one another; we always met for dinner or a movie in Boise or there in Latham. I know, odd, but for some reason at the time it seemed not out of the ordinary. Looking back on it, I must have figured she was just being judicious. Having been bitten by Mike Stanton, she was being careful, or so I thought. Besides, I was truly beginning to care for her, and in that state of mind one is not usually processing the practical side of a relationship.

I parked at the curb on Oak Street and got out of the Jeep. It was quiet, the temperature pleasantly comfortable, and the neighborhood was dark except for one house two lots away.

Ashley was on the porch hunched over, unlocking the front door. I stood watching until she opened the door, reached in to switch on the porch light, then waved me in.

It was very small inside, just four rooms and a bath, but cozy and cleverly appointed. I told her I liked it very much.

"It's one of those Sears bungalows. You bought the kit, and it arrived with everything you needed to build it, right down to the nails. This one is called The Brentwood. Think it was put up around 1934. This neighborhood has a bunch of Sears kit houses."

"Nice."

"Okay. How about some wine. Then we can talk."

She stepped into the small kitchen and soon reappeared with two glasses of red wine. We sat together on a short couch; we each took a swallow of wine and set our glasses on the coffee table in front of us. And then we were quiet. I turned to look at her; she was looking straight ahead.

I had reached out for my wine glass when she spoke. "I suppose we should delve into this." When she saw my curious expression, she added, "Shouldn't we?"

I retrieved my wine glass and took a good swallow. "This? By that you mean us?"

She studied my face as one would a Petri dish with an odd something growing in it. "Of course."

"So have you interpreted the indescribable something?" I asked. "You know, between us?"

"No. Nor have you, I would surmise."

I nodded. "Correct. So how do we define whatever it is?"

"I doubt that we have to."

I laughed and pinched my nose, erupting with a small snort. "Ashley, what the hell. How will we know if this, whatever it is between us, has legs?"

"Interesting turn of phrase." She turned sideways on the couch. "What is it you want, Ned?

I swallowed, still feeling the tannins of the wine in my mouth, and looked straight into her brown eyes, which were clearly evaluating me. "Isn't it what do we want?"

"Is it?"

I abruptly stood, stepped around the coffee table, and turned in a circle. She observed me as a cat would watch a dangling piece of string: curious but not sure it wanted to swat at it. I stopped pacing, shoved my hands into my pockets, and looked down at her. "Okay, here's the question. Are we merely filling time: dating, dining, you know, providing each other with a social agenda? Or is there something more?"

"I don't know. Is there? Do you want there to be?"

I shook my head and leaned forward. "Ashley. For me there is already something more. *You.*"

She smiled and cradled her wine glass in both hands. "That must feel nice."

"It does. Don't you feel it?"

Her smiled tailed off. "I wish I was that way, like you. I'm not."

I kept standing. My mouth grew dry. I was, I don't know, afraid: afraid of losing her or afraid that I wasn't good enough to count. I wasn't sure which. I hesitated, and we studied one another before I said, "Do you want this to go on?"

"Ned," she said." Of course I do."

"Why? Tell me."

Her eyes widened, and I saw confusion in them for the first time since I'd met her. "I just do."

"Not good enough," I said and waved a hand in the air. "Not by a mile."

She didn't respond, just looked into her wine glass.

"There must be a way to resolve this," I said. "A way to tell if, as you say, if there is anything to this. If not, then…best we call it a day."

"There is a way, I think, for us."

"What?"

Her smile was canny. "Two ways, actually. First, scent."

"Scent. Are you kidding?"

She shook her head. "No. Studies are suggesting that how we smell to one another is an important factor in human attraction."

I laughed; it was a relief. "So my body odor is on trial."

"Maybe."

"How am I doing?"

"Okay, I guess. I'm not repulsed."

I threw up my hands and laughed louder. "Thanks for the faint praise. Okay, what's the second way?"

She set her wine glass down and leaned back, folding her arms.

"Fit. How we fit together."

My mouth opened. "You mean?"

This time her smile was mischievous. "Yes, I mean."

And that's how our first sexual moment came to be. After a few minutes of self-conscious laughing, Ashley rose, looped an arm into mine, and steered us into her bedroom. She turned on a small lamp by her bedside, which cast a modest glow. We stood quietly looking at each other; then she began to disrobe without a moment's hesitation. She never took her eyes off me while she removed the belt from her skirt and began to unbutton her blouse.

It was the moment most people can recall when they and the person who loved them enough to want a life together willingly shared their bodies. By the time Ashley had undressed, I was down to my Jockey shorts. She stood quietly as I finished, and we observed one another in the low light. I must say that she and I were both average people; neither one of us would describe ourselves as voluptuous or physically stunning. However, to see her there before me, willingly revealing her total physical self, was the most lovingly sensual moment of my life. Her slender body was a gift; the curves of a female have always had a natural attraction for us males, the loveliness to which we are drawn and which our squarish, blunt shells can never equal.

So it was that night. Ashley remained still while I pulled off my underwear and stood before her. Let me explain what I may have looked like to her back then. I was around six feet tall, had blue eyes, thick brown hair that unless properly combed could resemble a brush, an average build with no extraordinary muscles but not overweight, a face with a high forehead, and a nose that was rather prominent (guess that's why I was taken by Ashley's). I'm not sure how I came across to Ashley at that moment, but to me she was beautiful, and I indeed wanted to find out if we fit.

Finally, she said, "Shall we do this then?"

I stepped forward and took her hands in mine. "Can I ask you something first?"

"What?"

"Do you love me?"

She hesitated too long. "I care for you, sure."

"Is that love?"

She raised her head and looked past me then said, "Do we have to go there at this precise moment...?"

"Of passion?" I finished her sentence.

She chuckled. "Ah, the complications of connecting."

I took the opening and said, "Is it okay if I love you?"

She tilted her head and smiled, "Can't we just do this?"

And we did. I remember even now the feel of her skin against mine, cool and smooth, her willingness to engage in an act to confirm what I'd hoped for. I can recall her breath against my face, how she held to me and how the paroxysm of her release moved me to completion. And that was it; we'd done it. We fit. Afterward, she kissed me gently on my lips, and we slept.

That was how and why Ashley and I cast our lots with each other. Now we both lie in hospital beds with perhaps no chance to absolve the slippage that had grown between us after that long-ago moment in Latham.

-5-

They let me out of the hospital the next day; rather, I was discharged the next day. It was like a restaurant eager to turn my bed for fresh meat—nice but insistent: sign here, verify insurance, pack your belongings, and take all of this hospital junk while you're at it. Dr. Sneed, the neurologist, came by for a few minutes to check on me and fill me in on Ashley's condition: his update from the neurosurgeon in Pocatello confirmed again that it wasn't a good story. She remained in a coma, and that test they called the Glasgow Coma Scale was in the severe range. After that offhand briefing, Sneed told me I was good to go, recited a list of precautionary steps I needed to be aware of regarding my own head injury, then tipped his head in adieu and evaporated from the room.

Jack Jackson, the managing partner of our small CPA firm, Jackson, Vogel & Pine, had been pacing around waiting for the doctor's departure. Afterward, he helped me wrestle into my pants, pulled my left arm into a shirtsleeve, and draped the right sleeve over the cast in a sling, then gathered my sundry belongings. He was my ride. I'd heard nothing yet from members of my family, all of whom lived elsewhere. None were in regular contact, nor I with them, so I wasn't surprised. By rule, I had to be wheelchaired out by a hospital aide; Jack followed along carrying a big plastic bag full of hospital stuff I didn't need or want but had to take anyway. John 'Jack' Jackson, our godfather, had founded the firm in 1977 at the tender age of 35. Now at 68 he hustled along beside my wheelchair, red-faced, overweight, and fussing.

"Ned," he said, "this is just god-awful." He was speaking through panting breaths. "I mean, it's been all over the news: papers, radio, TV—about the attack. You and Ashley." He trotted to keep up with the speedy aide. "How are you?"

"Have the mother of headaches," I responded. "And I've got this thing." I held up my cast. "But, Jack, she's really hurt bad, Ashley is. It's real bad." Without warning, I grabbed the arm of the chair and leaned forward as a howl of grief I'd been holding in roiled out. I couldn't stop the sobs as they convulsed in my throat. I gasped, almost unable to catch my breath.

The aide quickly stopped the wheelchair, locked the wheels, and squatted down beside me. She placed a hand on my back and stroked slowly. Jack dropped the bag and leaned over. "Oh my," he said several times. "Ned, Ned, Ned, oh my, is he okay?"

The aide nodded. "He'll be okay, I think. See this occasionally, pent up grief." She stood and stepped in front of me. "Mr. Pine, you okay?"

I nodded and inhaled deeply several times until my breathing was even again. "I'm okay," I answered. "Not sure where that came from."

"It happens," the aide said and began to propel me forward again.

I had to wait in the wheelchair until Jack drove his Lexus up to the waiting area. I felt able to walk to his car, but the aide insisted. Certainly more about legal liability than whether I was really able to walk. Jack plunged out of his car almost before it came to a stop and scurried around to help me as if I was his aging aunt. He stood by with a worried face until the aide had seen me safely buckled into the front seat.

"Violet has our spare bedroom all ready for you," Jack said as we drove away from the hospital. "Shall we go by your place so you can get some clothes?"

"No, Jack. I just want to go home."

"Not on your life," he responded. "You're in no shape to be

alone. We insist."

He pressed the point all the way to my house until he finally gave in—most reluctantly. He saw me to the door, hovered until I was safely inside, and agreed to drive me to Pocatello the next day. The house was a vacant thing, stone cold quiet, seeming airless and unwelcoming, as if I didn't belong there. I stood in the foyer and waited for a sense of belonging to come toward me, but it didn't. It came to me that I would have to assert myself and claim my rightful place at 4224 West Larchwood Court within the Whitewood Estates gated monstrosity. (I'd never wanted to live there, it was Ashley's desire.) I stooped to gather up the wad of mail that had been shoved through the mail slot in our absence. When I stood back up, my head swam and pounded; I had the sensation of the room spinning. Maybe I should have gone to stay with the Jacksons after all.

I waited for my equilibrium to settle, tossed the mail onto the coffee table in the living room, and went straight into the kitchen. I had to see it. Someone had cleaned up the broken dishes and wine glasses, made things orderly again, and performed minor surgery to the backdoor, including a piece of plywood over the broken window and makeshift repairs to the splintered door frame. I settled onto one of the kitchen chairs and felt the sensation of knowing what had happened there. I was seeing the attack in my mind's eye when the doorbell rang.

His name was Detective Morgan, Clarence Morgan, but professionally he went by C. T. Morgan. I knew him somewhat, but not well. His name was in the local paper whenever there was a crime of note that required criminal investigation. A tall, slender younger man was with him.

"Mr. Pine?" I nodded, and he said, "I'm Detective Morgan, and this is Detective Grimes. I checked with the hospital, and they said you had been discharged. We've been waiting to talk with you about the attack two nights ago. Is this a good time? I tried to call, but..."

I stepped back and let them in. Once the door was closed we stood in a tight group until I realized that nothing was happening and awkwardly led them into the living room. I gestured for them to sit down on the couch while I sank into one of the gray fabric club chairs Ashley had hand-selected. It was really her house. Everything about it had been her choice—after we'd discussed it, of course. A flash of humor crossed my mind: I could affirm that the chrome-and-black wastebasket in our home office was the one and only personal selection that had passed muster.

I came around to Detective Morgan's voice. "What? I'm sorry."

He flashed a limpid smile. "I was asking how you are."

I stared back at him, unable to smile in return. "Not good."

Morgan's face sobered even more. "Sorry to hear it." I managed a nod. "I can see that you've been through it," he went on. "What do the doctors say about...your injuries?"

I held up the sling. "Broken arm, concussion, and some defensive wounds to this hand. But that's nothing. It's my wife. Ashley. It's...well it's unspeakable. She's in a coma in Pocatello. Trauma center."

Morgan glanced at his partner, maybe to caution him to remain mute. "Sorry to hear it. We'll do all we can to track down the attackers. But we need your help. You up to answering some questions?"

Both men were leaning forward on their knees, eyes wide and antsy. I shrugged. Morgan pulled a notepad from his coat pocket and commenced: what time did the attack occur, were just the two of us in the house, how many invaders were there, could I describe them, how were they dressed, did they say anything, did we keep large amounts of cash or other valuables in the house, what was taken, did I know of anyone who would have reason to make such an attack, had I seen any suspicious persons in the neighborhood before that night, what did they use as weapons, and so on. I'm sure I was a disappointment to them; at least from my view what I gave them couldn't have indicted a neighborhood cat of an avian killing with a dead dove of peace in its mouth. They'd certainly gotten more information from my neighbor Guy Stewart; after all, he'd at least seen the perpetrators make their getaway.

Before leaving, the detectives dutifully thanked me, assured me of their commitment to find our attackers, and wished the best for Ashley's recovery. I closed the door on them, leaned my head against it, and said to no one: *Not a fucking chance.*

I wandered the disproportionately large house, entering each room, pausing and looking about briefly in an attempt to reclaim the square footage as mine—as ours. Didn't work. I was a stranger there, in that house of sticks and stones—had been from the beginning. Even with the heat ramped up, I still felt cold. The refrigerator freezer donated a frozen Stouffer's baked ziti pasta dish. I nuked it per instructions, procured a bottle of Chianti from the wine rack, sat by myself at the kitchen table, and felt very alone as I tried to eat. I drank more wine than I ate pasta.

Our landline phone message light had been blinking at me since I'd set foot back in the house; I'd opted to ignore the waiting missives until I was of a different mind. I wasn't there yet but was still curious. The collection of messages included Ashley's father, who had called three days earlier with a question about a contract, a reminder for a hair appointment, our neighbor Guy Stewart in a voice overcome with remorse letting me know he would do anything to help, and a couple of robo calls. No calls from our kids, not even to my cell phone, which held a bevy of messages left on it the night of the attack after I was taken to the hospital. The one home-phone message I chose to respond to right then was a brief call from my older brother, Harrison. All he'd said in his message was, "Ned, I heard about your break-in. Call me."

I listened to the voice I knew so well but rarely heard. I replayed the message three times, a total of fifteen seconds long. It had been, I guess, maybe five years since Harrison and I had actually been in each other's company. Hell, we were only four hundred miles or so apart. Probably take six or seven hours of hard driving from Latham to Baker City, Oregon, where he lived, still less than a third of a day. May as well be three thousand miles, as eager as he was to see me. Our disconnect got under way on January 10, 1987, the day Ashley and I were married, and went downhill from there. Not only was it the day of our vows, it was also when Isaac Tucker let me know in no uncertain terms how totally disapproving he was of his Ashley choosing me as her mate: *You are so low on my list of worthy choices for my daughter that you don't even register. Lower than zero. Understand? And yet she singled you out, so I'll live with it somehow. But never, and I mean never, assume that you'll gain my respect—won't happen. Got it?* He ended the invective by jabbing his right forefinger into my chest. I took one step back and held my tongue, something I regret. I should have matched the bastard's words in kind—which would have no doubt gotten me nothing, but I might have salvaged some self-respect. Regrets, I have many.

That was just for openers. My family had made the trip over from Oregon and showed up to witness our nuptials with a brave front. They came dressed in their Sunday best, as people used to say, but were given the famous cold shoulder from the Tucker side of the aisle. My brother, Harrison, was my best man, wearing his only suit, the one he kept in the closet except for church, funerals, and in this case, weddings. He was standing in among the Tucker men, who all wore tuxedos that day, me too, as I was so directed by my bride. It was rural Idaho, for crying out loud—tuxedos? My parents and my brother and his wife were farmers in Baker County, Oregon. They'd been farming a little over a thousand acres since back around 1947 by the time of the wedding. They were good people, straightforward, trustworthy—reliable to the core, the kind that got up at 5:00 a.m. every day to tend their crops and their animals. They had little tolerance or time to waste on foolishness, nor did they flinch in the face of indignity or countenance rudeness. And beginning on that day, after being exposed to the unique personality of Ashley Tucker, my betrothed, there began a downward spiral of mutual disregard between my family and my wife—a distancing that would never be resolved. Oddly, Ashley never got it; she would only look at me blankly when I asked her to be more open with my family or, on one occasion, to apologize for something misunderstood. The latter drew a raised eyebrow and a sly smile. Okay, yes, I deserve much of the blame for this rift. I should have asserted myself—I didn't.

So there had been this divide between my wife and me and my kin for the twenty-three years of our marriage. I guess you could call it estrangement. My parents were the gentle ones who still wanted to hear from me, at least my mother was. But my siblings, Harrison and my sister Corrine, would actually prefer I stayed out of their lives—so I was told by my sister some years ago now. And it all began on that day in January of 1987 when my family was looked down on in a very obvious manner: for what they wore, for their quiet ways, and perhaps for the men's strong working hands and farmer's hat tans. Even though Isaac Tucker had worked with his hands all his life, he seemed to find no kinship with my father or my brother. It was a painful day for me, all wrapped up in a faux celebration to which I was a party and participating celebrant.

Of course I believed there would be other times; we had endured just one awkward moment, an aberration. Surely Ashley and I would enjoy many years of loving familial interaction with my family. Such was not the case. I know now that I had learned to overlook Ashley's self-contained temperament for my own peace of mind. I loved her for all the other things she was to me; I loved her even though she never told me in ways I yearned for that she loved me back—equaling my total commitment. Over the years the times we spent with my side of the family grew less and less frequent until they no longer happened at all.

So on my wedding day, I was vilified by my pending father-in-law and stood by while my wife-to-be snubbed her future in-laws. How do they say it? Not my finest hour? Truly so.

-6-

It was after nine when I dialed Harrison's number. The moment the phone began to ring, I wondered if he'd still be up; usually he would have retired by that time, what with his alarm set as early as 4:30 a.m. But he was up. He even answered it himself, instead of Sybil, which in the past would have not been the case.

"Hello." His voice was cautious: *Who would be calling at this hour?*

"It's me."

"Ned."

"Sorry to call so late."

"That right?"

"Well, I know you go to bed early."

"Uh-huh." I heard my brother sniff. "I usually do retire before now, but Sybil had choir practice at church. She plays the piano. Anyway she just got home a bit ago. I wait up for her."

"Give her my best." I felt myself squinting, and my lips were pressed together. It was like I was expecting to be hit back when we were kids rough-housing.

"I will," he said. "So tell me, how are you?"

I paused, wondered how to go about this, and said, "I was released from the hospital today. I'm passable, I guess, have a concussion, broken arm, and some minor wounds."

"I see. And the wife?" He didn't say Ashley, hadn't for years; it was always *the wife*.

"Ashley," I said her name on purpose. "Very serious. She's in a coma at the trauma center in Pocatello. Real bad."

41

"That right? That must be hard on you. Have you seen her?"

"No. I'm going to see her tomorrow. One of my business partners is driving me down."

I felt Harrison wait a few beats. "What happened, then, the break-in? How'd that happen?"

We were quiet for a bit, the weight of familial history pressing down. Finally, I sighed and told him how we'd been invaded. He listened to the whole story without interrupting. When I finished, my big brother hesitated then said, "Quite something, quite something indeed. I've heard of home invasions but only in the abstract. And you're mostly okay?"

"Pounding headache," I answered. "But yeah, mostly okay."

"The police, they know who did it?"

"No. Working on it."

"Uh-huh. Well, hope they're successful." He paused, and I heard him say something that was muffled, likely behind a hand over the mouthpiece. He came back on. "Sybil says hello and God bless."

"Thank her."

"Uh-huh."

"How are Mom and Dad?" I asked in a tentative voice. My parents lived with Harrison and Sybil. I'd heard that my father was in the early stages of dementia, with my mother serving as his stalwart caretaker.

"You really want to know, Ned?"

I took in a couple breaths. His question was an accusation, a deserved one. With the severance between my marital family and my blood family had come a curse, which I regretted but had been unable to bridge—that being the neglect of my parents. At first it had been simply delaying contact while things related to my marriage quieted down. But time passed, and I did nothing. Oh maybe the occasional holiday phone call—that was it. So Harrison's pointed question hung there with justified implications.

"Of course I want to know."

My brother inhaled. "They're getting old. That's how they are. And Dad is losing it. If it weren't for Mom, we'd have to put him somewhere. That what you wanted to know?"

"God, Harrison. Is there anything I can do to help?" Was I sincere? I don't know. My father and I were never really close. He and Harrison were tough on each other but still simpatico; I was usually an irritant, catching the edge of his unpredictable temper. My mother looked sad on those occasions but never defended or consoled me.

Harrison breathed out a cynical laugh. "Really? You ask that now?"

I didn't know how to respond, so I didn't. I would have probably said the wrong thing.

"Ned, I'm going to go to bed now. Our day always starts early around here. Anything I can do for you?"

I said the only thing I had to say. "No, I'm just torn up about Ashley."

"Uh-huh," Harrison said with little feeling. "I imagine so. Best with that."

It must have been his placid response. I don't know. I just suddenly sobbed. "Harrison, I'm so scared for her. It's really bad. I...I could lose her."

"We'll pray that you don't," was his response. "That she recovers." With that he said good-bye and disconnected.

I sat in the dark, holding the receiver, the dial tone droning, my head aching, and let the tears form. I willed them to come; I deserved them, charged with wrong choices and neglect. The hour stretched out, and around ten o'clock I decided that I couldn't bear to sleep in our bedroom: the smell of Ashley on the pillow, her nightgown hanging where I could see it, her lotions and her toothbrush in the bathroom—couldn't do it. I had collected my pajamas and toothbrush and was heading for one of the extra bedrooms when the doorbell rang.

It was Guy Stewart, my neighbor. I switched on the porch light, and there he stood wearing his official dog-walking attire, a dark blue windbreaker and an English driving cap; at his feet was Joel, his white bit of fluff Maltese, all seven pounds of him. Guy, a seventy-year-old retired insurance company executive, was the only neighbor that we really knew, he and his sweet wife Nancy. His only activity since hanging it up, besides occasional trips to Nebraska to see kids and grandkids, was walking Joel twice daily and overseeing the weekly visits of the yard maintenance crew that kept his grounds and landscaping pristine.

"Guy," I choked his name out. "My god, man, come in, come in."

I reached out with my left hand and literally pulled him into the foyer. He stumbled in, the dog dragged along behind. He forced out an uneasy smile. I urged him to take off his coat and guided him into the living room. The dog danced around excitedly as if something fun was about to happen. Guy got him to lie down by his feet and be still.

"Guy, we are so in your debt," I said and leaned forward, the cast propped on my knee. "Really, if it hadn't been for you—"

"Ned." He raised a hand and interrupted my eulogy. "It was really a stroke of luck…" He paused. "I'm sorry, I didn't mean it like that. I meant my being out and happening to see those fellows come out of your house and speed away. I knew something was amiss." He paused again and wrung his hands while shaking his head. "And…and then I found you both in the kitchen. Oh my, it was just…it was awful." He looked at my cast. "How are you?"

I sat back and held up my arm. "Not great but okay."

"And Ashley? She…it looked the worse for her."

I hesitated. How should I tell this kind man how it was? "Guy… it's bad. Very bad." He squinted as if in pain. "She's in a coma. They moved her to Pocatello to a trauma center. I haven't even seen her. But I will tomorrow."

Guy reached down and patted the dog. He pressed his lips together and shook his head. "So she's still unconscious?"

I nodded. "Thank you, Guy," I said to change the subject. "I assume it was you who cleaned things up and patched the door. Right?"

For a moment, he just looked at me as if I'd made a social error. "It was Nancy. She cleaned things up. All I did was call our handyman and have him secure the door. Not perfect, but had to do something. I'm no good at that sort of thing."

"Sure. Bless you for that." He merely shrugged. "Can you tell me what you saw? Those bastards who were in the house? You saw them."

"It was like I told the police. I was out walking Joel for his nightly when I saw three men bolt out from behind your place and jump into a big pickup. It was dark, so even with the streetlight I couldn't make anything out. Couldn't describe them. All dressed in dark clothes, it seemed. I was startled, shocked really, and just froze. I mean, it's not like we see suspicious people wandering about. That's why we pay for the security guard."

I hadn't thought about that, and the detectives hadn't brought it up either. How did they get in without being cleared at the gate? I decided right then that I'd talk with the security company. "What about the truck? What kind was it? New, old?"

He smiled. "I never was good about cars. Not like the boys I grew up with. They knew every make and model. It was just a pickup, Ned: dark in color, big, stood on those big knobby tires, and the engine sounded powerful. That's it. Oh, it looked newish. It wasn't an old beater."

After that we sat looking at one another with nothing more to say. When Guy rose to leave, I asked if his handyman could repair the broken door like new. He said no, but he'd have a finish carpenter they had used call me if I wanted. He could do the job. I said I'd like that. Guy came to me and gave me an awkward hug and left with tears in his eyes, pulling the little bit of four-legged fuzz behind him. I stood by the closed front door after he left and felt again the lump in my chest that I felt every time I went back over that night.

I retired to a spare bedroom shortly after Guy Stewart left, to our son Michael's old room. It had been a very long time since Ashley had not slept beside me—I felt adrift knowing where she was: that I wasn't with her, that she couldn't communicate with me in any event, and worrying if we would ever share our bed again. At first I didn't sleep, just drifted in and out of consciousness. When I did sleep, my mind defaulted to Ashley and scenes from our less-than-perfect twenty-three-year bond. How often I had looked into her brown eyes and found nothing for me in them—only the pragmatic persona I'd come to know. In my stupor I was again in her presence on an occasion when she was looking at me as if perplexed. It was the expression of hers I'd grown so familiar with over the years, especially at those moments when I'd sought more between us but unfortunately lacked the persuasive skills to move her in my direction on demand. I know it seems inane that throughout a marriage a man and his wife would consistently be unable to seek out their passionate side. I did try my best to demonstrate that I was desirous of pursuing our carnal natures. Her response was usually one of pity—humiliating. I can count on two hands those times when we engaged in truly sensual sex, all prior to the births of our children and few after. Ashley had a plan, one I deemed *strategic sex*. I remember vividly those occasions when she allowed, even encouraged me to fondle her, to share her body with perceived enthusiasm. Each of those engagements are etched in my memory though I know that they were little more than scripted performances.

With Mike and Roz conceived and delivered, they became the endgame of our marital sensuality. I suppose that is how I justified succumbing to the warmth and openness of another. Gloria was her name, Gloria Denham. I never excused myself. I merely explored being close to someone who reciprocated and for some reason felt no guilt. When I once asked Ashley how it would be for her if we weren't together anymore, she merely said she would go on—no hesitation, no asking what did I mean. That cool response still rattled around in my head.

In my dream state, Ashley studied my face with no sign of emotion, no sign of judgment, no sign of caring, no sign of anything I could discern—except perhaps a trace of forbearance, which I interpreted to indicate her annoyance at being mangled beyond repair while I had escaped with less traumatic indignity.

Around five o'clock, I extricated myself from the twist of wadded blankets and tried to wash away the surreal mental images in a hot shower. Afterward I one-handed a pot of coffee and turned on the kitchen television. A cable news channel led with stories about President Obama visiting Capitol Hill for a final push on healthcare and Monarch butterflies suffering a population loss. I muted the sound, toasted a bagel, ate it with cream cheese, downed a second cup of coffee, and dressed to be ready for the trip to see Ashley. My stomach was alarmed.

———

Jack Jackson's Lexus was already at the curb when I came out. It was a sunny Friday, cool but pleasant—I truly didn't care. Jack was wearing a suit and tie. With only one arm, dressing had been a royal pain. I'd gone casual: fought into the legs of forgiving khakis, wrestled on a blue chambray shirt, forced the cast down an unbuttoned sleeve, then nestled my arm into the sling. Slipping on a pair of loafers had been the easy part. At the curb, I had to rotate my body into the car; a windbreaker hung cape-like over my shoulders. What an ordeal.

"Had to fight my way in," Jack said as the front seat accepted my body. "Security guard wasn't going to let me enter, but he finally relented when I used your name. Even offered his condolences."

"Sorry, forgot to call your name in. Preoccupied."

He reached over and squeezed my arm. "Hey, no biggy. You ready for this?"

I stared at the dashboard. His question was like a cattle prod to my chest. I straightened up and sat rigidly; my torso was in a vise. "I don't know."

Jack tightened his lips and started the car. "You'll be okay once you see her, don't you think?" When I didn't answer, he steered the car away from the curb. "I know it'll be tough," he said. "But we'll get you through it. Okay?"

When the seat belt beeper went off, Jack reached over and buckled me in. It would be an hour plus to Pocatello. I wasn't sure if I was desperate to be there or desperate not to be there. I sat quietly and watched the road ahead. Jack drove as he always did, conservatively; peripherally I could see him glance at me every couple of minutes.

Once we were on I-15 south, I felt him looking over at me again. "How's the season going?" I asked, referring to the tax season. "Shouldn't you be stroking client stress instead of being my chauffeur?"

He chuckled, ignored me, and softly asked, "How's everyone taking this, Ned? Your kids and in-laws?"

"You have any sunglasses?" I diverted his attention. "Must be this concussion. Seems too bright." He pointed to the glove box. I poked around with my good hand and found a pair of gold-framed polarized Ray-Bans and hung them on my ears. That was better, calming. My breathing seemed to slow. "That helps, thanks. They gave me this list," I said.

"List?"

"Yeah, of all the symptoms one might expect from having a blow to the head." I adjusted the glasses. "You know, everything from light sensitivity to feeling mentally foggy, dizziness, feeling queasy—long list."

"Really? So, how are you feeling?"

"In-laws?" I backtracked around his question. "I guess the best answer is that our particular brand of family misbehavior and neglect is alive and dysfunctional."

Jack gripped the steering wheel and stared straight ahead. He was such a *don't rock the boat* guy, always the one we sent in when a client was on a rampage. His soothing way almost always brought the crisis to ground with the client smiling in the end. Now he chose to just listen to me. He'd asked about something close to the bone and sensed it.

"It's complicated," I said. "Isn't that what people always say? You know, when they really don't want to answer or are unable to decipher their familial breakdown in a way that isn't embarrassing or weird?"

"Ned, you don't have to explain things to me. You have too much on your plate. Forget I asked."

I fell silent and asked myself Jack's question, especially about my children. How were they taking what had happened? What had my father-in-law told them? Isaac could have spun the story so that Mike and Roz thought I was responsible. Hadn't he said that to me in the hospital? I knew they hadn't called me because Isaac had persuaded them to leave me alone because of my injuries, the bastard. But why hadn't I called them? Couldn't blame everything on the concussion.

I edged my cell phone out of my pants pocket and palmed it. If Jack noted, he didn't say anything, just kept driving. I decided to call Rosalind first; she would be the most difficult. She was her mother's daughter, no nonsense, and would be the most likely to call me to task. I one-handed the phone and went into my contacts file, found her number, and looked at it for a long minute before I hit call. When it began to ring, I sat up in the seat and felt my chest tighten against the seat belt: her mother was in a coma—what now? After six rings it went to voice mail. I stumbled through some babble about it being *Your Dad*, things being terrible, me being on my way to see Mom, please call me.

Mike answered. I was relieved. "Dad, my god I've been waiting to talk with you, but Grandpa Isaac said to wait."

"I know," I said, restraining my urge to berate my father-in-law.

"We can talk now."

"Where are you?"

"On my way to see your mom. Jack Jackson from our firm is taking me since I can't drive due to my head injury and an arm cast. I'm grateful to him."

"Are you doing okay?" Mike's voice was up a notch and anxious beyond his usual bright tone.

"Not fully recovered but doing okay. Mainly I have to get to Pocatello to see your mom. It's been awful to be separated. I haven't even seen her since the...since the break-in."

There was a moment of silence on his end before he said, "I have to see her, Dad. When can I come see her...and you?" The dread in his voice was hard to hear.

"Anytime, Mike. You come as soon as you can. But you need to know that she is in a coma, a deep coma. Understand?"

"I guess."

"She won't be awake or anything, at least from what I heard last. From the doctors. We'll just have to be there and not expect her to know we're there."

"Okay, I understand...I guess." He hesitated. "I'll leave right away."

"Come by the house. You can stay there. You know where the key is."

"Okay."

"You have money for gas and food?"

"I'm good. And Dad, who did this to you?"

"No idea, Son. Not a clue."

We breathed in each other's ears for a bit before disconnecting. About half an hour out from Pocatello, Roz returned my call, her voice all elbows and fingernails. We traded information—that was all she wanted. Said she'd be out as soon as she could get there from Laramie, probably be most of a day by the time she got organized and hit the road. I figured Mike would get there first.

I put my phone away and sat back and calculated just what was waiting for me at the trauma center. For one thing, I knew Isaac Tucker would be on the scene, laying out his claim to be in charge of my wife's care. We'd see about that.

-7-

When I finally saw her, Isaac Tucker was standing on my right; Jack Jackson was on my left. I almost couldn't breathe, seeing her all wired and connected with tubes. Her eyes were taped down, the left side of her head and face was swollen and bruised, an IV line was inserted into her arm, fluid dripped from a plastic bag, a monitor blinked wavy lines, an airway tube had been inserted, a ventilator was breathing for her...she was a specimen. My good hand was fisted in my pocket so hard it ached. It was an otherworldly vision of someone I was supposed to know and love, but instead there was a manikin lying prone, representing a human female, its hair plastered down, its lips slightly separated by the tube in its mouth, merely acting out the role of one severely compromised. It wasn't her; it wasn't Ashley, couldn't be. But it was.

"My god." It was Jack Jackson who spoke those words, the ones I was thinking; he just said it first because I was too stricken to mouth them. "I'm sorry," he said. "It's just that..."

I turned to him. "That's okay."

Isaac stood with his arms folded across his chest, impassive; he'd already gone through the first moments of shock, so no emoting now from him. He had been the first person I saw when we approached Ashley's room in the ICU, seated in a side chair, his head back, chin dropped, asleep. Jack and I had entered the room and quietly stood at the foot of her bed, both of us stunned by what we saw. Our presence roused Isaac. He jerked awake, grunted, struggled up groggily from the chair, and stood with us but said nothing at first, until I asked about her status.

"Status?" he croaked. "Now there's a bean counter's word for you. Are you asking how she is?"

I bit down and took in a shallow breath. "Yes. How is she?"

"No damn good," he said. He hadn't met my eyes since we arrived. "That's what. No damn good."

"What have they said, the doctors?" I asked.

Finally he turned, towering over me. "And where the hell have you been? Not that it matters. I'm taking care of things."

"Mr. Tucker," Jack intervened, "Ned just got out of the hospital himself yesterday and is still feeling the effects of his head injury. He came as soon as he possibly could."

"Is that right? How brave of him. His wife, my baby girl, is down the well to hell, and he's got a headache." He glowered at them both. "I've been here watching over her, Ned. So you never mind. I've got her back. What good were you anyway when things got ugly?"

"My god, man," Jack said, his body stiffening, "have you no feelings? This man has been brutalized himself. What could he have done? They were attacked."

A mocking smile crested onto Isaac's lips. "That is the question, isn't it? What could he have done? Guess we'll never know, Jack. Guess we'll never know. I have my suspicions. I truly do."

"Unbelievable." Jack's incredulity hung in the air, a sour odor among them.

"Yes, isn't it?" Isaac retorted.

I nodded to Jack, waited a number of beats, and spoke to Isaac. "Who is the doctor attending to her?"

"Fella name of Small, Bertram Small. Neurosurgeon. He's a neurosurgeon. He's seen her several times."

"I want to see him," I said.

Isaac looked down at Ashley as she lay there unmoving and hooked to machinery. "He'll be along. Comes by frequent like. Besides, he's got nothing worth spit to say"

"No," I said, "I want to see him now. Is he in the hospital?"

"You'll get your turn," Isaac said. "He can't tell you anything he hasn't already told me anyhow."

A nurse in blue scrubs breezed into the room, checked a few things, looked at the monitor, and glanced at each of us in turn before exiting. I took all of that in and wondered what the nurse noted, if anything, and turned to my father-in-law. "I'll go to the nurses station and see if he can be located. Dr. Small, you said?"

Isaac looked at me as if taking the measure of someone he'd like to thrash and then merely shrugged. "Yeah, Small."

Bertram Small was a tall man, one who unlike me could look Isaac straight in the eye, thin, balding. While he had a good smile, he came across as a man who was all business and competent in his skill set. After being paged, he arrived at Ashley's room in about fifteen minutes and introduced himself to Jack Jackson and me. Isaac stood back, observing as I asked questions about Ashley's status and prognosis. When Isaac declared that he'd already heard what there was to know, I raised a hand, looked him in the eye, and let it be known that I intended to hear firsthand from Dr. Small what he knew about my wife's condition and discuss a few things in private. Isaac gave me his usual dominant male stare, which I ignored to the best of my ability.

Dr. Small led me to a small office just off the central ICU nurses monitoring station. We sat, and he studied me for a long moment. I waited for him to speak, my breathing shallow, my expectations low, and my fear on tenterhooks.

"How are you?" began Bertram Small. "I understand you were assaulted as well."

I assumed he was trying to put me at ease, but I wanted to hear about Ashley, not have him mess with my head about my own injuries. But I went along. "Concussion," I said, moved my arm in the sling, "broken arm, couple of scrapes and bruises."

"How do you feel?"

"Headache," I began, "look, Doctor, this isn't about me."

He smiled kindly. "I know. To tell the truth, it is often difficult to discuss the hard facts, so sometimes I take a softer route. Helps me ease into sensitive issues."

"That bad, huh?"

He slipped a pair of half-glasses off his nose and let them drop on a lanyard, folded his hands in his lap, and nodded. "Yes. Your wife's traumatic head injury is one of the most serious I've had contact with. You've heard of the Glasgow Coma Scale?" I nodded but didn't have a clue what it meant. He went on. "Ashley's reading after twenty-four hours was in the lowest range, which usually predicts an unfortunate outcome."

"Like?"

He waited a moment. "Like death or long-term coma that the patient is not likely to survive."

I blinked, looked at my hands, and experienced a swimming sensation in my head. "This can't be," I said, ridiculous of course. The doctor looked at me without responding. I couldn't focus my eyes, my chest tightened—every sensation of anxiety flooded my body. Dr. Small drew water from a sink in the office into a paper cup and handed it to me. I gulped at it, slobbering much of it onto my shirt.

There we sat, waiting for me to gather myself. After a bit I said, "Now what?"

Dr. Small seemed relieved for a question. "We wait," he said. When I just stared back, he added, "We won't know for sure if there is a remote chance that she may show some sign of recovery. Doubtful, but we'll still monitor her for some time."

"She won't come out of the coma, will she?" When he shook his head, I asked, "How long?"

"No way of knowing. Could be weeks." He raised his hands. "Might be a very long time, months, in some cases even years."

I looked into his eyes, which were filled with sympathy, and said, "There is something you need to know, something you may have already observed. My father-in-law, Isaac Tucker, is

55

dedicated to his daughter."

"Yes, I've noted that."

"And he assumes he is in charge of Ashley's outcome here. Frankly, he and I don't much get along. He even blames me for what happened. I want you and this institution to know that my wife and I had an advance directive drawn up several years ago after a friend of ours went through hell when her husband was dying and they hadn't gotten around to a living will. Anyway, I am designated to make decisions about Ashley's medical care through our durable power of attorney."

"Glad to hear it."

"The thing is, Isaac is not going to be happy to learn that he has no say in her care."

"I understand. I've been around such family discord before, many times."

I cupped my left hand under the cast. "Look, Doctor, I need to get something clear. No, more than clear, absolute, set in stone." When his eyes narrowed, I said, "At no time is Isaac Tucker to make independent decisions about my wife's care."

"I'm sure that won't be—"

I held up a hand and stopped him. "Not to be rude, but my father-in-law has a way of getting what he wants. He can be aggressive, threatening even. I don't want one of your nurses or colleagues to be swayed by him at any time. He can be persuasive. He'll certainly assert that he is her father and will expect his wishes to be granted. Can't happen."

Dr. Small nodded. "You get us a copy of your advance directive, and I'll see that it is put through channels and in her records. And I'll pass the word to all concerned here." He rose from his chair, ready to return to his duties. "Of course at this point there will virtually be no options to consider, for some time anyway. Your wife will remain in her coma, so there will be no assertions your father-in-law can make that will have any legitimacy."

───────

I returned to Ashley's room; she was alone. Nothing had changed, nor was it likely to. I understood that then. The *being* on the bed was only vaguely reminiscent of the woman I'd had dinner with just three nights ago—my wife in form only, breathing with artificial assistance, unable to give me the atonal greeting I had grown accustomed to. I moved closer to the bed and looked down at the damaged face until it began to assume familiarity. My eyes were dry. It dawned on me that I had moved from agonizing grief to the sober realization that everything had changed and I had no control over my wife's terrible prognosis, and with it my own life.

She was in there; I just couldn't get to her. It came to me right then that Ashley was the person I was meant to be with. In spite of the gulf between us much of the time, I truly sensed that we were preordained in some way. At least that is what I felt at first blush. And there were elements of our relationship that linked us with no relief—those aspects restrained us from dissolving our "us" in favor of our separate selves. I knew it was Ashley's separate self that was paramount for her. As I had revisited in my dream, I loved her even while I was purely a chess piece in her life, or at least I thought so. It wasn't that our marriage ever decayed. It began on a certain note for her, and there it remained; there was no degradation between us because her opinion of me was locked in and never rose beyond her assumptions, or fell short for that matter. She'd held me in a sterile comfort zone from which I never strayed. At that moment, I wondered if Gloria Denham had heard what had happened to us. I shuddered at having such thoughts as I peered down. It was not guilt so much as it felt like a social error. My god man, I thought, get a grip.

Jack Jackson came back into the room and stood beside me; he held a paper cup of coffee. "How'd it go?" he asked. "With the doctor?"

"She's never coming back."

Jack's eyes widened when I turned to him.

"That's how it went with the doctor."

"Surely there's some hope."

I used my free hand to knuckle an eye. "No. Like Isaac said, it's no damn good. Injuries are too profound."

Jack sipped from his cup and stood silent. We both did for several minutes. "What's that mean?" he asked finally. "If you don't mind my asking."

I looked into his soft bulldog face and smiled. "It means nothing right now except that she will not recover, ever."

"Like hell." It was Isaac. He stepped past me closer to the bed. "You don't know shit." He looked down at Ashley's inert form. "That what the doctor told you? Well then, he don't know shit either."

The man's face was lined with his years and from long-term exposure to the out of doors. But now there were more wrinkles crimped tightly in defiance of an actuality he'd not yet accepted, maybe would never accept. At that moment, my feelings actually went out to him; I felt a lump in my throat, and a small wave of empathy passed by.

Isaac pulled a handkerchief out of his back pocket and snorted into it. "And if that's the way you feel about it, get the hell out." When he saw my expression of incredulity, he squared up before me and added, "I mean it. Ashley should never have married you, you spineless example of a man. Look at you. Just when she needs a husband to stand by her, she has you. Pathetic. You... you just never mind. I'll take care of her and see she recovers. Now git."

I sensed Jack's umbrage beside me. He was no doubt waiting for me to respond. And it was true, I was fighting my own nature, that of going along to get along. I stared into Isaac's bulging eyes and wished for that moment to evaporate. The three of us stood as if hypnotized, counting our breaths and exacerbated heartbeats. Isaac stuffed his handkerchief back into his pocket, the ventilator continued its methodical cycle, and we all stood stark still.

"No, Isaac, you won't," I said after too much time had gone by.

He threw his head back. "I won't what? I'll take care of my girl, not you."

I nodded. "Of course you will care about her and be here for her. I understand and welcome that. As her father you have that right. But I will be the one to make decisions about her care."

"Like hell," he came back.

"As her husband, I am her next of kin and legally appointed to make decisions about her medical care. You must accept that." I could see the rage build in him as I spoke.

"That is not the way it is going to be," he said, emphasizing each word.

"Yes, it is," I responded, offering him a sympathetic smile.

"Wipe that silly-ass grin off your face, you prick. You have no right to say how my child is cared for, no right."

"I do. Legally I do."

"Legally?"

"Yes, Ashley and I drew up our advance directives a some time ago and assigned each other to be the one who would make our medical decisions if the other was unable to. It's called a living will and durable power of attorney for health care."

"I know all that. Isobel and I had them." He raised a finger and pointed it at me. "But we'll just see about that. Just saying it don't make it true."

"It's true, Mr. Tucker," Jack spoke up. "I know for a fact because I was their witness when the documents were finalized. Ned's clearly named as Ashley's health care agent."

Isaac looked back and forth between us, eyes widened. "Don't make no difference. I'm not allowing you to decide what's best for her. No way. You...you have her already dead. Well, I don't. She'll come out of this, and I'm gonna make sure you don't keep her from being taken care of proper."

"We both want the same thing, Isaac," I responded. "You think I want her to die?"

He stepped close and put a forefinger against my chest. "I do think that. Get her outa your hair. Get rid of all the watching over her, maybe for a long time until she comes around. Yeah, I think that."

"That's reprehensible." Jack spoke with more strength to his voice than I'd ever heard.

"You think so," Isaac said, raising his voice. "We'll just see about all this. I've got lawyers."

We glared at each other and fell silent. Isaac returned to the chair he'd been in and dropped down like a sack of cement. After another visit from the nursing staff, I told Isaac that I was leaving but would return tomorrow with our kids, who were on their way.

He thought about that, nodded, said that would be good. He was close to his grandchildren. "But don't you be brainwashing them about their mom. Making them think she's got no chance to come back. Don't you dare."

Jack and I left with Isaac slouched in the chair, peering over at his daughter as if he could rouse her by merely willing it. When I told him again I'd be back with my kids, he didn't react. I felt sadness for the man, but I had to come to grips with the fact that our long-term dislike of one another was about to intensify. How long could Ashley linger, and how much animosity could we all endure?

Jack drove me home. My kids were there. And there was a potted plant on the porch with a gift card attached.

-8-

I entered the house carrying the flowering plant; the tag said it was a gardenia. Never liked the way that particular flower smelled. I set it on the hall table and headed for the sound of voices coming from the kitchen. I saw them a moment before they caught sight of me. They were seated at the kitchen table; they had liberated a couple of beers from the refrigerator, which they were quietly consuming. It was always amazing to see them now as the adults they had become, each unique, each so much a part of us, and yet fully their own beings; it made my heart ache.

"Hey!" I said too loudly. "Here you are."

They started and jumped up. "Dad," they spoke in unison and came to me. Rosalind ducked under my raised arm in the cast, actually grabbed me, and held on in a very strong embrace. She wasn't usually the huggy type; she was her mother's child in that regard and usually had little patience with her father. I'd often been an embarrassment to her with her friends. I hugged her back hard and relished the moment, holding my cast away from our clutching. When she let go, my son grabbed me in like manner, and we swayed back and forth until he stepped back, tears glistening in his eyes.

Roz was sobbing now, her arms crisscrossed over her chest. She so resembled Ashley with her ash-blonde hair, blue eyes, and lovely wide mouth. It seemed surreal to see her in such an emotional state, not that she wasn't moved by dramatic events, but mostly she handled crises coolly, just like her mother, controlling her outward response. But right then she was visibly heartbroken.

Mike wiped at his eyes. "So you saw her?"

I nodded and couldn't speak for a long moment. "Just got back. A man from my office drove me down and back." When they looked at me expectantly, I said, "It is very bad."

"She'll recover though," Roz said, eyes wide. "Right? She'll come out of the coma?"

I smiled at her through my own bubbles of tears. "No, honey, they don't think so."

They fell silent; we stood in a semicircle looking at one another, at the floor, at anything. At one point, Mike smiled and reached out to thump a loosely held fist against my cast. I grinned and brandished it like a weapon. For a while we all sat at the table, finished a few more beers until I suggested we order in a pizza; no one was interested in going out to eat, and the larder was all but depleted. When I alerted security at the gate for the pizza delivery, I remembered that I was going to find out how our attackers gained entry. Just the thought of that gave me a chill.

The three of us consumed much of a large combo pizza from Luigi's but stopped short of the total annihilation that we would normally have exhibited. My kids seemed to want to just sit in the kitchen and be together. They asked about the attack after seeing the crude repairs to the kitchen door. They wanted to know if I was okay and seemed relieved that other than the broken arm and a grudgingly persistent headache, I would be okay. Eventually I told them that their grandfather was staying in Pocatello to be near their mother.

"I came back because I knew you'd be arriving soon." I waited, wiped some pizza residue off my face, considered how to say what had to be said. Instead I vacillated. "I...well, I'm glad you both arrived safe and sound." My made-up grin was worse than frowning.

"What?" Mike asked. "Dad?"

Roz studied me in I her serious way. "What aren't you telling us?"

I pushed the pizza box aside and leaned my good arm on the table. "I'm sure it's no secret to you that your grandfather and I have never been best buddies."

"Like yeah," Roz said. "Like forever. That's not news, Dad."

I chuckled from a sense of relief. "Right."

"So, what?" Mike asked.

"Isaac. He and I are in disagreement over your mom's condition." Their eyes were boring into mine. "I had a discussion with the neurosurgeon who is overseeing her treatment—if you can call it that. It is his opinion, following their complete medical assessment, that your mom's traumatic brain injury is so severe and the early testing so conclusive, that it is almost a certainty she will never recover."

"But Grandpa isn't buying that, is that it?" Mike said.

I nodded. "That's right. And he thinks I'm caving in, accepting this Dr. Small's evaluation, which your grandfather thinks is bullshit."

"Could he be right?" Roz asked.

"There's this test they run on anyone who has had a traumatic brain injury. There's a scale that tells doctors after twenty-four hours what a person's outcome is likely to be."

Mike looked right into me. "And this doctor says Mom's chances are really bad?"

"That's right."

"So Grandpa is just hoping." My son took in a deep breath. "But that's okay, isn't it, him not wanting to give up even if the odds are all bad?"

"Of course. I want the medical assessment to be wrong, too. But you also need to know that I am legally in charge of making the final decisions on your mother's care."

Roz leaned back in her chair. "That must not set well with Grandpa, I'm guessing."

"He's livid on that point." I smiled. "His long-held disapproval of me has found added traction. He feels he should be the one to make all decisions about his daughter."

"Why shouldn't he?" Roz said in her blunt way.

Mike put down a cold piece of pizza he'd bitten into. "'Cause that's the way it's supposed to be between a man and his wife."

"Do you love her?" Roz asked as if she were asking me how I liked the pizza.

For a moment all I could do was look at her, into those blue eyes, which had turned into marbles. "What?" That was all I could get out.

"It's…well I mean I've always felt that there was something not quite right between you and mom."

I looked back and forth between them. Mike was looking at his sister as if she had cursed at me. Who knew? She might yet. "Yes, I love her." The pitch of my voice rose. "Of course I love her. How could you ask me that?"

She tipped her head the way she had done as a teenager when she was in her resentful mood. "Because, I knew how it was."

"What was? What are you talking about?"

"Remote," she answered. "That's what I'd call it, remote. You and mom were distant like. Never saw you hug except on special occasions when it was expected, anniversaries and the like."

"We hugged."

"Uh-huh," she smirked.

"Roz," Mike came in, "what are you doing? So what if they didn't hug every minute? How about you and the plumber? You have hugging marathons back in Laramie?"

"Fuck you."

"Stop it." I slapped the table with an open palm. "Your mother is lying in a coma in a hospital bed and here we are sparring. We're feeling helpless, I know. We cannot fix her. Maybe no one can fix her, so we need to be good to each other."

Roz stared at me as if she wanted to slap me. "That night," she said, "when those creeps broke in here, what happened?"

I shrugged. "It was like I said, fast and terrible."

"You couldn't stop them?"

I bit down. "We were cleaning up after a late dinner, both of us with our hands full. The damn door blew in, and they charged in swinging bats. Aluminum bats."

"Did you fight with them?" she pushed at me.

"Fight with them? How? It was a crash, two, three ticks of the clock, lights out, wake up in the hospital."

"So you didn't try to stop them. I know you said too fast, but still—"

"Damn it, Roz, you sound just like Isaac."

"Oh yeah, how so?"

I cursed myself. "Never mind."

"Roz, leave him alone," Mike broke in.

"No," she raised her voice. "I want to know what Grandpa said."

I held up a hand. "All right. Okay. When I woke up in the hospital, he was there in my room. He didn't want to be there, but he came by to tell me what had happened to your mom and where they'd taken her." I inhaled. "That's when he said I should have protected his little girl. Kept her from harm was how he put it."

"Could you have, Dad?" It was Mike asking. "Saved her? Sounds like it was too fast."

I clasped my hands on the table and massaged them. "It was... it was too fast. Still, ever since Isaac threw that guilt trip at me, I've gone back over that night, every second, and wondered. If I'd only acted more quickly, maybe if I'd thrown myself at them, between Ashley and me. You know, what if?"

When I stopped, we all sat frozen in place, pondering our own thoughts. I guess I'd given my two children a spoonful of doubt about their father's courage and if the impossible had been possible—me saving their mother from injury.

Roz pounded a clenched fist on the table. "So maybe you could have saved her!"

"Roz, honey."

"Don't you *Roz honey* me," she barked. "Not with mom off

somewhere with tubes in her and maybe never coming back to us." She shoved her chair back and stomped out of the kitchen, throwing the word *coward* behind her.

Mike ran a hand through his tousled head of brown hair and pulled on his prominent nose. We sat looking at each other like two people who had just heard their dog had died. Mike got up and cleared the pizza box and beer bottles then came back and sat down.

"You know, Dad, she'll have forgotten all that by morning."

"No, Mike, she won't."

My kids slept in their old rooms. I went back to the master bedroom and felt Ashley's presence all over again. Before retiring, I'd listened to the messages on my phone; there were a dozen or more, most wishing me condolences, and Jack Jackson had called to see if I was okay and to remind me that my cell phone was off. There were two calls in particular that brought tension with them. One was from Gloria Denham, with whom I'd had the brief affair some time ago, but not all that long ago, come to think of it. Her message was warm and sympathetic; there was no suggestion that we see one another, even to commiserate over my predicament. The other was from Sylvia Winters, a woman who had become a client of the firm and was someone I had to hold at arm's length. She had clearly become attracted to me, and her message of condolence was syrupy and too familiar. The gardenia plant was from her; I would trash it the next morning.

I tried to read in bed to get drowsy. A novel, written by a local author we knew, only served as a blurry bulletin board; my mind stared at the pages, nothing registered, and I was still wide awake. Besides, my head was hurting. I gulped down two prescribed pain pills and lay back. After an hour or so of staring into the dark, I got up and went into the living room. where I finally fell asleep on the couch. It had not been a good day.

A pain in my back stabbed me awake. The soft couch hadn't

been my best friend. I sat up to find Mike seated across from me in a club chair dressed in Jockey shorts and a Montana Griz tee shirt; his mop of hair had a bad case of bed head, with strands wildly askew. My receding hairline was jealous. He held up a cup of coffee. I nodded. He left and returned with a cup emblazoned with our company logo and sat back down. The acrid bite of the black brew acted like smelling salts, clearing my head. It was quiet in the house, so I assumed he and I were the only ones up. According to the mantel clock, it was only six thirty.

After a couple of swallows, I looked at my son. "Roz?"

"I looked in. She's dead to the world."

"You sleep okay?"

"No," he answered. "Not a wink." He crossed his legs and sat on them as only young joints can do. "This is so surreal. You and Mom being attacked in quiet old Latham. You know, when I was a kid, we never locked the front door when we lived on Tyler Street. Remember?"

I nodded and smiled as best I could. "I do. And you always left your bike lying in the front yard."

"Right, that's right. And now this. And Mom, the most can-do person I know, in a coma and maybe never coming out of it. I can't get my head around any of it."

I stood, holding my empty cup. "We'll go see her today. It will be hard, Mike, but maybe seeing her will help you experience the reality of it, and you'll be able to come to grips with it in some way."

"No," he said. "I'll never come to grips with my mom gone but not gone. No. Have you...come to grips with it?"

I saw the question in his eyes and realized that he, like Roz, was weighing his estimation of my culpability in the upheaval they had been handed. My answer was likely one he'd latch on to and keep in his memory of this time forever. I juggled my response before blurting, "Of course not. Why do you think I was on the couch? You mother is right here." I tapped the side of my head. "I had to get out of our bed, the one we've slept in together, to get away from that space we shared. But I've also seen her. I've gone through the gut-wrenching anguish you've yet to experience. At some point, I'll have to absorb my agony so I can concentrate on overseeing her care." I stepped toward him and looked down as he uncurled his legs. "Do you understand what I'm saying?"

My son stood, took the cup from my hand, and said softly, "I don't know what to think." He walked off, taking our empty cups into the kitchen, and all I could do was watch him. I felt it: he doubted me and perhaps didn't even trust me.

"I'm with him." It was Roz. "I need to see Mom. See how she really is and what Grandpa has to say."

I talked them into having breakfast in town at Rudy's Diner, where we ate without any conversation except for Roz telling me she wouldn't be riding with Mike and me to Pocatello.

She would take her own car in case she wanted to spend more time with Ashley, but mainly she wasn't coming back to our house. It was clear she had no interest in spending any more time with me. The day was off to a grand beginning.

The moment we hit the road, Mike loaded a Lady Gaga CD into the player in his Volkswagen Jetta, and we rode the entire eighty miles with the music buffering the fact that we had nothing to say to each other right then. Parents never know for sure how their children regard them—especially fathers. Of course we all go through that phase when our teenagers declare their hatred of us and when we are nothing but an embarrassment to them in front of their friends. Beyond those laughable moments, when our offspring move on into adulthood, we can only wonder how we are perceived: our values, our strength of character, our choice of career, our bodies, and most importantly our demeanor—are we joyful to be around or not? But when a catastrophe occurs, that is when the parental traits of courage, trustworthiness, and honor are put to the ultimate test with children—I can verify that fact. That day in March, I was filled not only with remorse for my wife but in addition I had to accept that my children thought less of me than I could have imagined. With the music playing and my head aching, I sat still, fixed my eyes on the highway dividing line, and floated in a cloud-like realm, assessing who I really was. I was still in that sphere when Mike parked in the hospital parking garage and finally disengaged Lady Gaga. A minute later, Roz pulled in right next to us in her big SUV. She sat in her vehicle with her head down. Mike and I waited. Finally she got out, and I led them into the hospital.

At their mother's room, I stood back and let them enter on their own. Both were hesitant, but it was Roz who stepped forward and walked in and went up to the bed. Mike stood back a bit. I know the shock they were feeling, seeing the same medical trappings I'd been exposed to; it had been a blow to me, and now to them in turn. After a minute or so they grabbed onto each other. Their sobs cut into me, all the more so since I knew they weren't sure if I'd done right by their mother. As I stood back watching, Isaac strode by out of nowhere and wrapped his long arms around Ashley's children.

I watched but then couldn't stand to see their emotional outpouring, especially knowing that I was excluded, an outlier at that moment. While they embraced and cried and circled about, I went out to the nursing station and found the acting nurse supervisor. She accepted the copy of the witnessed advance directive I'd brought from home and agreed to see that it was processed properly. It was clear that she knew the implications of that document in our particular case and reached out to touch my arm; it was the only sign of empathy I was likely to receive that day.

———

It was after five o'clock that afternoon when Mike and I started the drive back to Latham. Both he and Roz had been thoroughly indoctrinated by their grandfather and hung tightly to the hope that their mother could recover—beyond hope, expectation. I tried to be wallpaper as much as possible and did nothing to counter Isaac's tirade about his daughter certain to make a full recovery. I wasn't convinced that my kids bought fully into their grandfather's assertion, but they were so freshly wounded they needed to believe in some form of positive outcome. His block-headed stubbornness didn't seem out of the realm of possibility to them.

Roz had decided to drive straight back to Laramie, seeming to understand that there was little of anything she could do for her mother at that moment. Maybe later, she told Mike, later for sure. She gave Isaac an enormous hug before leaving. In the parking garage she hugged Mike good-bye. They cried some more; then she gave me an obligatory squeeze and drove away. Mike drove me home, playing Lady Gaga once more, and headed back to Missoula the next day. It was Sunday, and I was alone again. It was three and a half weeks until the tax deadline, and I didn't give a damn.

-9-

The next three months went by like a slow-moving freight train that never reached its destination. In that time, I had been to see Ashley twice a week in the beginning, but nothing changed. She remained in a deep coma. Dr. Bertram Small usually came around whenever I visited and updated me on my wife's status and prognosis. It was never good; I guess I had already accepted that her outcome would not include recovery. Not so Isaac Tucker. He remained adamant that his daughter would awaken from her unconscious state and prove the doctors wrong and me to be a pathetic weakling. He had prowled the hospital corridors many more times than I had, until even he realized that if his Ashley was to recover it would a very long process, so his visits slowed to once a week. Likewise, I began going to Pocatello less and less, eventually limiting my conversations with Dr. Small to brief phone calls. The thing facing me then was how long before I had to move Ashley to a long-term care facility. The medical implications were that her persistent state hadn't been showing any signs of improvement, nor were they likely to, and before long she would have to be transferred out of the hospital.

There were only three things on my to-do list; those included my visits to see Ashley, persistently pestering the police about their investigation into the attack, and avoiding going to work. I had no social life, even though in the beginning there had been a few invitations. My partners at Jackson, Vogel & Pine had given me a long leash and a great deal of sympathy; I took advantage of them. Once a week either Jack Jackson or Claude Vogel would call me to see how I was and ask if Ashley's condition had improved. I could count on a call from one of them every Wednesday about mid-morning, that being the day and time we always held our weekly partners' meeting.

It all began in 1986 when Ashley and I were in the throes of infatuation. It was obvious to me that I wanted to spend my life with her and just as obvious that I would never get her to leave Latham and working with her father. Shortly after I'd been let go by Laxell & Crowne in Boise, I received a phone call from Jack Jackson of the then Jackson & Associates CPAs. Amazingly, he had heard that I had left Laxell & Crowne and was interested in meeting with me to discuss a position with his firm. I puffed up with my own self-esteem and agreed to a meeting; only afterward did it dawn on me how improbable it was that Jack Jackson could have heard of a lone green associate in Boise who'd just lost his job. Later when I accused Ashley of setting things up with Jackson, she merely said, *So what? We're a client, so why not use a little leverage?* I met with Jack in his storefront office of those days and sheepishly tried to act as if the meeting hadn't been wired. He and I have laughed many times about that trumped-up job interview, and yet we were both glad it happened. Later he brought in Claude Vogel as his first partner, a man with considerable experience, and they both agreed after three years that I should be on the letterhead as well. I bought into the firm with a loan from my wife; of course all parties concerned knew where that money came from—and how reluctantly it was given. But Isaac Tucker never denied his Ashley anything, even if he had to swallow the sour taste afterward. The part of that story I'm proudest of is that I long ago paid off the money owed to my father-in-law.

———

Matters grew more convoluted by mid-June that year. To begin with, the time had come to move Ashley out of the hospital. Dr. Small and his colleagues had determined that her coma was a persistent state and that they did not expect any improvement. It was time to move her into a long-term care facility. I chose the Garnet Skilled Nursing & Rehab Center right in Latham. Isaac Tucker was irate at first because he saw moving Ashley out of the hospital as giving up on her ultimate recovery, something he would never accept. The saving grace was that she would be right in town where he could see her whenever he wanted to without eighty miles of highway to navigate again and again. The staff at the care center accepted Ashley with intense grace and treated Isaac and me with kindness and understanding; they became familiar with Isaac's demanding ways and accepted his crusty nature as that of a devoted father. They absorbed his bullying better than I would have. He and I sort of adopted a schedule for our visits so we didn't have to run into one another often. He preferred mornings; I visited in the afternoons.

———

My other primary pursuit was the investigation into the attack. Police Detective C. T. Morgan had gotten used to my calls, and I'd gotten used to his claims of no progress in locating the men who had invaded our home. "There is so little to go on, Ned," he said again and again.

"What about the security guard on duty that night? Anything on him?" I'd always ask. A couple of days after the kids had gone, I went out to the guard station, to inquire about the guard who'd been on duty the night of the attack—he'd quit. The police tried to locate him, but he had skipped town. The company, A-Ball Security, had no forwarding address.

"We're still looking for him," Detective Morgan would say again. "So far no leads."

"He has to be somewhere," I'd retort. "Didn't he have family here or friends?"

"No. He was a loner. But we'll keep looking." That was as far as I got each time.

———

That's how I spent time back then, until the day after the Fourth of July, a Monday, around lunchtime. I was eating another of the turkey sandwiches I'd perfected, when the doorbell rang— odd, because there had been no call from security at the gate. I hated the enclosure thing, but you did get used to the privacy part. I wiped mayonnaise off my fingers and went to the front door, and there stood a worst moment. Sylvia Winters, one of our most prized JV&P clients, was all teeth and smile; my gut took a turn.

"Hi Sylvia," I said with feigned pleasantness. "How did you get in?"

"You mean the guard shack guy?" She laughed. "I'm your sister from out of town, didn't you know? I put on my saddest face and got right in."

I nodded. "I'll have to have a talk with that guy."

"Now, don't ruin things," she said. "May I come in? I have something good." She held up a casserole dish covered with aluminum foil. "My famous beef stroganoff."

Sylvia Winters was modestly striking to look at. She wasn't beautiful or sensual but had the best smile of any woman I knew: very white teeth, nice-to-look-at lips, and a *here-I-am* attitude that culminated with flashing brown eyes that crinkled at the corners when she was energized. That day she was energized; I didn't want her to be. I didn't even want her there.

I was more or less forced into meeting Sylvia when Claude Vogel cajoled me into taking her on, moving her account under my client banner to help alleviate his overload—that was the story. Sounded good at the time, since Winters Fine Foods was a linchpin among our client base. Sylvia had assumed control of the food processing company when her husband, R. J. Winters, known to one and all as Reggie, had died suddenly of a massive heart attack; that had been over ten years before. She took the small but successful company, which had been primarily known for its wholesale frozen potato products, and had grown it into a major player in the prepared foods industry: everything from gelatin salads, slaws, desserts, potato salad, Mexican foods, baked sides and dinners—over five hundred products—were distributed in all western states and Canada through major grocery chains and independent outlets.

Sylvia Winters was a local icon in our small city. She gave money to local charities, saw the Winters name emblazoned on civic buildings, and was sought after to be on local nonprofit boards. Winters Fine Foods had become a power broker in Latham and beyond, so why did Claude Vogel hand off such a prized client to me, the junior partner? That was a question I pondered, but just for a moment before my avarice took over and I readily agreed to Claude's proposal. My portfolio just expanded exponentially.

"I asked for you, you know." Those were the initial words out of her mouth on my first visit to her office.

"Really?" I replied. Right then I had a tingle of wariness flit across my back. "Why's that?"

She flashed the smile I would come to know so well. "Oh, let's just say that Claude and I were getting a bit stale. He's been our go-to guy ever since we moved to your firm. What's that been? At least seven or eight years I'd say, you think?"

"You'd know," I responded.

"Yes, it's been about that long since we made the move from the Carson group. You know them?"

"I do. Good firm."

She puckered her face and shook her head. "Stodgy. Out of touch. We were looking for a progressive CPA firm. Would you say you're progressive?"

I squirmed. What was the right answer for this woman who represented the second largest piece of business for the firm? "What does progressive mean to you?" I ventured.

"Good comeback," she said. "For one thing, it means that I will see you more than once or twice a year. You know, no just stop in once a year, churn out an audit report, stick your head in the door and say ta-ta, and the rest of the time all we get is one of your bright young associates on site. I want a CPA firm that is proactive, is able to provide consulting services—in other words hold our hand on these matters. We're a growing concern and need accounting and business services to keep up with the pack." She leaned her arms on the desk and looked right at me, eyes twinkling. "You going to hold my hand, Ned?"

"Of course, I'll work with your CFO as often as necessary and find ways to improve your company's performance."

She slumped back, and I watched her face lose its sparkle. Sylvia was just short of fifty, but she worked very hard at looking younger and for the most part succeeded. She knew how to dress, packaging her body to its best advantage; her makeup was expertly applied, accentuating her assets and shading over her less pleasing facial features. Clothes, jewelry, and all other accessories were the best money could buy. Needless to say, she didn't shop for her wardrobe in Latham.

"That's not why I asked for you, Ned," she had replied. While I waited for her to disclose her reason, she pulled a lipstick from her center desk drawer and made a run over her lips. "I'm wanting a more one-on-one relationship with our lead financial guru." When she spoke, her freshly glossed lips shone with a red coral hue.

"I see."

"Do you? I hope so. You see, Ned, with our company growing as it is, I need to be in constant touch with every aspect of our financial structure." She paused and seemed to examine my face. "You follow?"

"Of course. A good practice."

Her smile back at me was mischievous; at least it felt that way, and I would be proven right. "And practice makes perfect, as they say. So you agree?"

"I do." Where was this going?

"All right then, I look forward to seeing you...and often."

As I left her on that first visit, she followed me to the office door, took my extended hand, and held it between both of her hands until I gently pulled away. She smiled, knowing that I was caught off guard, placed an open palm against my chest, and whispered that she would see me again. I queried Claude Vogel about his professional relationship with Sylvia Winters—had it gone beyond business? He hadn't a clue what I was referring to. Did I mean socially, he asked. He recalled being invited to the company Christmas party once or twice. That was about it.

And there she stood at my front door, splendidly attired as usual, holding out a casserole dish. After an awkward stretch of hesitation, I stood back. She stepped right past me, asked where the kitchen was, and marched off when I gestured. Had she ever been in the house? I guessed not and followed along, struggling to quash my feelings of being caught in the grasp of a least-favorite moment. I grimaced when she looked around for an open space to put the casserole down: there was none. Dishes, pans, coffee cups, wine glasses, and encrusted silverware covered every inch of surface. After my apologies for the mess and an ungraceful attempt at decision-making, I agreed that the dish should go into the refrigerator to be warmed up later.

Whenever a woman enters another woman's home, she gives the domicile her personal appraisal, an assessment of domesticity that cannot be denied. I observed Sylvia Winters doing that as I led her into the living room. It is always subtle, that reckoning: eyes moving deftly from room to room, artifact to artifact, perhaps comparing the surroundings with those of her own, for better or worse, whatever the equation. After a bit of standing in place, we settled into club chairs separated by a lamp table; I looked into my lap and clasped my hands as Sylvia Winters adjusted her skirt and looked about.

"So," she spoke first, "how are you, Ned?"

"Oh, I'm doing okay."

"Fully recovered?"

"Mostly." I raised my atrophied arm. "Cast has been off my arm for a spell. Still have headaches a little. But, yeah, mostly good."

"But not back at work yet?"

I crossed one leg over another and gripped my knee. "That's right, not yet." When she studied me without further comment, I went on. "Not quite ready."

"Doctor's orders?"

"No, that's not it."

She smiled without showing her big white teeth. "How is your wife doing?"

I swallowed and looked across the room at a photograph of Ashley that stood on a bookshelf. I sensed that Sylvia saw me; when I turned back, she too was studying the photo. Her face was unsmiling when she looked at me again.

"Not well," I said, my voice tightened. "I just moved her into the Garnet nursing home two weeks ago. Long-term care."

"I heard. But she'll recover?"

My teeth clenched involuntarily. "Actually, it's very unlikely that she will recover, ever. She's still in a deep coma. The kind very few people come out of."

She remained poised, sitting straight and calm in the chair, and seemed to consider her words before she spoke again. "But it can happen, recovery. Even after a long time, I read somewhere."

How odd to hear that from this woman. "I suppose," I said. "But the neurosurgeon has cautioned me to not raise my hopes in Ashley's case. The rarity of recovery is such that the cases where people have revived after months or years are very few and scientifically historical."

"You've given up, then."

I felt my face flush both from her accusation and my resentment. When I didn't respond, she apologized. "No," I said, "you're right, I suppose I have—given up. I don't know what else to do."

"Oh, Ned," she uttered, her face sagging into a mask of concern. "I'm so sorry for you. You've been on my mind constantly since I first heard of it, the attack." When I shrugged, she said, "No really. Claude and Jack were besieged by my calls." Suddenly she stood and walked over to Ashley's photograph and picked it up. "I wanted to come by, to see you. So many times I started to drive over here, so many times. But it didn't feel right. I had to wait a decent amount of time—don't you see? I just couldn't barge in on your pain."

I nodded. "Sure. I understand. I'd have done the same thing."

She put the photograph down and walked back toward me. "I've missed our one-on-one sessions. Claude, he's been filling in, doing a good job, but it isn't the same."

"He's a good man."

"He is, it's just that…"

"Sylvia," I said, standing, "thanks so much for coming by and for the casserole."

She was caught off guard by my abrupt leave-taking utterance but after a blank moment regained her composure, smiled, and said, "Of course. My pleasure. Be sure and reheat the stroganoff in the oven at 325 for about twenty minutes."

"I'll try and remember."

"You will." She stepped up and grabbed me in a hug then took my face between her hands and kissed me full on the mouth until I carefully pulled away. The scent of her tangy perfume hung around for some time after she had gone.

Sylvia had first come on to me a month after I had begun meeting with her professionally. It had become obvious that she was flirtatious and enjoyed being with me. In the beginning I accepted her advances as part of the business relationship and perhaps as the result of her having been solo for so many years. On that first occasion, we had completed a long post-audit session, and I agreed to join her for dinner at the local steak house. We'd finished off our meals and a bottle of excellent red wine and were both feeling the effects. After a trip to the women's room, she came back and slid into the booth on my side, pushed her body right up against me, and hung a slobbery kiss on me. I went along with it but was not interested in more of the same. My reluctance earned me a bleary-eyed forewarning, which clearly meant Mrs. Winters was not to be denied. It took every bit of my artful discretion to maintain the business side of our connection and not get tied up in an ongoing liaison.

So that day, the hand delivery of homemade stroganoff reignited a long-held wariness when it came to the queen of prepared foods.

-10-

As the days passed, I became nothing more than a hermit, a strange man who let his facial hair grow a week at a time, whose wardrobe consisted of the same three pairs of Levi's worn in rotation with a fine selection of weathered tee shirts, battle-scarred running shoes, and a faded Boise State baseball cap. I shopped once a week at Albertson's to stock up on food needing no culinary expertise; ironically I was losing weight on that fare. The only other regular stops were for a breakfast burrito at Juan's Mexican Grill when I felt like it, sit with Ashley for an hour every Monday, Wednesday, and Friday afternoon, and drop by the police station once a week to harass Detective Morgan. When C. T. Morgan saw me coming, his shoulders would slump, and then he'd rise from his desk and follow me back out to the coffee shop located across from the station. It was merely a ritual by then. I knew he would have nothing new to tell me about the case; he would have called in a heartbeat if even a shred of new evidence had surfaced. He never commented on my slovenly appearance, though I noticed him noticing.

I suppose I was lonely. Not sure how that was supposed to feel, but guessed I was close to fitting the definition. Have you ever thought of what it would be like if the most important person in your life was snatched away? I hadn't either. The only people I saw with any regularity were my neighbors Guy and Nancy Stewart and Alejandro the yardman. I had to keep Alejandro on or risk the homeowner's association giving me grief about an unkempt yard. However, I kept an eye on the bank account, which was diminishing bit by bit. I was continuing to receive compensation from the firm, but to live in the style Ashley coveted required both of our incomes. For a while, Isaac Tucker had kept paying his daughter's salary, but that stopped abruptly one day; he'd stuck a note in with the usual check that said it was the final compensation for services rendered by Ashley Tucker-Pine. I found out why he chose to do that when the Garnet Skilled Nursing & Rehab business manager asked me to stop by his office one day. He informed me that Tucker Construction carried Ashley's long-term care insurance. I knew that. What I didn't know was that the plan Isaac had purchased was limited to two years then would no longer cover her care. Isaac discussed the insurance plan's limitations and he said he would establish a fund to cover Ashley's care after the insurance had expired. He asked the business manager to be the one to tell me about his intentions. It all made sense to me; after all, Ashley was no longer working for Isaac, and I was grateful that he had the resources to pay for her care over time. Then again, I'd have to make long-range economic adjustments without her income.

On one forgetful Wednesday afternoon when I arrived for my usual quiet time with Ashley, I found Isaac Tucker waiting. He was thumbing through an old copy of *People Magazine*, which he set aside when I filled the doorway. We looked at one another for a long moment before he turned his gaze onto the still-life form of his daughter then back at me; his eyes were hard.

"Don't you look special," he said, scanning my disheveled condition. When I flushed, he added, "She'd be proud of your appearance, now wouldn't she?" By contrast he was attired in pressed khaki pants, a starched white button-down Polo shirt, and polished loafers. In comparison to my ragged mane, his granite gray hair was close cropped and neatly trimmed.

I eased into the room and stood at the foot of the bed. "How are you, Isaac?"

"But you're right," he went on, "Ashley can't give you *what for* anyhow now, can she?"

I didn't respond. My heartbeat had come up when I saw the man and now remained that way. "I got your note," I said, "the one in the last check."

"Did you now? Good. That's sort of why I'm here crowding in on your time with my daughter. It's good of you to keep up your regular visits, taking time away from your other important duties, I'm sure."

Ashley's face had its usual pallor. Her eyelids remained permanently closed, hair lifeless, as was everything else about her. I sat on the foot of the bed and looked over at my father-in-law. "What's on your mind?"

"Be careful where you're sitting there."

"I'm fine. You have something to say to me?"

"The accountant fellow, he talk with you? The business manager?"

"He did."

"Then you know. About the fund I'm setting up." I nodded. "Okay then. I'll be covering her care here when the policy runs out."

"That's a good thing," I said as carefully as I could. "It will be costly."

He turned again to Ashley; I saw him swallow hard. "That's no never mind. I want her back no matter the cost."

"We both do."

"That right? The difference is that you don't think she'll ever recover."

"Doesn't mean we can't hope," I said.

"But you don't think she'll be back, damn you."

I reached out and touched the blanket covering her legs and patted gently.

"Stop that!" he snapped. "Don't you touch her…not while I'm in the room."

I lifted my hand; the flare of anger filled my face. I squinted at him. "Are you deranged?"

"Disgusting," he grunted. When he saw my eyes open wide, he added, "Yeah, disgusting. You don't deserve her—you never deserved her. And now here you are, a slob, revolting."

I rose from the bed. "She chose me, Isaac, me." I walked over and leaned down, the only time I'd ever been above him, and thumbed my chest. "Me. And we loved each other."

"Bullshit. You were a miscalculation. A blunder. I tried to talk her out of it, marrying you."

"You couldn't though, could you?" I boasted.

"No. I couldn't. Know what she said? Said she'd live with it." He gave me a cynical grin. "She'd live with it. Feel special now?"

I choked a gasp. "She never said anything of the kind, you son-of-a-bitch."

"Think not? By your way of thinking, you'll never know. Me, I'll be here to welcome her back. Then she'll set the record straight, you waste of a life."

"I'd like you to leave now so I can spend time alone with my wife."

I could see from the crimped expression on his face that he was considering telling me to go to hell; instead he stood and once again looked down at me. "Fair enough," he said and started for the door. "Just one more thing. With me setting up this fund, I'll be making all the decisions for her from now on."

He turned to leave, and I said, "Not on your life. Set up the fund. That'll be good. But I'm still her legal arbiter and designee of her durable power of attorney."

Isaac froze in the doorway and came back right up to me. "Listen, you son-of-a-bitch, she's my daughter. I'll be making the calls now."

"No, Isaac, you won't."

He grabbed my shirtfront in two fists and drew me in. Even for a man nearing seventy, his body was muscular, and he was angry. I decided not to resist; I knew he wasn't going to actually strike me, not there, not in his daughter's space. "I will not have you deciding her medical care—do you understand? She will recover, and you will not stand in her way."

"Isaac, stop," I said and took ahold of his wrists and pulled his hands away. "You can't believe that I want anything less than you want."

"Oh but I do. You want her gone. I know it. I feel it."

"My god, man, are you out of your skull? I love her, same as you."

He pointed a thick forefinger at me. "I've got lawyers."

"You've said that before. Have you talked with them about this?" When he didn't respond, I said, "You have. I know you have. And did they tell you that you could override a durable power of attorney and my spousal rights? I thought not. Now let's just get along and see to Ashley's best interest—together."

He stepped back and squared his big shoulders. "Never. You don't believe, and I do." He turned to go then spun around, "By the way, they're bringing a special mattress in."

"Why?"

"See, you don't know everything. The director here, that Mrs. Carrington, she told me the doctor says Ashley needs to be moved regular like. Rotated so as to keep her lungs clear and stop bed sores and the like.

My face burned. "She never told me that."

"So what? Needs doing. This mattress will turn her automatically, every two hours. I okayed it," he said and walked out.

When he left the room, I felt the absence of his force of will; it was a relief. I sat with Ashley in the quiet, again knowing that she wasn't really there but still needing to be in her physical presence. How long would I feel that way? I didn't know. I stopped by the administrator's office on my way out and let Mrs. Carrington know my displeasure in not being advised about the rotating mattress. She apologized but thought Isaac's approval was all that was needed. She still didn't get it. At least it was being covered by the insurance for the present.

I wasn't really surprised when Jack Jackson called asking me to meet with him and Claude; I'd been expecting a summons. When I entered our office, it was alien space to me. The receptionist was a new, young face. I assumed Dorothy, who had been threatening to retire, had made good on her intention. The dark-haired, slender woman in her place gave me the kind smile extended to an unfamiliar face. When I pointed to the wall sign behind her and said I was Pine, she turned red and said, *oh, oh, oh,* as if she'd committed a sin. I patted the air to soothe the moment and walked away, leaving her unsure and embarrassed.

We gathered in Jack's office around a mahogany table. I'd actually showered, shaved, and put on a suit; I felt strangely constrained. The young receptionist appeared, carrying a tray laden with coffee service. In that moment of distraction, we each poured ourselves a cup, doctored our drinks, and retreated into our own thoughts. I felt Claude watching when I added cream and sweetener to my cup; I knew it would be his assertions that would set the tone for what was about to happen. After we had each taken a swallow, set our cups down, and looked at one another, he dutifully asked about Ashley. What else could I say? I hesitated, looked between them, and told them the truth: Ashley remained as she had been, no change, nor was there likely to be. Their facial expressions reflected their unique individualities: Jack was visibly stricken, Claude's expression implacable.

"My god, Ned." It was Jack who spoke first. "How can you handle that?"

"You don't," I answered. "I'm not. Not if by handling it you mean sleeping through the night, functioning at any useful level, and understanding what it all means." I took in a breath.

Neither man responded. "I see her. Three times a week I see her, sit with her, then promise myself I will come back again...see her one more time and the time after that."

Claude studied me over the rim of his coffee cup. "Makes one wonder," he said, "how a man can plod through daily life knowing that his life mate is out of reach and will never be back."

I heard Jack suck in a breath at the blunt reality of Claude's measured utterance. My response was, "It is not something you can train for. It is the finality that gets to you."

Claude nodded. "You've lost weight."

"Amazing, isn't it? Shouldn't be with the food I'm eating. I know the frozen food aisle at Albertson's intimately." They chuckled. "Used to run, too. Haven't done that in months."

"But you're fully recovered, aren't you?" Jack asked. "From the beating and all."

"Mostly, yeah. Broken arm is healed up and the concussion. I just get a headache every now and then. Guess that's some sort of residual from getting clobbered in the head."

Jack jutted his head out cautiously and asked, "Any news from the police...you know, about who did it?"

I shook my head, and they fell silent, acted like they were interested in their coffee, and glanced at one another. When Claude cleared his throat, I knew it was the moment I would learn what was on their minds. Of course I knew. I hadn't been a productive member of the firm for months. I had it coming, whatever it was.

"We've been wondering," Jack opened, "when you'd feel up to coming back to work?"

I looked at each of them in turn and smiled. "I can expect that's been on the agenda for a while. Surprised you haven't been after me before now."

"Come on, Ned," Jack countered. "You needed time."

"You've been more than generous. I'm sure your workload has been brutal."

"As a matter of fact, it has," Claude said. "We've added a couple of new associates, but they don't have your experience and contacts. It can't go on like this."

"Now wait, Claude," Jack said. "We've been doing okay. We're just saying it's time to discuss your plans, Ned."

"More than that, Ned," Claude said. "We need you back or…"

"Or what?" I asked.

Claude leaned on his forearms and looked directly into my face. "Look, there are some client issues that need your attention. We're on the verge of losing some significant ground."

"My attention? Okay, spell it out."

"Winters Foods, for one. Sylvia Winters wants you back on her account. I've been covering the bases, but she drank the Kool-Aid when you took over, and she wants you back—and now."

I thought of all her phone calls over the past weeks: invitations to join her for dinner, to attend a play at the community theater, or be her guest at a gala fundraiser for the Latham County Museum. I'd managed to politely refuse on each occasion, but Sylvia Winters was losing her patience, and Ashley's condition was wearing thin as an excuse.

"I see," I said. "What else?"

Claude looked at Jack and nodded for him to speak. "Isaac Tucker," Jack said. "He's taking his account to the Carson Group. Frankly, we were shocked by that one."

"Don't be," I responded. "Isaac and I, we have no fondness between us. Not a shred. Never have had. Hates my guts, if you want to know."

When the two men said nothing, I nodded. "Not news to you, then. Fact is, Isaac despised the fact that I married his daughter. Now we're at loggerheads over Ashley's care. He thinks I'm denying that she has any chance of recovery. I'm not denying anything. There's nothing to deny, because it is a medical impossibility that she will ever recover. So you see, me being Isaac's son-in-law gives this firm absolutely no influence on retaining Tucker Construction as a client."

The coffee grew cold. I could sense the polarity between them, Jack the peacemaker, Claude ever the bottom-line absolutist. It took about an hour for them to go through their list of clients and work-related assignments that my absence was impacting negatively. I listened, took a few notes, but in the end I didn't care. And I could tell they saw that in my face: an obvious disconnect, the abject passivity I knew I was conveying through my flaccid facial muscles, and my minimalist responses to their questions.

In the end, I decided that there wasn't any one of the dilemmas they'd laid out that really needed my golden touch—not one, not even Winters Fine Foods. When all of their complicating factors had been vocalized, both of the men leaned back in their chairs and studied me; Jack had sadness in his eyes, but Claude was exasperated. Of course I felt some guilt. After all, those men had taken me on when I was green and untested and we'd built something together.

I smiled lamely, stuffed my folded notes into an inside coat pocket, and said it was a lot to think about and I'd get back to them. Claude let the pen in his hand drop onto the table, a move I took as a sign of pique, and said, "Make it soon." I nodded, and he added, "You might think about getting a haircut."

-11-

As soon as I got back home, I stripped out of my suit and tie, got back into a pair of Levi's, a Seattle Seahawks tee shirt, and a light-weight runner's jacket, and went out for an early night at Little Ray's Barbeque Pit. I hunkered down in a back booth where a man alone could feel comfortable and devoured a huge Texas-style beef brisket sandwich and washed it down with three Idaho Pale Ales. I began to feel almost content.

That was until I parked my SUV in the drive back at the house, belched in honor of my good feelings, and sort of weaved for the front door, keys in hand. My comfort zone was about to be tested. Her voice came out of the dark.

"Had a good time, did we?"

I jerked up, keys extended. "God, Sylvia, scared the hell out of me? What are you doing here?"

She rose from sitting on the edge of a terra cotta planter, brushed the back of her slacks, and said, "If the mountain won't come to Muhammad, Muhammad must go to the mountain."

"Whatever that means," I said. She stepped forward, and in light from the street lamp, I saw her profile: head raised, shoulders back, dressed in a stylish beige jacket, a black mock turtle sweater, and a gold chain necklace. She had her hair pulled back. She wasn't smiling.

"It means I'm a bit tired of being—how shall I say it—spurned? Yes, that's the word for it, exactly the word for it."

"Like I've told you, I'm just not up to big social outings. My mind is consumed with—"

"Okay, dinner then. Looks like you managed to eat out. Let's do that."

"Sylvia."

She came right up close. "Don't you *Sylvia* me, Ned." She softened her expression and put a hand on my chest, a gesture I'd gotten used to. "Look, sweetie, you need to give yourself some space from all of this, this stress. It's way past time."

Just then a car turned onto the street; its headlight glare swept across where we stood, and I was struck by the tautness of Sylvia's face as she stared at me. I jiggled the keys in my hand. "It's time," I repeated. "For what?"

"I don't know." Her voice dropped. "Time for to you step away. To forgive yourself."

"Forgive myself?"

She placed both hands against my chest. "Don't you need to? It wasn't your fault, now was it?"

"So you think I'm suppressing guilt over what happened?"

"Aren't you?"

My head began to swim, and not from all the ale I had consumed. The allegations from Isaac, even my own daughter, tumbled back: Could I have saved her? "No," I blurted. "Not really."

"What's that mean, not really?"

"Damn it, Sylvia." I stepped around her and stuck my key in the lock, fumbled the door open, and spun around. She was right there behind me, her mouth crimped in a self-satisfied smile. "What is it you want?"

"Can we go in, out of the dark?" she asked in a soft but assured voice. "Please?"

I balked at first, my body planted in the open doorway, until finally I turned and went inside. I tossed the keys on the hall table and heard her close the door. Suddenly I felt claustrophobic, a prisoner in my own house.

I reluctantly acquiesced to her request for a glass of wine and opened an Italian red. I'd had enough alcohol for the night and waved her off. We sat quietly at the kitchen table while she sipped from her glass; it was a wooden feeling for me, as I had no desire to engage with her about my life, my sense of guilt, or anything else about Ashley.

"How is she really?" she asked without warning. "Your wife."

I studied her face, trying to comprehend her intent. "Ashley," I said.

"Yes, Ashley, how is she?"

"You mean her prognosis? Is that what you want to know, Sylvia?"

She tipped her head. "I suppose that's the right question. Sorry if I'm being blunt."

I leaned over the table on my forearms, getting close to her face, and breathed through my nostrils for a few inhalations. "She's gone, and she isn't coming back. That what you want to know?"

She drew back from my proximity and held her composure. "I see. That must be more awful than I can imagine. Having her present but gone at the same time has to be excruciating. At least when I lost Reggie I could grieve his absence and finally keep going with my life. What can you do?"

I sat up and folded my arms. "I have no idea."

She poured herself more wine and took a modest sip. I had nothing to say, though I suspected she did—I waited. When she asked to use the restroom, I got up and began to gather the residue of my kitchen clutter: dirty dishes, frying pans, and cups with cold coffee remnants in them. She returned and watched me without comment for a time.

"Have you spoken with your partners recently?" she asked finally. "I understand you've been on leave of absence. Is that the right term?"

"Close enough," I said. She waited for the second half of my answer as I finished my cleanup. "And yes, we spoke today as a matter of fact, but I think you know that."

"I do." There was the trace of embarrassment in her smile, a sight not often seen. "How did it go, the meeting?"

"Fine. They were just getting me caught up on business matters."

"Of course. So you'll be returning to work then?"

"Sylvia," I said, "let's sit down. I want to tell you something." I hesitated until we were once again facing each other over the table. "My life is a wreck right now. You know that, my partners know that, hell, everybody in town knows it. And you know what? There's no handbook on how to survive, stay alive and thrive after something like this. I don't even know who I am."

She reached out and put a hand on my arm. "You'll be fine."

"You don't know that. How could you know that?"

"I just do. I felt some of what you are when Reggie died. It took time, but I came out the other side pretty much okay."

"That may happen," I said, "but for now, I'm not going back to work. Haven't told Jack and Claude yet, but I'm not ready, wouldn't be an asset for the firm."

"But you must. I need you."

"You don't need me. Claude can handle your account every bit as well as I can, probably better."

She played with bracelet bands on her left arm: every other band gold, every other one black; there must have been five of them, maybe six. "They didn't give you the word then."

"The word?"

She held up a forefinger and shook it. "Ah, they were bad boys—very bad boys. The word. Well the word is *no*. No Ned, no Winters account."

I must have looked dumbfounded, because that was how I felt. Stupefied. The smile formed on her lips as if on a drawstring then remained locked in place. "You can't be serious," I said.

"Oh, but I am." She picked up her wine glass and twisted it by the stem. "I most assuredly am." She lifted the bottle and poured herself another half-glass of wine.

"But the firm is doing a great job for you. You've said so yourself. This is tantamount to bribery, underhanded bribery." I dragged my free hand across my face. "Damn, can't believe this." When I opened my eyes again, she still had on that ridiculous smile. "Okay, do what you want. It makes no difference to me because I'm not going back to work...for now anyway. They're doing a good job for you, and you know it, Sylvia. You damn well know it."

"That's not it," she said. "I want you."

"Sylvia, like I said..."

She reached out and gripped my arm again. "Don't you see?" She shook my arm. "I want you."

I was stunned. "You want me?" I squinted. "You mean on your account."

"No, Edward Longren Pine, I want you...you." Her voice had gone throaty. When I could only stare at her, she said, "I've been waiting, for all these months I've been waiting. I know how long it can take for the shock and the pain and the grief to run its course. I know. And then I know that beyond those passages of trauma that loneliness creeps in and corrupts your life. You see, I'm an expert on these matters."

"You can't make up for losing Reggie by doing this."

"Yes I can," she responded. "And so can you."

I felt spacey; my head swam. I grabbed the bottle of wine and gulped from it directly.

This was not going any further; I stood and looked down into Sylvia's face. "My wife is still alive. She is still breathing. Her heart is still beating." I leaned down. "And I still have her in my heart." I tapped my chest.

That drawstring smile returned. "No. No you don't."

"You know nothing. How ghastly."

"I doubt that you've loved her for some time. When was the last time you felt real passion for your wife?"

"I want you to leave, now." I extended my unrestrained arm, a social traffic cop pointing the way.

She remained seated. "I know that to be true, Ned."

"Leave, Sylvia, now please. Just leave."

"Do you want to know how I know about your domestic wasteland?"

My arm was still extended. I didn't respond.

"You do, don't you. I can see it in your eyes." I gritted my teeth, dropped my arm, and shook my head. "Of course you do. How could you not want to know how I learned of the most intimate part of your life?"

I dropped back down onto the chair. I was angry, so very angry, and yet my desire for reprisal was paralyzed by fascination with her deplorable assertion. Did I want to know? Of course. How had the dead zone of our lives become known outside of our bedroom?

"Is that a yes?"

I didn't react because I knew that Sylvia Winters would be unable to restrain herself. She had to tell me.

She studied me for a bit, sipped more wine, and said, "Big Isaac."

Blood rushed to my face. My heart thudded its vexed outrage. My eyes glared their question.

"Yes," she said. "It was some time ago at the annual Chamber of Commerce Harvest Gala. Isaac Tucker and I ended up at the same table together. Both of us were without spouses or dates. Naturally, we struck up a conversation. We danced a little, had more wine than we should have, and ended up afterward at the hotel bar."

I listened with my hands clasped on the table, squeezing the blood out of them, and let her go on. She learned about how much Isaac hated me and never wanted me to marry his Ashley, all of that. But it went deeper, and I was eviscerated. My internal organs seized when I was told that my wife had revealed to her father that she never was in love with me, that I had been merely an expedient choice. I knew of our passionless life—I lived it, for god's sake—but that was private, not even discussed between us. To have our apathy toward one another disemboweled, dissected by Ashley and her father, unbeknownst to me, was vile. How often had she rued her decision to marry me and wallowed in her mistake with him?

When Sylvia had finished her accounting of my life, I had finished off the wine. She fell quiet and smiled benignly at me before saying, "How long has it been since you've been with a woman who wants to be with you?"

I laughed through the veil of red wine and gripped my forehead. "You mean ever?"

Her eyelids closed and reopened. "If you want."

"Ashley wanted to be with me when we were making babies. That count?"

"Wasn't that synthetic?" When I shrugged, she answered, "Then no, doesn't count."

I felt myself smirk. "Then I think it was with Penelope."

"Penelope."

"Yes. Penelope Cross was her name. Damn, we had fun. My senior year of college. She was a junior. Can't even remember how we met, but we sure spent a lot of time together."

"And you were sure that she wanted to be with you?"

"Oh yeah." I laughed again. "We both wanted to be together."

"Why?"

"Why? Hell's bells, we were given carte blanche to field test brand new equipment. And we did, even worked without a manual or a net."

The benign smile remained on Sylvia's lips. "But that was one of those youthful intersections of life. It was a game. We all played that game before life kicked in."

"Oh, you want life," I said. "Then the answer is no."

"We can change that."

It wasn't in our bedroom. Did that make it less despicable? Did I do it for revenge? Damn, I don't know. I know how it felt to have that woman, whose body and smell and breath were unfamiliar next to me—different. Her skin was different; her energy was more evident. Even as my own body reacted so differently, so sexually on cue, my mind was in lockdown. Ashley was there, even in her dispassion, and in her comatose state, she was there, watching, judging—I knew that.

Then it was over. We lay side by side in the suffocating quiet of the house and waited while our body tempos subsided. My head throbbed from too much, just too much. At some point Sylvia slipped away to the bathroom. I looked up in the dark of the room and listened for the sounds of another person in the house, something I hadn't heard in a while: the sound of someone's footfalls, of a toilet flushing, water running—none of that. She returned, resumed her place beneath the covers, moved up next to me, and placed an arm across my chest. It was an oddly awkward moment—the aftereffect left me wondering and mentally adrift.

We remained in that position for an amount of time, probably less than it seemed; neither of us moved to continue the experience in any way. It was like that until she rose on an elbow and kissed me on the cheek. I reached out and touched her on the arm; both were perfunctory attempts at tenderness. She whispered something: *nice* and *better go*. I remained on my back, arms folded across my body, and listened as she dressed.

Before leaving, she leaned over the bed and placed a hand on my cheek. Her parting words were nothing more than a soft breath into my ear: *This is the beginning.*

I was about to drift off after she was gone when a chill flooded my torso.

-12-

The next morning, I threw the covers off after hours of rolling about but not sleeping—it must have been no later than five o'clock. I sat on the edge of the bed and had a run-through of the previous night's recklessness. I shuddered and tossed my head side to side when her words replayed: *This is the beginning.* What a fool I was. I paraded around the house in my shorts, room to room, stopping only to curse myself. The hottest of showers did nothing to wash off the residue of the lowest moment in my life.

The image in the bathroom mirror was recognizable but barely, looking more like a boxer on the wrong side of the count. The long examination, as I stared into my puffy red eyes, did nothing to improve the sight. After a breakfast of raisin bran and coffee, I donned a pair of running shorts and a sweatshirt and set off on a brisk walk about the neighborhood but gave up on that ruse after a few blocks and circled back to the house, snagged the paper still on the front porch, and went back inside to beat up on myself some more.

The landline phone was ringing. I wasn't up for taking any morning-after calls from Sylvia Winters. But the caller ID window said something else; it was my baby sister, Corrine. It came to me right then that she had never called me after the attack. In all the weeks, now months, she hadn't called, emailed, or texted—certainly hadn't written. Why now? She and I had quietly slid away from one another into that confused region of estrangement a long time ago. It had crossed my mind that I'd never heard from her after Ashley and I had been beaten, but while that was disappointing, I hadn't given it much thought actually. I know, sad, but the long-held disaffection had turned into a cauterized scab from way back.

I lifted the receiver reluctantly and spoke softly into the mouthpiece. "Yes."

"Hello, Ned, it's me, Corrine." Her voice was throatier; she hadn't quit smoking, I could tell.

"Hi."

"Hi," she tossed back.

"This is a surprise," I said.

"I know." I waited for her to speak more. "Yeah, it is for me, too. A surprise."

"It's not my birthday." I was trying to be breezy.

"I know that. Wouldn't call you then anyway."

I absorbed that small jab and waited her out.

"So...well, how are you anyway?"

"I'm doing okay," I answered, neglecting to add that I'd fucked a woman other than my comatose wife last night.

"How's your wife, how's Ashley?"

"The same."

I let her ponder my answer. "I don't know what that means."

"I'll bet you do."

"No, no I don't. Why would you say that?"

"I just assumed you've talked with people."

"People?"

"Harrison or my kids. Have you?"

There was a long pause. I pulled the newspaper from under my arm and laid it next to the phone, noting a story below the fold about Tropical Storm Hermine headed for Texas.

"All right, yeah, I have," she said finally. "Checked in with Harrison a couple of times. Even had a powwow with Uncle Floyd. Always a trip talking with Floyd."

"That it is," I said, smiling and processing a flashback of the phone call I received from my favorite relative, Floyd Pine, my

99

father's younger brother. Floyd had always been the family's outsider, not a black sheep, just an unconventional member of the clan, a man who went his own way. He dropped out of high school in the sixties, joined a commune named the Tolstoy Farm in Davenport, Washington, where all devoted followers espoused peace and love. Uncle Floyd, like every other member, disavowed all regulations, tolerated drugs, sex of all kinds, nudity, and just about any imaginable thought and behavior. With no rules restricting sexual activity, my uncle, according to family lore, fathered several children. Where they were and who the mothers were, all of that, lost in the antiquity of free love.

Floyd called shortly after my conversation with Harrison. He hollered over the phone, wanting to know if I was okay. And how was that woman I had been living with? Floyd had never gotten on the marriage bandwagon. He prattled on, warned me to keep the doors locked and told me to come on out to Portland and spend time with him.

"Then you know," I said to Corrine.

"You're not gonna make this easy, are you?"

"Not sure I follow."

She laughed into my ear. "Same old Ned, nothing's changed."

"Why'd you call, Corrine?" She forced another laugh. "After all this time?"

"Okay, truth is Harrison told me to. Said it was time to bury the hatchet. So here I am doing what my big brother tells me to do. Feel special?"

"Not really, but if it works for you, fine. I have a question though."

"What?" she asked.

"What was it ever about? This long drought we've endured?"

I could sense she was taking a drag on a cigarette. "Planet earth to Ned. You're as thick as a Christmas gourd. No one ever liked her, Ned, not for a New York minute. Talk about your cold fish, your wife was the coldest, most disingenuous bitch I've ever met."

"No one?" I said.

"Not in our family. Not after the first fifteen minutes at your wedding. You know how we were treated that day and later on."

I had to admit that I did. "I guess," I maneuvered.

"You guess, my ass. You know damn well."

"So now you're wanting to know how Ashley is, or you've been instructed to find out how she is."

I heard another drag on her smoke. "Okay, so how is she?"

"You already know how she is. You know that she is in a place she can never come back from. You know that she'll never recover. That's how she is, Corrine."

"That's tough, Ned. No matter how I feel about her as a person, it's got to be harder than hell for you."

"So now what?" I asked.

"I don't know," she replied. "Maybe...since she's like that... maybe now we can connect again. Be a family again."

I could feel the pulse in my temples. "So let me get this. Now that my wife is lying unconscious like an eggplant, you are suddenly willing to talk with me again. That it?"

"Jesus," she said in her raspy voice. "How can you talk like that about her?"

"Because, baby sister, that is exactly what you meant. Tell Harrison that you did your duty. Think I'll pass on the family reunion." I didn't wait for her response.

After I hung up on Corrine, I noticed that I had a missed call on my cell phone from Claude Vogel. He wanted me to call him immediately. I didn't. I knew what he wanted, and I wasn't ready to go there yet, almost but not yet, not for sure. Instead I got dressed and drove to the care center to visit Ashley—fulfill my sense of obligation.

It was the same. Her body hadn't moved an iota. The new rotation thing, the air mattress, hadn't been installed, I could tell. An IV drip was feeding her nutrients. At other times, I knew she was fed via something called a nasogastric tube through her nose down the esophagus into her stomach—that and the catheter for urine and diaper for fecal matter were way more than I wanted to know. It was beyond sadness; it was repellent to me. The bedclothes were unmussed; her blanket was without wrinkles, smoothed over her torso and legs like a cocoon. She lay perfectly still on her back, her face muscles intransigent, eyelids down as if glued, and her lifeless hair brushed back. I never asked the nurses or the aides if there had been movement, any sign of life; I did at first, as if I would be judged uncaring were I not to angst over her condition on every visit. That day, I sat in the chair like always and finished reading the paper while my internal clock ticked off the minutes biding time until something akin to an hour would pass.

After about forty-five minutes, I rose and stood beside her bed, ready to leave. Her barren face was merely an artifact now; there was nothing of whom she had been to relate to anymore. But I was provoked regardless of her literal absence, provoked by another woman. I leaned down, closer to her inanimate face.

"Ashley," I said, my voice sounding intrusive in her space. I looked around to see if I had been heard; I hadn't. I twisted the newspaper in my hands and turned away. If I turned back, would her eyes be open? Would she challenge my right to speak to her?

When an aide walked into the room right then, I was still facing away. She went to the bed, ran a hand over the blanket, checked the IV, and asked if everything was all right. I nodded, but my smile was synthetic. The aide exited as if on air. I waited for a moment and returned to the side of the bed.

"Ashley," I said again. But then my eyes glazed over, her face went out of focus, and my mind locked up. I couldn't do it, though I sorely wanted to. I was at the door when Sylvia Winters self-satisfied revelation of my passionless marriage returned.

I spun around, looked again at the inert presence, stepped back into the room, and shut the door behind me. The stagnant quiet closed in. After standing still for a moment, I approached the bed again. I said her name for the third time. I waited; then I spoke, and it all came out.

"I hope you are listening," I began. "I really do. They say that unconscious people can still hear. I pray that is so, Ashley. Because," I whispered "last night while I was fucking another woman, I learned how little you thought of me. We were never anything close to a match made for the gods, I knew that, but last night before bedding this eager woman she told me that you thought of me as merely an expedient choice. Guess who told her that?" I popped the folded newspaper into my hand. "Isaac. How often did you and Isaac discuss our personal lives? Often enough that he knew you didn't love me, never had, and regretted your decision to marry me? And often enough that he felt no compunction in sharing our tale of disappointment and hollowness with anyone who would listen?

"God damn it, Ashley. There you lie, immovable, unreachable. I can't get to you. I can't retaliate or defend myself of all your charges. I loved you. I did love you. Now you're gone, and I can do nothing to alleviate the pain. Hell, I can't even repair the damage to my ego, to my reputation. I wasn't perfect, but I mostly liked myself. But you've taken that away."

The door to her room opened, and the aide came in looking perplexed. "Is there a problem?" she asked, eyes widened.

"Leave us be." I muttered. "Please."

She stood stock still for a moment but then quickly backed out and pulled the door closed.

In the vapid confines of the room, I took several short breaths to regain my equilibrium and looked upon my wife, wondering if indeed she had been able to hear me. How was I to know? But then, I thought, if she will never recover, what difference does it make? Perhaps none. Maybe it was time to finish it between us.

"Ashley," I said. "It is me again, Ned, in case you can hear this." I pulled a chair over and sat close to her. "You know ever since the night of the attack, everything has changed. You're gone, never to return. That leaves me flying solo here. And let me tell you, being out here all by myself twisting in the wind is hell. In one sense, you got the cushy part of this. I know, spiteful, but that's how I'm feeling." I leaned right up close to her face. "So listen up. I've made some choices, and they don't include you anymore, except for the legal part of being in charge of your health decisions. I'm keeping that part. It'll drive Isaac berserk, and I like that.

"Mainly, I want you to know that this will probably be the last time I'll see you. So take one last look at my handsome face. You'll be in good hands here. Your care is being paid for. Isaac will take over paying for things once the insurance runs out, so you're good. Keep breathing as long as you want, but I'll not be seeing you. I have a life to find out there somewhere. Thanks for listening and helping me decide what to do next." I planted a kiss on her cheek, patted an arm, and told her good-bye.

The air seemed cleaner when I walked out of the care center; the sun was high and shining, my lungs filled easily, and I felt just damn good, if you want to know. Damn good. I knew exactly what I was going to do, thanks to Ashley. I drove straight to Jackson, Vogel & Pine, waited until Jack and Claude were both free, and pulled the plug. I wanted out, I told them. I asked them to activate the partner buyout clause of our partnership agreement. When Claude balked at the suddenness of my departure, declaring that it would place financial and business hardship on the firm, I assured them that I would be reasonable. A lump filled my throat when I saw Jack's eyes water and his face slump sadly. Those men had been good to me, they had given me a rewarding opportunity, and I was opting out. I should have felt like a defector, abandoning my trusted colleagues with no warning; I should have felt like Judas. I should have, but I didn't.

Damn it all, I felt no shame. After dragging things out, engaging in an awkward discussion, I gave Jack a big hug, shook hands

104

with Claude, and left, taking one last look at my name on the wall. There was a twinge in my stomach, realizing that it was over.

Shortly after I drove away from the office, a black pickup riding on huge tires crossed in front of me at an intersection. I jabbed at the brakes and lurched to a stop. A horn blared behind me as the truck disappeared from sight. The temptation to go after it rose then fell away. What would I have done if I had caught up to the pickup—wave the driver over and demand to know what he'd been doing the night of March 17? Attacking people on Larchwood Court? The driver behind me laid on the horn again; I waved apologies and drove on.

Still shaky from encountering the black pickup, I stopped for a late lunch at Rudy's Diner; over a garlic mushroom burger I considered what lay ahead. I knew what I intended to do, the very things I'd alluded to when I'd whispered to Ashley. I had made choices, and they wouldn't include her anymore—never would. That self-made ultimatum knotted in my throat; I swallowed it away and considered my intentions. Telling her good-bye had been number one; resigning from the firm had been number two.

I had to laugh when it came to me that I was more or less creating a business plan for myself; there was abandonment, divestiture, capitalization, market analysis, and a loosely formulated set of strategies.

For the next step, I needed Gloria Denham.

-13-

Sure, I had slept with Gloria Denham; I enjoyed it, and so did she. But it was never only the sex for either of us, or so we rationalized. Gloria was our real estate agent when we bought the Whitewood Estates house. The first thing I noticed was not just that she was pleasant to look at but that she handled Ashley's dispassionate manner with aplomb. No doubt she had mastered the art of dealing with prickly home buyers: nonetheless, I was taken by her poise and amicable manner.

On the day we surrendered to our mutual attraction, I'd been given my marching orders to have one last walk-through of the house and pick up the key—Ashley had decided she was too busy. Over the course of our many trips to view the house, I'd learned that Gloria had been married, shared two children with her ex-husband, with whom she had endured a bitter divorce, and once emancipated had reinvented herself as a Realtor. I was impressed by her temperament and just how accessible and warm she was.

That day, she and I toured the house one more time, noting how often we'd seen everything, and ended up in the master bathroom to check out the drawer and cabinet pulls that were scheduled to be changed to those selected by Ashley. Thankfully, the conversion had been completed. When I saw that, I burst out laughing and yelled *Thank god!* That tickled Gloria, and she began to laugh; soon we were both gasping, almost unable to breathe. At one point, she collapsed against me, spent from laughing, and I inadvertently wrapped my arms around her.

It was one of those moments when something unexpected but not unwanted suddenly occurs. And within the grip of such an occasion your mind swirls about until it decides to relish the moment or reject it. Neither of us fell away in embarrassment. Nor did we laugh it off. Maybe we should have. Instead I stepped back, as did she. Her face was open, holding an expression of curiosity but not of dismissal. A slightly crooked front tooth shown through her parted lips, which were poised in a cautious smile. It was the first time I'd really noticed the hazel of her eyes beneath the graceful arch of her dark eyebrows. After an unsure passage of time, seconds running on, I reached out to touch her face; she didn't pull away. Impulsively I put a hand beneath her chin and leaned forward; our lips met. It was an unexpected act of surprising acceptance.

When we eased back, nothing was said. Later we would discover our mutual need to be totally wanted by someone. But at the moment, we said nothing of that, just found our way to the master bedroom, where the model home bed was still on display. Afterward we dressed and then embraced again; no comments of regret or shame were uttered—ever—between us. Eventually we ceased our lovers' ways and rarely saw each other. I suppressed those indiscretions as best I could, but I never forgot.

─────────

I called Gloria the day after resigning from the firm. When she answered my call, I could hear her take in a quick breath. She said my name twice and expressed deep regret over what had happened.

"Thanks for your call, Gloria."

"I should have come by. You know, give you my sympathies in person, but I just couldn't," she said. "Can you ever forgive me?"

"Nothing to forgive," I replied. "Everybody processes bad news in their own way. Last thing I would ever do is judge you, Gloria. You know that. Don't you?"

"I suppose," she said. "But I haven't forgiven myself." She paused. "How is she?"

I told her. She sucked in another breath of regret and fell silent. I was out on the patio; it was sunny, and I was stretched out on a chaise lounge, another piece of home décor selected by Ashley. "I need you," I said, pressing the cell to my ear over the lawnmower noise from a neighbor's yard crew.

She was quiet for a moment. "Ned, I...really I don't think that's a good idea. Do you?"

I chuckled. "Gloria, my dear Gloria. I...how sweet you are. I need to make myself clear. I'm calling your real estate side. I want you to sell this house for me." I waited while she processed and added, "I can't stay here."

"Ned," she said with the tone of a worried friend, "what is going on? Really?"

The yard noise next door ceased. I sat up on the edge of the lounge, told her of my leaving the firm, and made an ambiguous statement about future unknown plans. I knew what I was thinking, but I didn't know if it had legs. I stumbled around, citing that I needed to sell the house now for cash flow reasons. She promised to get things started but cited the down real estate market as a deterrent; I said I understood the challenge. Then we listened in dead air while the intimate moments we'd once shared floated by.

"I've never forgotten," I said.

There was a sigh, and she said, "I know." A lag followed before she said, "I'm seeing someone."

"Great."

"He's a good guy. Another Realtor." I chuckled, and she added, "Looks like we'll be getting married before Christmas."

"Sounds like a collaboration. Which house will you put on the market?"

"You are so bad," she laughed and promised to get going on the house. We agreed on an appointment the very next day, and that was it—all very professional.

That same evening, Sylvia Winters called my cell while I was watching CNN's coverage of tornados knocking over buildings in an industrial complex in Dallas. "What the hell's going on?" she barked into my ear.

"Hello Sylvia."

"Don't you *Hello Sylvia* me. Just what are you up to?"

"Right now I'm watching tornados tearing up Dallas."

"You know what I'm talking about. You're leaving the firm?"

I hit the kill switch on the remote, and the television went black. "News travels fast."

"You can't do that!"

"Really? Why's that?"

"Because...you just can't. I need you."

I caught my breath. "You need me?"

She grunted over the line. "You know what I mean. Our company needs you. That was our deal, once you returned to work. Besides now we...I mean now there's more."

I closed my eyes and clamped down on my teeth. The words, her words, came back: *This is the beginning.* The knot of spaghetti I'd tossed together for dinner took that moment to express itself. My stomach was agreeing with my assessment: *This can't be.* "I know it's a shock to everyone," I began to explain. "But I had to do it. My life...it's not what it was, and never will be again."

I could imagine her processing, finding her words. "Ned, listen to me. That's why you need to keep your roots down, keep yourself engaged and involved."

"I've decided."

"Oh, you've decided," she chided. "Just what will you do with yourself? Play golf?"

"It's done, over. Besides, I don't play golf."

"But we've just begun, you and I."

My god, I thought. "Sylvia, listen, that was a mistake. It was a moment lost in the throes of despair. It shouldn't have happened. I'm sorry," I said in an attempt to derail her intent.

"You're sorry." Her voice was vinegar. "You wanted that. You know you did."

"We'd had too much wine."

"Don't give me that."

"It shouldn't have happened," I repeated. "I have a wife, I was wrong."

"You don't have a wife, Ned. You know that. She is gone."

"Damn it, Sylvia, for god's sake."

Her sigh flooded my ear. "I'm sorry for that, truly sorry. But Ned, you know it's true. And you have a life to live. *We* have a life to live."

I stood and walked into the kitchen just to move and somehow fend off her objective. "Sylvia, don't do this. I need time to decide what I will be doing from now on. I can't deal with what you're suggesting."

"Suggesting?" she almost shouted. "You didn't need any suggestion when it came to bedding me."

"Good-bye, Sylvia." I ended the call and tossed the phone onto the kitchen counter. It began ringing right away, but I just let it ring. A minute later I got a text from her apologizing and saying *We can fix this*. I found a dusty bottle of bourbon in our thinly supplied liquor cabinet and filled a tumbler half full and drank it without ice. Never a solo drinker, I'd found reason to engage in that act—or so I thought. Of course it made no difference in my foreboding; all I got for my diversion was a head full of rolling marbles.

One thing I noted after Ashley had been moved into the long-term care center was a considerable drop-off in contact from what had been our finite social circle. The food offerings had ceased about the time word was out regarding Ashley's condition. It might as well have been a death in the family; first there's shock, the outpouring of food and sympathy, the funeral, the church potluck, and a plot at the cemetery. After that, everyone goes back to living their lives, hoping they aren't next. It has to be that way; otherwise, we'd cease to function as people.

The thing was, Ashley hadn't done the decent thing and died. When someone is comatose, what do you do? At first there were a few visitors at the care center, female friends of Ashley's, but after seeing her unresponsive and deathlike, they never returned. Closure was an impossibility. Who wanted to visit living death on a regular basis? Those who knew her couldn't even celebrate who she had been; you know, the fond memories, humorous stories, and shared photographs of a previous life. Those observances were reserved for the finality of life.

When I'd see people on the street in town or at the grocery store, people we'd socialized with, the only thing they knew to ask was how I was doing; then they'd hesitatingly inquire if there was any news of the unspoken tragedy—repeatedly, was there any news? Perhaps they had been chatting with someone over the avocados, smiling, laughing, until they caught sight of me. Then their faces would flatten out like cold mutton. Frankly, it was a downer to have me walk about town, the dark cloud that wouldn't go away. I had learned to absorb the discomfort I saw in those faces of regret, but the disassociation had begun to eat away at me after three months, around the middle of June. It had taken that long for busy details of the attack to subside: my own injuries, the hospitalization of Ashley, the medical outcome to be determined, the police investigation, placing Ashley at the Garnet Center, and just coming to grips with my own despair.

It had been near the first of July when I began to really assess my life: just what the hell was going on, who would I become, and what did it matter? It was the day that Sylvia Winters had shown up with her casserole. When I opened the door and saw her, it somehow clicked in my brain that this woman, whom I didn't want to see, represented my nonexistent human interaction. I began to process those people I never saw anymore. Their names and faces came to me. There were friends who had been important in our lives; where were they? Then again, why hadn't I reached out to them? I knew, I guess, it was because none of us knew what to say or how to get past the horribleness of the villainous act: *Hello Ned, say is Ashley dead yet? Hi Ralph, it's just me now. Ashley can't join us, still in the coma.*

Right then, with Sylvia Winters' beef stroganoff casserole in the freezer, was when I began to disengage from my life as it had been. Leaving the firm, saying good-bye to Ashley, deciding to sell the house, and considering what would be next. I had some piecemeal ideas, nothing more.

With Gloria Denham scheduled to put the monster edifice on the market, I felt it, the tide of cutting loose. It was happening. I walked about, entering each room, straightening things, tidying the kitchen, and putting dirty clothes in the laundry room hamper. That house, which had never liked me much, and hadn't warmed to me after the break-in, seemed even more aloof that day. I felt more like a museum guard than its rightful inhabitant.

I dispensed with my usual slovenly ways and showered, shaved, put on some fresh chinos along with a yellow polo shirt and tasseled loafers. By the time Gloria arrived, I had paced the house several times, had three cups of coffee, and read the paper front to back. When the doorbell rang, I was halfway through the crossword puzzle, thinking of a word for *mistletoe piece*.

We stood looking at each other across the threshold: smiling, remembering, managing our expectations. To me, she appeared the same; three years had passed, but it was as if I'd seen her only yesterday. She was dressed casually, wearing blue jeans and a white smock shirt not tucked in. Her smile showing the crooked tooth was the same—the prospect of seeing her as I wanted had been met. She looked wonderful.

When I stepped back, she strode by, patted me on the arm, then turned and expressed her regrets again. I thanked her, and that was it. After an hour, it was done. A selling price had been set, a property management crew would be engaged to clean and prep the house, and the house would be listed as soon as possible. Gloria promised to get the wheels rolling on Monday, but when she asked what I would do with all the household furnishings and personal items, I didn't know. She told me that for a fee the people who would get the place ready for sale could also pack up everything in the house—just as if I was moving across the country. I was ready to act; I told her to set it up. That was when she looked me in the eyes and asked me the loaded question: *What about your wife's things?* I stood flat-footed, staring at her, and realized how little I had actually thought things through.

Gloria very kindly advised me to take care of Ashley's clothes and personal effects on my own. She was right. I should have thought of that. I would surely reap the whirlwind if I ignored the slice of her life represented by what hung in her closet, filled her jewelry box, or anything else that was personal to her. Following Gloria's advice, I dropped by the local U-Haul rental store and bought a selection of moving boxes and packing tape.

I lied when I told Sylvia Winters that I didn't play golf. What I left out was that I didn't play it well. And frankly didn't play it often, usually just with clients of the firm. With that off the table, I had even less reason to play. It was a beautiful day, and with the house business all set, I left the confines of that damn place, drove by U-Haul and got the boxes, then drove out to the Latham Municipal Golf Course and knocked three buckets of balls out into various abstract placements on the driving range. I saw no improvement in my swing, and after watching my final ball sail off in a big-time slice, I headed for the clubhouse and sat at the bar over an IPA and watched the windup of a tournament sponsored by BMW someplace in Illinois. The only thing of interest was that Tiger Woods hadn't made the cut; guess he was human after all. Too bad.

I felt rather than saw someone slide onto the stool to the left of me. Keeping my eye on the television, I ignored whoever it was. The bartender came over, dropped a coaster down, and asked what the person wanted. I recognized the voice when he said he'd have the same as I was. Detective C. T. Morgan looked sideways at me when I turned my head.

"Mr. Pine," he said. "How was your game?" He was dressed in the full golf regalia, plaid red, blue, and yellow, pants, blue polo shirt, yellow cap, and a golf glove on his left hand.

"No game," I responded. "Hit some balls on the range. Didn't improve."

He chuckled and pulled off his glove. "Brutal game, most unforgiving."

"That's mostly why I don't play it. Just a nice day, and I felt like hitting something."

The bartender brought Morgan his beer and plunked it down; foam swirled then oozed down the sides of the glass. "I have days like that, most days, in fact." He took a long drink.

I looked up at the television. Guy name of Dustin Johnson won the tournament by one stroke. He was grinning and holding up the trophy.

"Johnson," Morgan said. "He can hit the ball a mile."

"Never heard of him," I said, swallowed the dregs of my beer, and started to slip off the stool.

"Hey, let me buy you another," Morgan said. He raised a hand to the bartender, so I stayed on the stool. "If I may, how's your wife doing?"

The inevitable question or the inevitable question not to be asked, depending. "No change," I answered.

"Sorry," he said. My beer arrived; Morgan spun his glass on the coaster. "That mean what I think it means?"

"Likely it does." I sucked the top off my beer. "Means she's gone and won't be back."

"Jesus." He worried his glass some more then took a deep

swallow. "Don't know what to say to that, you know. Mostly I see finality or survivors, not the in-between thing."

"Just seems in between. Takes more than breathing to be alive." I sort of enjoyed the grunt that got out of him, telling a cop something heavier than he's used to.

We both fell quiet, looked abstractly at the television; another tournament, this time from Utah, was in progress. Looked like all the rest to me, a lot of green and crowds of people watching other people hit a little white sphere then run after it. "Any news?" I said finally.

Detective Morgan bobbed his head. "I was wondering when you'd ask. Haven't seen you much of late."

"You missing my pestering coffee breaks?"

He coughed a laugh. "I don't know about missing, but I was getting used to them."

"I figured you'd call if you had a breakthrough."

"True. Fact is, I've been seeing more of your father-in-law of late. Comes by about as often as you did there for a while."

"Isaac being a pest, is he?"

"You might say. Bit testier than you."

"Anything to tell him...or me?"

He pulled his cap off, laid it on the bar, and ran a hand over his head. "No, not really."

"Not really? Now that has more to it than a flat no. Something you want to tell me?"

He swiveled on his stool and faced me squarely. "Look, the only thing I can tell you is that we are continuing to pursue the security guard angle."

"You were already doing that. What's new?"

He studied me and pursed his lips in and out. "Okay," he said. "No big breakthrough, nada. But... and this is only a maybe, the security company has been more aggressive in trying to track down the guard who went missing. You know, the one that was on duty the night of the attack."

"They found him," I declared.

He shook his head. "All I'm telling you is that I've been leaning on them more lately, and they've agreed to do some internal inquiries and look farther afield than they had been."

"Doesn't sound like much of a change."

"I know, but they've been very laid back about helping us find the guy. Now that I have their attention, they've agreed to be more cooperative."

I raised my eyebrows at his curious statement. "Now that you have their attention? You didn't before? What's changed?"

His smile was impish. "Nothing."

"Nothing?"

"Nothing except that—and this is just between you and me—they sort of got the idea that if they don't apply more diligence to locate their former employee, future calls for assistance from their security staff may receive a lower priority rating by us."

"You can do that?"

Morgan smiled a broad Cheshire cat smile. "Not officially, and you never heard it from me. But if it gives you any comfort in all of this, we can do it and will. Imagine if word got around that A-Ball Security has a strange disconnect with the local police. May not be good for business."

"So it's just your threat, not any progress then?"

"Let's just say we have their attention. My thinking is they know more about where the guy is or at least have more connections than we do in finding him. They were dragging their feet, and now they're not, so we'll see. I'll be in touch soon as I know anything."

I shrugged my grudging thanks and bid farewell. When I left, Detective C. T. Morgan was reliving every stroke of his last game with a couple fellows; all three had produced their scorecards and were brandishing them as if they were important legal documents.

On the way home, I drove past the Kokanee Center shopping mall and noticed a big Tucker Construction sign next to the building site where a national brand sporting goods store was being erected. I was glad to see Isaac's company doing well; I wanted to be sure that he could keep paying for Ashley's care when the time came.

The house was impassive when I returned, as if it knew that I was about to abandon it, as if it had ever welcomed me at all. That night, however, the place seemed to echo even though it still held the full complement of our possessions. It was another lonely moment, the kind that I brought on myself because I never reached out to old friends who had faded away once the newness of our tragedy had played out and Ashley was unavailable to visit with and receive pity. Like I said, I would occasionally see an acquaintance somewhere about town; we would dance around our discomfort with smiles and nervous laughs and good wishes. But that night it was just me alone in that damnable house.

It was after dark when I carried the stack of cardboard boxes into the house and began the surrealistic chore of disemboweling that place and my life of Ashley's personal possessions. The act took longer than I thought it would; I left nothing behind, nor did I throw even the smallest items of hers in the trash. I retained it all. Into the early hours, I removed her things from closets and drawers, folding and packing it all. It was sobering; the smell of her was on everything I touched.

When I'd finished, a sense of accomplishment flowed through me. The boxes, all folded shut and taped, were stacked neatly in our bedroom; I slept soundly in Mike's old room.

-14-

The next day, however, I had to face up to the hastily contrived decisions I was making to revise my life; I had no time to feel lonely. I'd showered, dressed decently, and was finishing a spartan bagel and coffee breakfast when the doorbell rang. It was a skinny young fellow in jeans and a tee shirt from Gloria Denham's real estate company asking for permission to sink a post in my lawn with a For Sale sign attached. I'd urged Gloria to put a sign up right away, to not wait for the MLS listing. An hour later I received a phone call from the property management company to schedule a time for a crew to clean and prep the house; I would, of course, have to be off the premises. Gloria was making things happen; perhaps she'd sensed my craving to be rid of the place.

I must admit that the flurry of activity did give me pause that day. When everything I was changing had been solidified, then what? No job to go to, no house to call my own, and no wife to discuss the transition with. It was eerily transforming. I was going from being a solid performer in a respected firm, living with an intelligent and accomplished wife, having a tight circle of special friends and acquaintances, and being a parent to two strong offspring. I would still be a parent, but all else aforementioned would dissipate. On top of that, there had been no end point to the attack that had precipitated the implosion of our lives. I was living it; Ashley would never know. Maybe she got the best of it. Those who terrorized our lives and ruined everything were still unknown, as were their intentions. So nothing made any sense, not the travesty of why, the gutting of our lives, nor my clueless-ness now that I had cut myself loose. I was both shattered and invigorated.

That Monday afternoon, there was another ring of the door-bell; a courier delivered an envelope from Jackson, Vogel & Pine CPAs. I signed for it and read the enclosed letter of proposal, out-lining the partner payout formula in legalese. It was off-putting to be communicating with my friends and colleagues in such an antiseptic fashion. I read the document through three times and found nothing to dispute; they were offering to pay out my part-nership share over a six-year period. If I concurred would I please make an appointment to come to their offices to sign the agree-ment at my earliest convenience? Why wait? I called and told the young woman at the front desk that I'd be in around two o'clock if acceptable; she checked and confirmed that Jack and Claude would see me then.

My name was still on the wall. The new receptionist smiled sweetly and led me to the conference room, where I paced the familiar space for longer than I knew was necessary. When they finally entered, Jack offered me a nice smile and his hand. Claude merely nodded, spread some papers on the big walnut conference table, and handed me a pen. So that was it, I gathered, no friendly farewell chitchat, just business; I was back in my car in less than fifteen minutes. It was all very odd.

The day ended quietly. I popped a frozen chicken enchilada din-ner into the microwave and consumed it with a glass of Chianti while Rachel Maddow dissected the current political scene on MSNBC. I had just rinsed off my dinner plate when the land-line started ringing. I muted Rachel and answered on about the fourth ring. Don't recall who I was thinking it might be, but I was caught off guard when I saw F Pine in the caller ID window and heard my Uncle Floyd's raspy voice tickle my eardrum.

"Hey Nedder," he all but shouted. He'd called me Nedder since

I was a boy. Started when he actually showed up for a family Thanksgiving gathering at the Baker County farm. I was about nine, and Uncle Floyd seemed a most fascinating creature to me: rustic looking, always grinning, loud, and with tales to tell of his life on the commune up in Washington State. Still in his twenties, he was already losing his hair, but he'd offset that with a bushy, reddish-brown beard. He had what I would now call a loamy aroma about him; his smell made him seem manlier to me, silly boy. But I was instantly connected to him.

I remember how much fun he was but also how condescending everyone else was to him. I guess all families have a member or two who are out of the loop—you know, those who never quite fit the generic mold of the clan, who went their own way, not expecting to be heaped with praise from their gene pool but at least welcomed home. That was Floyd. He messed around for those two to three days, tried to chat everyone up, but got the message that his lifestyle no longer meshed with that of his kin. I still remember Floyd shouting his good-byes, ruffling my hair with a calloused hand, calling me Nedder one more time, and driving off in a rattletrap International Harvester pickup.

To my undying regret I had acquiesced to the family's disavowal of my most genuine relative. We'd kept him at arm's length all those years. My father, Hugh Pine, Floyd's sole sibling, was the only one who had sporadic contact with his younger brother; it was the decent thing to do. And then my phone rang.

"Uncle Floyd," I said as if responding to a telemarketer.

He laughed. "I wake you?"

"No, no," I fumbled, "just a surprise to hear from you. How are you?"

"Hell's bells, I say to that. Bigger question is how are you? How's your...how's Ashley?"

"Ashley? Ashley hasn't improved."

"That's a damnable state of affairs. Gonna get better though, right?"

"No," I answered carefully. "No, Floyd, she isn't. She's in a permanent coma."

"Permanent? You don't say. My god, boy, where's that leave you? How you coping?"

I took the portable handset into the kitchen and sat at the table. "I'm mostly sleepwalking. You know, getting along day by day... that's about it."

I heard him take in a ragged breath. "I tell you, this isn't what I expected to hear. How long's it been now?"

"Four months and a couple of days." I surprised myself by knowing the count.

"Four months. Wow. I'd heard of how bad it was and all but wasn't even thinking of things not getting back to normal for you all. You know. Like maybe you were getting ready for a big trip to Paris to celebrate, but not this. At least you got your work though. A big accounting company, right? You're an owner and all, ain't that right?"

"Was, but I'm selling out."

"You don't say, selling out. Well, guess you know what you're doing. With all that's happened, maybe the right thing to do. So what'll you do?"

"Not a goddamned clue, Floyd." When he laughed, I added, "Selling our house, too."

"And selling your house," he hooted. "Whatcha gonna do, get a tent and live in the woods?"

"Might. Hadn't thought of that." I laughed. "Not a bad idea."

"Yeah it is. I done that back in the day. Sounds like what's his name. Thoreau. Sounds like Thoreau but wouldn't be nothing like he wrote. Guarantee it, nothing like *Walden* for sure. You'd go bonkers in no time."

"I'll take your word for it."

"Okay, glad we got that outa the way." There was a rustling sound. "Wait a second, this is making me thirsty. Need me a beer." I waited, and he finally picked up the phone again. "That's better. Okay, Nedder, no job, no house…and seems like no wife. Sorry."

"It's okay, Floyd. You're right, not a lot left."

"So," he said "you planning on traveling maybe?"

"Nope. That doesn't sound appealing in the least right now."

There was a pause; I could tell he was taking another swallow. "You know, I'm just thinking. I never in my life experienced what you're going through. Hey, I've been footloose, but this, what you're experiencing—losing your wife, no responsibilities, no plans, just time and lots of it—not so much. What I'm getting here is that you don't have any idea what to do next. Right? Am I right?"

"Hadn't thought of it that way, but you just put a lid on it. Guess I'm just twisting in the wind. Feels like that some, too."

"You know, Nedder, I'm thinking here. Getting an idea. I have a notion forming in my head."

"Should I be worried?" I laughed.

"No, just hang with me now. This could be good. I'm liking it. I truly am."

"And?"

"I got it. Here it is: You're moving out here to Portland to live with me and help me out. Damn if that ain't brilliant, don't you think?"

"Floyd, are you nuts?"

"Surely I am, but not about this idea. I'm thinking you need to get away from things, go someplace where you can sort of re-charge your batteries."

"And that's with you?"

"Why not? I've got room, and I can give you stuff to do to keep you from going round the bend."

I pinched my nose and chuckled. "What kind of *stuff?*"

"Come on, you know I have this retail business. Nothing too challenging to it, but you'd fit right in."

I had no idea what his business was; I knew once maybe, but it never registered. "I'm sorry, what business, Floyd?"

"I'm crushed. You don't recall my thrift shop? Floyd's Stuff?"

"Sorry, I don't."

"Hell, man, it's been a mainstay in the St. John's neighborhood for going on two decades. I bought it from an old guy about eight years ago, changed the name, and sell all kinds of shit."

"Why'd you do that?"

He hesitated. "Well, 'cause I was just like you are now back then. Had nothing going, no plans, my woman left me, and one day I told myself, I said, *Self, you can still be of some use.* Read about this place in a Nickel Ads, dropped my savings into it, woke up the next day, and got back in the game."

"Good for you. But to tell you..."

"Listen Nedder, answer me this. What do you have going on in that town you're there—Latham is it? Yeah, Latham. You sold your business. Gonna sell your house. Your wife is sadly no longer available, you say. So you got nothing to do, and soon no place to live. Tell me this—how's your social life going? Seems like maybe you're gonna be adrift in a place where people will give you a smile in passing—in passing, but you'll be a sad case they talk about but won't want to associate with."

"What, you a shrink now?"

"Not on your life. But I've been through all of that—in my own way, of course. Oh, and another thing, has our family closed ranks around you, offering comfort and support?" A moment of dead air passed. "Thought not. You and I, we suffer from the same malady—we're outcasts: me because I've lived an offbeat life, you because you married an offbeat wife. Our people, they never cottoned to her."

"I know, been reminded of that."

His laugh was a burst of air. "You and I, we've been rowing in the same damn canal, nephew, and never considered our parallel universes. Hot damn. I must say, it's a real nice feeling, being up close to a family member—ain't had any of that. I know that sounds bad, but it's true. So whatta you say? Want to take an open-ended vacation out my way and help me sell stuff?"

"Floyd, I'm sorry."

"You don't want to do it? Helluv an offer. Even comes with penthouse quarters above the shop. Plenty of room."

I laughed. "Sounds regal. But I'm sorry, you know…"

"I get it, kiddo. Why you think you were always my favorite? 'Cause you were fair and honest with me." He fell silent, and when I didn't jump in, he said, "Okay, now, you comin' out here for the good life or what?"

I pulled at my nose again, closed my eyes, and imagined living over a thrift store in Portland, Oregon. No images came to mind, so I laughed at myself, and Floyd he laughed right back. In the end, I said I would pack up and be in Portland as soon as I had tidied up my affairs; maybe two weeks, maybe a month, whatever. He said, *I'll be damned* and promised to clean up his digs enough for a respectable person before I got there.

-15-

The next morning I slept until around eight o'clock, skipped breakfast, donned some running attire, left the newspaper on the porch, and went for a jog around the Whitewood Estates. All was quiet. I likened the scene to that of a modern ghost town: lawns manicured and excessively green, sprinklers turning on and off on their own, driveways empty of cars either gone for the day or hidden away behind multiple garage doors, windows peering out blankly, unretrieved UPS packages resting placidly on porches, but no barking dogs or signs of human life. I felt like I was the only person who hadn't gotten the notice to vacate the neighborhood in advance of some cataclysmic event.

I labored around a complete circuit of Carriageway, a pompous name for the development's boundary road, amused at how those impeccable environs might compare with my supposed replacement habitat above my uncle's secondhand store. Panting, and grateful that my house was again in sight, I slowed upon seeing a white Ford pickup parked out front. I knew without seeing it that the side doors would carry the Tucker Construction name and logo. Isaac Tucker was standing on the front porch, peering into one of the sidelight windows and jabbing at the doorbell. I stood out in the yard and leaned over on my thighs to catch my breath.

Eventually, Isaac stopped jabbing and knocking and turned around to find me drenched in sweat staring at him. "Isaac," I said.

At first he didn't move or say a word, merely stood like a pole, his splayed feet planted, and studied me as one would an invasive species. After several deep breaths, he stepped off the porch and came toward me in long strides; I straightened up and tried to gauge his body language.

He came right up to me and looked down—the tree to the bush. "What the fuck do you think you're doing?" He pointed a forefinger toward the For Sale sign.

I used the tail of my tee shirt to mop my face; my cheeks were aflame from the exertion of the run. Twisting my neck, I looked over at the post and its placard. "Just what it says."

"You can't do that," he sputtered. "This is Ashley's dream home." His face was rigid with anger, more than anger, fury.

"One person's dream can be another person's nightmare," I said, stepping back from his close proximity.

Isaac turned to face the house then spun around, his gnarled hands squeezed into clumps of bony flesh. "You bastard," he seethed. "You goddamned bastard. This is the home my daughter will come back to. You are not going to take that away."

Sadness is what I felt right then, sadness for this man whom I disliked so very much. How did he get through the gate anyhow, I wondered. Then of course I remembered he'd had his own gate card ever since we'd moved in. Ashley had insisted. But since the attack it seemed that anybody who showed up at the gate could get in by simply giving the guard the name of us poor unfortunates. The irony was that gaining access should have become more difficult not easier, damn it all.

I was beginning to cool down. My face was drying, and the salt-laden sweat was crystallizing on my forehead. I rubbed at it while readying myself to do battle with the towering force before me. How could I say what needed to be said? My wife's father, broad shouldered and angry, was hyperventilating, breathing hard through his nostrils. I said it straight out. "Isaac, she's not coming back to this house."

"She will. And you will not sell it."

I smiled as kindly as I could muster and shook my head.

"Ashley is gone." I spoke those words in a quiet tone, hoping to disarm his anger. "You know that...don't you?"

His shoulders rose up, and his face beheld me with absolute disdain. "I'll never quit on her," he said. "You have already quit on her, you son-of-a-bitch. You never deserved her, and now you're proving how worthless you've always been by deserting her." He stepped toward me again. "And when she recovers, we will rid you from her life like that." He snapped a thumb and finger.

I decided I'd heard all of that ad nauseam and started to walk past him. He grabbed me by an arm and spun me around. "You will not sell this house. You hear me? It's not yours to sell."

"It is mine to sell, and I need to sell it. I can't sustain the financial overhead this place demands. It was tough enough on two incomes, but on my own, not a chance."

He studied me. "I'll pay her share, Ashley's share of the expense. I'll pay it."

"I don't want that. I need to move on. Isaac, Ashley is not going to recover. Haven't you spoken with the doctors? Haven't they told you that medically it is over? She may be alive like she is for another week or two years, who knows? But she is gone."

"They don't know everything. Plenty of times people come out of these comas. I've read about it on the Internet."

I heaved a sigh. "You believe what you want, Isaac. I know you will. But I've listened to the evidence, and I know what I know. My wife, my Ashley, isn't coming back to me."

He came at me, grabbed a fistful of my tee shirt, and yanked me toward his face. "Get it through your thick skull. She's not your Ashley, never was. She's my Ashley, my little girl. And you, you worthless piece of shit, are not going to sell her house. I'll see to that."

I slapped at his hand, and he let go of my shirt. "Isaac, I have the authority and the right. I will sell this house."

He marched out onto the lawn, yanked the real estate post out of the yard, and threw it all into the back of his pickup. After he'd gone, I walked out and looked down at the hole in the grass and had to laugh. When I looked up, my neighbor Guy Stewart was standing in his driveway holding onto his fluff of a dog by one of those retractable leashes. I raised a hand and waved; he did likewise and yelled over to ask if I was really selling the house. I called back that yes I was, though I was temporarily without a For Sale sign. He laughed politely even though I was certain he didn't have a clue about what had just happened to his strange neighbor. He'd quit asking about Ashley, and his promised invitation to have dinner with him and his wife Nancy had faded away, replaced with cordial greetings.

I went back into the house of my disdain, stripped out of my still damp running togs, laughed when I saw that my tee shirt was emblazoned with that Nike line—*Just do it!*—and took a long, steamy shower. My lunch consisted of chicken noodle soup out of a can, complete with a stack of stale saltines and a diet Coke. While consuming those delicacies, I left a message on Gloria Denham's cell phone that I needed a new yard sign because mine had been stolen; I didn't say who the culprit was. The newspaper held little of interest except for a story about a one-vehicle fatality crash out on Arrow Rock Road. A man I had known, Ralph Stokes, 56, failed to negotiate a curve; his pickup had gone over an embankment and landed in the rocks 100 feet below. He had died at the scene. That sobered me. Stokes Equipment Company had been one of my first clients when I joined the CPA firm; I knew Ralph Stokes very well. I emailed my former partners with my condolences. Jack replied right away: *Many thanks, Ned. It is a sad day.* From Claude all I got was *Duly noted.* Obviously the umbilical had been severed with Claude. The realization of being *officially* out at the firm was clear.

After that communiqué, I stood in the foyer and considered that I'd never really felt despair before, let alone isolation. Being a loner had always felt comfortable to me—even preferable at times. But I felt both of those sensations right then. Who was I, after all? Without Ashley, without my position at the firm, and with the only person who did want me being a predator, what was left? What to do now that my life was totally mine for the first time in a very long time. How does a man go about reinventing himself, forming an assumed role, broad jumping from an ambiguous youth, past years of being defined by a stiff marital contract, to a borderless domain that is his to define? That's just it; I had no experience of deciding for myself—not the big stuff anyway. Ludicrous.

I rubbed a hand against a cheek, felt the emerging stubble, and pressed my eyelids closed. My torso had a band around it. If I'd been felled right then, stricken, how long would it be before I was found? Would it be because I was missed? No. No, I would be discovered there on the floor for one of three reasons: a crew came by to prep the house and found my stone-cold body, the foul odor of my decomposing carcass aroused suspicion, or Sylvia Winters was relentless in her rapacious pursuit.

I stumbled into the kitchen, banging a shin on something on the way, splashed water on my face from the tap, and gulped down a full glass of cold water. I leaned forward, propped my arms on the counter, drew in a full breath, and let it out slowly. It was quiet. My mind was in neutral. Then a foregone conclusion spoke to me: *You are gone.* When it hit me, I stood up straight and waited for it to hit me again. No need to wait; in fact, I needed this to be over. The janitorial guy wants me to be out when they swoop in. Well, okay!

A sudden surge of energy entered my body as if I had been rebooted. I went around the house considering my plan of attack, put several Rachmaninoff CDs on the stereo player and ramped up the sound. With the house vibrating, I dragged out all the suitcases, duffle bags, and boxes we had (anything that would hold stuff) and began filling them with clothes, shoes, toiletries, towels, my laptop computer, CDs, and lots of other stuff

I'll not bother to list here—leaving the rest for Gloria Denham to dispose of. I backed the Explorer into the garage and loaded it to near capacity. I hadn't felt so motivated in a very long time—maybe ever. Yes, *ever*.

It was a transcendent moment when I slammed the rear tailgate down on the SUV—done! Seeing the vehicle stuffed to the roof was a sight; it made me laugh. I would giggle, stop and take in a breath, then shout out a burst of laughter until I had to lean over on my knees. Damn, the release was something I hadn't expected, right then—I'd moved on. Like an iguana shedding its skin, that's how I felt.

Before driving away, I decided to leave a message with Gloria Denham, giving her complete instructions and authority to do whatever it took to sell the house—including selling the furniture, packing and storing whatever didn't sell, securing separate storage for Ashley's things, prepping the house for sale—and telling her I would pay her well for all of it. With the finality of that call, I felt a rush of heat and a shudder; it was really time, time to vacate the place, give it the finger, take Floyd up on his offer—no waiting two weeks or whatever. Just go. In fact, I picked up my cell again, dialed my uncle, and told him I wasn't waiting. I'd be there in a few days after I stopped off in Baker County to see the family. He just giggled.

I took one last piss, turned off the lights, activated the garage door opener, and pulled out into the driveway. I stepped back into the garage where Ashley's silver Audi sedan sat unused, paused for a long moment while my mind ran through the unpredictable course I was setting for myself, then carefully set the door opener on the hood of the Audi. I'd have to decide what to do with her car later, not a priority right then. I hit the switch to close the door and ran out before it came down with a thud.

On the way out of Whitewood Estates, I gave a wave to the security guard on duty and drove away, I hoped, for the last time.

How do I describe it, the way I felt right then? It was weird. My breathing seemed shallower, my head was swimming, and there was tingling in my hands as they gripped the steering wheel. I lowered the driver's side window and let the warm summer air brush my face. After a mile or so, my equilibrium all but stabilized. At the entrance to the Garnet Skilled Nursing & Rehab Center, I slowed, thought about just continuing on, but finally drove in and parked.

At the reception desk, I signed in, nodded to the attendant, and walked the hallway to Ashley's room; the familiar antiseptic odor, human murmurings, and bleakness had become the norm. Her room was the same, always the same: a bed lamp cast a gauzy illumination over the inert human presence on the bed, and the same light blanket covered her—the same.

I stood just inside the doorway and drew in a breath, held it, then let it escape slowly. Ashley was in the precise position she had been in on all other visits. An IV was still attached to an arm, feeding her nutrients, liquids, and electrolytes. The ventilator had been suspended; Ashley needed no assistance to breathe. A thing called a pulse oximeter was clipped to the forefinger of her right hand, monitoring heart rate and oxygen saturation. And a new mattress had been installed; I guess it was the rotating kind that Isaac had told me about. I didn't sense that it was doing anything right then. What would it do, jostle her up and down? Regardless of the sophisticated warehousing, she was still just a breathing hunk of meat. No alarms ever went off, neither did she have rare moments of movement, nor did an eyelid ever rise or even flutter. The Ashley I'd known wasn't in there, a fact known to me from the very first time I saw her after the break-in.

So why did I visit? Why had I stopped on my way to elsewhere? Obligation. Guilt. To verify her permanent lack of consciousness, an absence of mental presence. Assurance that after I left our local environment she wouldn't suddenly pop up in bed cursing me, proving her father right after all. What it really was, and I knew it to be so—I needed to be sure, of course—was that mostly I wanted to tell her good-bye on my own terms. To hell with Isaac, our friendless friends, and the malignant specter of Sylvia Winters.

"Ashley." I said her name on a breath; the sound hung there just past my lips. After that I moved to the side of the bed and looked down at the semblance of a face once recognizable but now just veneer, a mask, slack and inert. I reached out and laid the back of the fingers of my right hand against her brow. By holding them there for a time, I felt the warmth of blood through her skin. There was life but no cognition; there was no cognition because what made that part of her function had been irreversibly destroyed. That I knew well. So why was I there?

I pulled a side chair up to the bed and sat down, resting hands on my knees. "So," I began. "Here I am…why? Last time I was here, I told you I wouldn't be back." I looked at that face, steadfastly, my eyes refusing to blink. "One more time. I'm here one more time because…because it's really over, our life. It is done, even if you sat up in bed right now. And I'm here to say out loud that I am leaving this place to try something else. I resigned from the firm. I'm selling the house and—you'd laugh—moving in with Uncle Floyd out in Portland."

I stood, put my hands in my pockets, and waited for something else to come to me, something more than a list of actions taken and pending, something to tell myself in the guise of conversing with her.

"Okay," I said on a steady voice. "All right. I want to say some things out loud without you being able to take them in. Just for me." I squeezed my hands into fists inside my pockets. "I loved you," I said. "I did." I hesitated. "Something's just coming to me, a remembering, an example of how we functioned, I guess. It was our last anniversary, January 10, twenty-three years gone by. And how'd we celebrate? You had Isaac over for dinner with a bunch of his construction buddies. Remember? Never once was our anniversary mentioned. Not once. But you know what was chilling…for me anyway? It didn't mean anything to you."

I leaned over her. "I share the blame of course because I said nothing either. I was once again weak. I could have lobbied for us to have a nice dinner somewhere—just the two of us. I didn't. Oh, I brought home flowers and a sweet card, and you did pat me on the arm for being thoughtful. But you know what?" I sucked in a breath. "I wanted us. For there to be an us that night, not a bunch of good old boys horsing down our food and telling raunchy stories. Even more, I wanted you, your body, our bodies together—to verify that we belonged together. We never did though—verify *us*—did we? Not in twenty-three years. I guess I got what I had coming."

I rose back up and took another long look at her. "Good-bye Ashley." The obligatory farewell rose from my chest but meant nothing, of course.

I passed the nurse's station on the way out, advised the person stationed there that I would be leaving town for some time. Reminded her that they had my cell phone number if anything came up needing my attention. The woman stared at me calmly, took in what I was saying, wrote something on a pad, and thanked me. That was it.

————————

I sat in the parking lot behind the wheel and wondered again how it had all come to this. Life had just happened, in segments like it does for all people, segments that streamed by without being noticed: a quarter here, then another until you realize that you've more or less reached the halfway point—maybe—much of it wasted time. Or maybe not wasted but gobbled up without it seeming to be happening. So there I was, much of my life already spent, looking at the last half to be covered in one slow leap; there'd be no more time for quarter notes.

I started the car, thought again of Ashley: permanently inanimate, with her final days an unknown sum. After stopping downtown to fill up at Express Gas and buy road food at their convenience mart, I had one last duty to perform before moving on. Detective C. T. Morgan answered after four rings.

"Mr. Pine," he said with more energy than I expected. "To what do I owe the pleasure?"

I chuckled and responded, "Honor indeed. Catch you at a bad time?"

"No. Not at all. I'm actually having my lunch. My bride makes a terrific sliced smoked turkey sandwich with cheddar, lettuce, onion, and tomato—on whole wheat, too. I'm hunkered down in the station's fabulous break room enjoying life."

"Makes me hungry."

"Sure it does. What's up?"

I took a sip of coffee from a paper cup and set it in the armrest holder. "Leaving town."

"That right?" I could hear him chewing. "Taking a trip?"

"More'n that. Pulling up stakes."

There was a pause before he responded. "Oh? Mean leaving for good?"

"Maybe. Selling my house and heading west, out to Portland."

"Hmm." I could sense him pondering my disclosure. "Surprising. What about your wife?"

"She's being cared for. Like I told you before, my wife's gone."

"Yeah, I recall. Bummer."

"I can't keep wallowing in it forever. Need some new scenery."

"I hear you. Don't you have that accounting company?"

"Did," I answered. "Selling out. To my partners."

"Hmm," he uttered again. "Big changes. Well, I wish you all the best."

"Thanks."

"So why'd you call me on your way outa Dodge?"

"My wife's no longer viable, but I still want the animals who killed her found."

"Killed?"

"I know she's breathing, but she is in fact dead."

"Sure," the detective agreed. "Not sure what the law says about that, but I understand where you're coming from."

"Keep looking," I said.

"We will."

"Anything brewing on this?"

"Nope. Nothing to report. Still leaning on A-Ball Security."

"You have my cell number. Call me whenever you do have news."

"Sure, will do." Morgan chuckled. "And I suspect I'll be getting occasional calls from you on the subject."

"You will. Enjoy your gourmet sandwich."

"I am. Happy trails."

It felt odd, unreal in its own a way, to pass the Latham city limits as if never to return. Even knowing I would have to come back on the occasion of Ashley's passing, whenever that might be, there was nothing left for me in the town—not anymore.

-16-

By the time I hit Twin Falls, it was nearing 4:00 p.m. Since I had intentionally passed on lunch so as to put Latham in my rearview mirror, my stomach was knotted in hunger pangs, and I had been close to nodding off for nearly fifty miles. I nosed the Explorer off an I-84 exit in search of food and found Mel's Café down in town, a square box of a structure with a slope roof. The place was still open, empty except for a booth with four men wearing shirts with White Satin Sugar logos on them; I recalled that Amalgamated Sugar was a big employer in Twin Falls. Our firm had made a run at getting them as a client to no avail, out of our league. The men eyeballed me for a moment then went back to their coffee and conversation; their words were being doled out one at a time, it seemed—no long sentences. I took a backless stool at the counter and decided on the special: a ham and cheese sandwich and a cup of split pea soup. Big-bodied Mel himself took the order just before my cell phone began a relay of calls: my brother's wife Sybil was first, responding to my earlier voice mail. Yes, it was fine for me to stay at the farm that evening, her tone was nice but not enthusiastic. Then Gloria Denham was all over me for just leaving in the middle of things but agreed to all I asked, for a fee. By the time Uncle Floyd called, I was getting glares from the sugar guys, who evidently didn't approve of my answering service interfering with their coffee break.

"Hey Nedder!" Floyd brayed. "You on the road or not? Got a bunk all ready for you."

I smiled as my food arrived; my stomach rumbled in anticipation.

I lowered my voice. "In Twin Falls as a matter of fact."

"Driving through or taking a leak?"

"Having a late lunch."

"All righty, all righty, then," he laughed. "So when will I see the whites of your eyes?"

"Maybe tomorrow. Stopping to see our kinfolk in Baker City. Staying the night."

"Now that sounds reasonable. Give everybody my best, you hear. And my big brother, be sure and tell Hughby hello for me."

"Sure thing." I hadn't the heart tell him of my father's dementia.

"I just know it will brighten their day." His laugh was small, sad.

I was handing Mel my credit card when the next call came; it was Isaac. With his voice blustering in my ear, I signed the receipt and hustled outside. He was on the attack.

"Where the hell are you?" Those were his first words. "You there?"

I didn't answer until I was out of earshot of the White Satin crew. "I'm here."

"I was over to the house early this morning. You didn't answer the bell," he was nearly shouting. "We need to talk."

"About what, Isaac?"

"Whatta you mean, about what? That house you're trying sell out from under us, me and Ashley. That's what."

I leaned up against the Explorer, the afternoon sun glaring against my face. I stepped around to the shady side of the vehicle, let a few heartbeats pass, expelled a calming breath, and said, "What about it?"

"It ain't gonna happen, that's what," he grunted. "You hear me?" Isaac's voice poked into my eardrum.

"I heard you." I counted to five. "Look, Isaac, like I told you before, the house is legally mine to keep or dispose of as I see fit. And I see fit to sell it."

"Like hell you will. God damn it. That's the house Ashley's coming home to."

"Heard that before…"

"And you ain't gonna deprive her of that, no siree."

"Hey," I raised my voice. "Listen. Just listen. Get this through your thick head. Like I've told you any number of times: durable powers of attorney, durable powers of attorney. Signed and sealed years ago to give the surviving spouse total control over health determinations and all of our assets. Get that through your head."

"You fucker. I'm coming over there and beat the holy shit out of you."

"Good luck with that," I laughed. "I left town today. Moving on, old man."

"You what?" His voice sounded as if he'd been strangled. "Where?"

"You're not on my dance card."

"Bastard. You're abandoning Ashley?"

"Ha. Thought I didn't deserve her. I went by this morning, spent some time with her just to clear my head. Nothing's changed. She's not there, just the remnant. But I told her good-bye."

I could hear him groaning his anger. "You…you worthless piece of cow dung."

"Gotta go, Isaac."

"I'll find you, you son-of-a-bitch."

"Then what?"

His hesitation was prolonged; then, "I'll kill you."

I held onto the phone for a chilling moment before ending the call. My father had said that to me once in the heat of rage: *I ought to kill you.* I had been negligent in my duties of overseeing the birth of a calf, which ended up stillborn. The mother was what they called a first-calf heifer, needing more assistance. I'd left the barn on my watch to visit with a friend of mine who'd come by in his recently acquired custom '50 Mercury. By the time I returned to the barn it was too late. Even though a certain percentage of first-calf heifer stillbirths are a given, my father saw it as clearly my dereliction. He and Isaac Tucker might well lift a beer on the subject of my demise. My father had never forgiven me for that lapse; likely Isaac would never absolve me of guilt for Ashley's loss either. I felt special.

———

The year was 1896 when the farmhouse was built; our parents had assumed the ranch in 1960 when Harrison was a two-year-old. I came along four years later, my little sister Corrine four years after that. My parents had been methodical in their procreation. Driving up the gravel road with green center growth between the tire runs, a feeling of déjà vu flooded through me. I'd been there before of course, had grown up there, but I'd been away so long it was as if I was visiting some alternate life. I recognized the white box two-story house with its red metal roof looming up at the end of the drive, all right, but from someone else's scrapbook. Strings of barbed wire fence ran parallel to the lane; in the pasture to my left a small herd of Herefords grazed nonchalantly in the diminishing light of the day.

It was nearing 8:00 p.m. when I pulled the Explorer off to the side of the house, parked, and stepped out. It was one of those special summer evenings in Baker County, a hint of gossamer light, cooling with a gentle breeze rustling the aspen trees that had bracketed the house for all those years. I stretched my back and did a 180 turn, taking in the panorama of the place from which I'd long been separated.

The porch light came on, and the screen door opened against a groaning spring; an older woman emerged. She stepped to the edge of the porch and stared out at me. My mind tumbled about for a moment until I was assured: it *was* my mother. She seemed smaller. Even in the low illumination of the porch light, her hair was whiter, her face more lined, flesh looser; she moved easily but with caution. Rosalind was her name, Rosie to all who knew her well. I raised a hand, spread a smile on my face, and moved toward her. She hesitated, waiting until I drew near and came up the steps.

"Mom," I said with a catch in my throat.

She looked into my face as if I was a stranger. "Ned," she answered after a moment. "It *is* you. Sybil told us you were coming." She was wearing a flowered housedress and cotton apron like always.

"And here I am." I held my arms out, confirming my arrival. I expected to give her a big hug, I wanted to, but the idea just stalled between us.

"Yes. This is a surprise. How are you?" Beneath the porch light, I couldn't really make out her once bright blue eyes, and strangely, she looked at me with a form of suspicion.

"I'm doing pretty well."

"That is good to hear. It has been so long since we've seen you."

"Sorry about that. But I'm here now."

She nodded and looked at my vehicle and back. "Well," she said at last, "you'd best come in. Your father is watching the TV, and Harrison and Sybil are with him." She paused, holding the screen door part way open. "He's not fully himself these days, Ned. Your father. "

"Harrison told me."

She looked into my face and studied me for a long moment. "It's good that you know. Come in, now."

My father was in his mid-seventies, I guessed; damn, I should've known that. Hugh Pine had been a man of the soil all his life. And like his wife he had a nickname that had followed him since childhood; to one and all he was Hughby. I followed my mother into the house, unprepared for my father not being himself. He and Harrison were a matched set in many ways: both were taller than me, had similar square faces, the same ears that clung close to their heads, identical hairlines, and most telling, the same terse, no-nonsense personalities.

I heard sound from the television before I saw him. He was seated in a big recliner with his eyes locked onto the screen; a game show was on. I froze in the doorway to the living room, totally

140

unprepared for the effigy of someone I'd known whose once broad body was now a diminished likeness of what had been. Harrison and Sybil sat side by side on a couch; they turned away from the television screen when I entered, each offering me low-wattage smiles. I looked again at my father and sucked in a breath. My mother reached out and patted my arm. He was dressed in every-day clothes: worn Levis, plaid short-sleeved shirt, but slippers not boots. My mother walked over to him and touched an arm. He didn't respond. His eyes remained glued to the flickering screen. A woman had evidently just won a set of appliances and was jumping up and down; my father's face remained placid. I instantly thought of Ashley's catatonia and her total lack of responsiveness to stimuli.

My mother stepped between the television and my father. His eyes stared ahead for a long moment before he slowly raised his head. "Look who's here," she said, her tone even and forbearing. "Hughby. Look, it's Ned. He's come to visit." She gestured toward me as she would a stranger, which in many ways I was.

I took a couple of shuffling steps toward him, my torso bent at an angle, and pasted on a painful grin. "Hi, Dad."

He did look my way but seemed to find me uninteresting and waved an arm for Mom to quit blocking his view. She gave me a patient smile and ushered me out of the room; Harrison and Sybil merely observed. In the hallway my mother dropped a hand into her apron's patch pocket and brought out a hanky. "He has some good days and not so good days," she whispered and daubed her eyes. "Today he's not having much clarity. I'm sorry, Ned. He didn't seem to recognize you."

This time I stepped forward and gave her a hug; my arms easily reached all the way around her and even had some overlap. My mother had always been petite but strong, erect and hard work-ing. But now I was aware that, due to the time that had gone by without seeing her, I had missed witnessing the gradual incuba-tion of her aging. She allowed me to embrace her but reciprocated with but a light pat to my chest. Then she blinked, smoothed her apron, said she would fix me something to eat, and marched off to the kitchen.

It was nearly the same kitchen I had grown up in except for newer appliances. The long farm table sat where it always had, next to a span of four double-hung sash windows that looked out onto the wide back porch. Ladder-back chairs were still gathered around the table, and the wooden hutch handmade by my father held the family dishware. The old maple butcher's block squatted on heavy wooden legs in the center of the kitchen, just like always. When I was about twelve, I'd driven a nail into its hard grain for some harebrained reason and caught holy hell.

I sat at the table as my mother bustled about. It felt abnormal being a stranger in my boyhood home, backtracking on slips of memory, grasping at scenes that flitted by but did not remain, knowing that I no longer belonged. That seemed to be my mantra those days: no longer belonged.

My mother was well underway to fixing me a plate of leftovers evidently from the evening meal when Harrison and Sybil came in and took seats at the table.

"Ned," Sybil said in the soft melodious voice I'd almost forgotten. "It's good to see you." Harrison hadn't spoken yet and didn't right then either; he just studied me.

"Good to see you," I replied through a tight smile.

She nodded. "You caught us at a busy time. Potato harvest starts next week: three hundred acres of Russet Burbanks waiting to be dug up. Almost nonstop now that we've begun, not much time for socializing. And we hit the hay pretty early, I'm afraid." She looked up at the kitchen clock. "Getting on bed time."

I raised my hands, palms out. "Hey, that's all good. I just appreciate seeing you and having a room for the night."

"That's right." She rolled up the sleeves on her blue chambray shirt. "Flying through, huh?"

"Yeah, only here for a hot and a cot. Just the one night." I laughed. No one else did.

My mother set a plate in front of me heavy with two pieces of cold fried chicken, fresh green beans, and mashed potatoes. She added a side plate of sliced wheat bread, butter, and a glass of milk. I nodded my thanks and picked up my utensils.

"How's the old place look to you?" Harrison suddenly spoke. "Feel like home sweet home?"

"Been awhile," I said, "but, yeah, brings back memories."

"Been awhile. Hear that Sybil?" Harrison chuckled and folded his arms. "It has been years, little brother. Years."

My mother and Sybil looked at Harrison. "What?" he said.

"We agreed to not go there," Sybil answered.

"Prodigal son honors us with a visit, and we have to play nicey nice? That it?"

I felt my face flush. Sybil glanced at me, measuring my reaction, I guess. I raised my eyebrows and smiled benignly. She looked away then back at me.

"How's your wife?" she said. "Audrey, isn't it?"

"Ashley," I responded. "There's no change."

Sybil's face flushed. "I'm sorry, her named slipped my mind."

"That's all right, Dear," Harrison said. "Can't be blamed. When's the last time we saw *Ashley*? Quarter of a century, something like that?"

"Damn it, Harrison!" Sybil glared at him. "He's gone through hell. Show some empathy."

My brother reared back in his chair. With his cap off, his farmer's brow shown bright white above his weathered face. He let out a disgruntled sigh. "Empathy." He ran a hand over his salt-and-pepper short hair. "All right," he said, nodding. "Guess your wife isn't going to make it. Sorry about that."

"Harrison," I said, holding up a hand to stop Sybil from weighing in again. "The torment of what happened to Ashley and me back in March gutted me. It eviscerated me. Those bastards intruded into our lives and ruined everything." When he opened his mouth to respond, I said, "Look, regardless of how we lived our lives, regardless of our flaws, I have lost her. There's no waiting things out until she's all better. Not gonna happen. So whatever I had with her, it's all gone…never to return. Got it?"

He tipped is chair back down, studied me for a long moment, and nodded.

"I'm empty." I made a fist and thumped my chest. "Nothing in there. On my way to…what? I don't know, a resurrection, I guess. Stopped by on my way to see how life ought to be lived."

Harrison snorted. At that moment our father wandered into the kitchen and blurted that he wanted food. We all paused in our thoughts and looked at him. His presence changed the mood, sure did for me anyway. I watched him shuffle forward in his slippers and sit in a chair next to me. My mother was quickly at his side; she whispered that he'd already eaten dinner.

He sat calmly then said, "More."

My mother patted his shoulder and quickly buttered a piece of bread off my plate and handed it to him. After looking at it, he bit into it. The rest of us sat quietly. Harrison looked down; I saw his jaw muscles pulse. Hugh Pine chewed the bread methodically and after his first swallow turned to me.

"You're Ned, aren't you?" he said.

I started, hearing him suddenly address me. "Yes, Dad, it's me all right," I managed to utter. I smiled limply.

He looked at me, his face non-expressive. "You let us down." The silence among the rest of us thickened. "Leaving the farm. Taking up with that woman. Shameful."

My mouth grew dry. Would he hear me if I responded? He turned away from me. Mom brought him a glass of milk; he drank from it in long gulps and seemed to have retreated into his own space, wherever that was. I reached out and touched his arm. When he turned toward me again, I said, "I'm sorry, Dad." His expression told me that whatever moment of lucidity he'd reclaimed had passed. Silence hung over the table as we all abided his presence in our own ways.

My father finished the bread and milk, looked about at those seated, except for me, and pushed his chair back. When he tottered to his feet, I took ahold of one of his hands and gently squeezed it. Gone was the hardened farmer's hand I remembered. In its place was a veined, splotchy, and thin-skinned hand of age. He looked down at my grasp and oddly considered it before pulling loose, his expression one of annoyance. His glare at me was that of a stranger. I watched him shamble back to the living room. The man who was my father had morphed into someone else. I stared after him, at the empty doorway.

"Reruns." It was Sybil who spoke first. "That's all he does, watch reruns. He especially likes *All in the Family*. Don't think he gets the punch lines, just drawn to the ruckus Archie Bunker stirs up. And game shows."

"But he knew me," I said.

-17-

I had just made the most unfortunate of observations about my father's cognizance.

"For that moment, he knew you," Harrison said with resignation. He gave up a small laugh and added, "He recognizes me and Sybil on occasion. Mom, she's the only one he responds to most of the time. Even she can be a stranger to him sometimes."

"Oh, Harrison," my mother said. "Your father has many good days."

Harrison pursed his lips, shrugged in my direction, and shook his head a bit. Our mother took that as a cue to clear the table and escape further assessment of her husband of nearly fifty years.

My big brother and I stared at each other; Sybil, sensing the awkward moment, rose and helped with the cleanup. "So, obviously, you're running things now, right?" I said.

"Ha!" He laughed and slapped his hands together. "You bet. Presiding over this mega cattle and potato operation. That's me." I blushed; he leaned forward on his arms and looked hard into my eyes. "Here I am, fifty years old. You know how long I've had a free hand to run this place, little brother?" I shook my head. "Less than eighteen months, right up until the very last moment before he didn't know up from down. I've been sucking hind tit all these years. Waiting. Waiting my turn. I've been doing all the heavy lifting—making the place run, keeping it solvent—but with no authority, none."

"But why?"

"Why, he asks." He stood and hammered a fist into the tabletop.

"Because that old man in there kept me on a leash, treated me like a hired hand. And that leash was a promise that the place would be mine to own and run once he decided to step aside."

"That was good, right?" I said stupidly.

He barked again, clapped his hands together. When he spoke, his face was a mask of indignation. "But he would never give me the reins. Never. I've been his subservient child all, these years. No one ever did business with me. Only with Hughby. I was never a co-owner of this business, not even a cosigner on day-to-day business."

He leaned over the table, frowning at me. "And you know what?" he said, his voice hard-edged. "Now that he's lost his marbles, I can't even tell him to go to hell."

He rose from the table and went out the backdoor. It jumped in its frame when he slammed it.

In Harrison's absence I joined my mother and Sybil back in the living room where we sat quietly with little to say and endured the television programs that kept my father transfixed. When he finally dozed off, Sybil and Mom got him on his feet and guided him into what used to be the dining room. It had been converted into a bedroom so that my father, in his diminished capacity, could be kept in a separate space for his frequently troubled slumber. It also meant that my mother had her own bedroom—her own space. They had acquired a baby monitor system with two audio units; that way both Harrison and mother could hear when Hughby woke up in the morning or caused a disturbance during the night.

I watched as the once robust, self-assured man I'd known was led away like a drunken person. I found the remote and fiddled with it until I managed to turn off the television. There was a low murmuring between my mother and Sybil while they shared the duties of getting the impaired being they were devoted to undressed and prepared for bed. I cringed hearing the humane struggle going on, realizing that such was the case each and every day—whether I was there or not. While that was going on, Harrison came back into the house. He stood in the doorway to the living room and witnessed my reaction.

"Yeah," he said. "It's like that every day and every night." His crimped smile offered me no solace.

All I could muster was an anemic smile in return. "Is he getting worse?"

"Sure, what do you think?" he said, turning his head toward the makeshift bedroom and back. "He is. At first it was just moments of blanking out on a name or being unable to finish a sentence—then he'd laugh and make light of it. We all did. Doesn't seem that long ago, really."

"But it's been...coming on for some time?"

"Right."

After an uncomfortable length of time, my mother and Sybil returned and rejoined us. Harrison pulled the dining room pocket doors shut and sat down beside Sybil. She patted him on a leg, and he asked if everything was okay.

"Who knows?" she shrugged and looked in my direction. "We got him tucked in—once again. Best we can do...best we can do."

Harrison squeezed his eyes shut then reached up and knuckled them as if he were kneading dough.

I decided to keep my mouth shut. My mother sat in the old upholstered rocker, hands folded in her lap, eyes closed, and tipped back and forth gently. Time has a way of controlling the moment. If something is urgent, time often lingers, forcing its linear power to withhold any solution or remedy needed apace. Counter to that, a matter better dealt with over a longer term frequently forces its will on those concerned well ahead of an arbitrated outcome. The latter was staring us in the face that evening. It began with Harrison.

"So, Ned," he said, a quiet length of time after our father had been put to bed. "You said something earlier about dropping by to *see how life ought to be lived.*"

I grinned a shrug. "Just pondering out loud."

"No. You meant it. What exactly?"

"Oh, I don't know. Guess I was feeling torn asunder following the wreckage I've been swimming in."

"My, my, asunder, is it? You were assuming that life on the farm must be more solid, tried and true? Like that?"

I scooted back in the armchair I was seated in; the leather upholstery groaned. "I suppose. It was just a loose assumption falling back on memories of times past."

"Guess we put that myth to rest," Harrison said. The dimple in his chin stood out in stark relief beneath a cagey smile. "Wouldn't you say?"

I leaned forward on my knees and clasped my hands in a knot. "Look, Harrison, this place still has a certainty about it. I...I, well, what I mean is that in spite of that," I nodded my head in the direction of the improvised bedroom, "you know what you need to do every day. You know these walls and this acreage will be there when you wake, even if it all demands much of you. Maybe too much in your estimation." Off to my right, I saw Sybil's face contort.

"Oh my," Harrison said and looked at his wife. "So you know what this life is all about now after being AWOL for years? Damn you."

"Harrison." Sybil spoke softly.

"No," he responded. "No. I will not sit here and let this absentee analyze my life. Telling me I have it better than it seems."

We stared at each other; I absorbed his glare. "By comparison," I whispered.

At that moment our father reappeared, his big bare feet showing beneath pale blue pajamas that hung on him like a tent. He stood on unsteady legs and looked about, then spoke saying, "No, no, no." His voice wasn't loud, just persistent.

Our mother rose quickly and went to his side. She took a big hand in hers and purred words into his ear. He stood stark still for a moment then let her lead him away, back to his bed. Harrison rose and closed the sliding doors again.

My throat swallowed involuntarily. I clinched my eyes shut. "It's okay," Sybil said. "Rosie will lie with him until he goes back to sleep. He does this sometimes."

I nodded as if I actually understood. "Did it mean anything? What he said?"

Harrison settled on the couch again and uttered a heavy sigh. "I doubt it. He can get agitated when things get out of order. Maybe that's it."

"Like me showing up?"

"Could be," Harrison said and looked sideways at Sybil.

"So I've upset him," I said.

"I wouldn't know," Harrison responded. "Maybe."

"In the kitchen he…"

"That's over, Ned," Sybil chimed in. "Hughby's memory can dredge up stuff from years ago but not yesterday. You know, like they say about recent memory and all."

My father's most indelible recollection of me, maybe his only remembrance, judged me shameful in his frail mind. And there it hung, and would until nothing of his cognizance remained. At that moment, the disheartenment I was processing must have made itself evident via a slight upturn of my mouth; it was not of humor, mind you, but may have seemed that way.

"That funny to you, Ned?" my brother prodded.

I was startled by his question. "No," my voice throbbed. "No. Of course not."

"Why the smirk, then?"

"There was something else," I said. "Something related to…all of this about Dad."

"Want to share the joke with us, then?"

I scooted forward and yelled. "It wasn't a joke, damn it!" For once Harrison didn't have a retort. Sybil placed a hand against his arm and pushed several times in attempt to quell his vexation. "It wasn't a joke," I repeated. "Not a joke."

Harrison reached up and pushed Sybil's hand away.

I sat back. My eyes were moist; I felt stranded, alone within myself. "What it was…what came to me just then, was that I am no longer able to communicate with two very important people in my life. They are unreachable. They're alive—technically. My wife is breathing but nothing else. And my father, functioning on the fringes, only recalls the worst of me."

No one spoke, neither they nor I. We remained that way for some time. It was Sybil who broke the silence. "Ned." She spoke in a kindly manner, one she hadn't often given me in years past. "How about we set all of that aside and you tell us of your plans?"

Harrison looked over at her, grunted, and shook his head. Heat came to my face. I locked onto to his blue eyes beneath shaggy eyebrows and said, "You know, I'm not sure what the fuck I'll do with my life now that it's mine for the first time ever."

Sybil flinched at my profanity.

"Ned's going to hook up with Uncle Floyd." Harrison's voice practically warbled his amusement. "Speaking of plans, isn't that the plan?"

"That's where I'm headed," I answered.

"Uh-huh. To what, be controller for his junk yard?"

"What is it, Harrison. You want me to fill in for Dad? Go ahead, tell me to go to hell. That work for you? You want to make someone the scapegoat for you not being able to give that old man what you think he has coming? Okay by me. I can take it."

Harrison reared up and put his hands on his knees. "You…you—"

"Harrison, stop!" Sybil raised her voice.

"Stay out of this, Sybil," he responded and waved a hand at her. "I mean it." She sank back on the couch.

When I just sat still and didn't engage him, he leaned toward me as if he'd like to reach out and grab me. "You don't need to stand in for Dad. You've got enough stink on you of your own.

You cut yourself loose from us, got a college education on family money, married that bitch, and we never saw you again. And now," he raised an arm above his head, "since that woman is brain dead, or whatever, you're running away again."

I stood and looked down at each of them in turn. "I shouldn't have come." Their reaction to that declaration was conjoined: she the humiliated host, he full of sibling animus. When Harrison nodded in agreement, I asked where I would be sleeping. My mother had prepared my boyhood bedroom for me. I apologized awkwardly and climbed the stairs. The room was not actually as I recalled it. The furnishings were different, maybe the same bed, but there was no other semblance of my childhood; it was not a return to my place of youthful slumber. Someone, my mother no doubt, had placed my travel bag on the bed. I closed the door, turned on the lamp on the nightstand, and stripped down to my underwear.

The tap on the door brought me out of my detachment as I lay staring up at the ceiling, lamenting my return. After a second rap, I invited whoever it was to come in. My mother pushed the door open slowly, hesitated, and asked if she could come in. I scooted up in the bed.

She approached. I asked, "How's Dad? He okay?"

"No," she said, sitting on the edge of the bed; she held a photo album in her lap. "Of course not. But we are managing…mostly."

"Not what I expected," I said. "I mean, I knew something was wrong but…"

My mother smiled and patted the blanket I was under. "It is what it is, Ned. He's not going to get better and will only drift farther away from us."

Her face, the face I had lived with, the face I had grown so accustomed to when I was a self-absorbed young boy, seemed strange to me at that moment. It was as if she was a neighbor lady visiting. And her words just then were unlike words my mother would have spoken. *It is what it is.* My mother had never talked like that.

"I understand," I returned.

"Yes. I'm sure you do, more than most, I think." She took in a breath and asked me, "How is it now? With your wife? With Ashley?" she added.

My arms were on top of the covers. I put my hands together and squeezed. "Erased," I answered. My mother's sad expression coerced me into softening my tone. "She's still in a coma from which she will not recover. That's the flat answer."

The woman who bore me studied my face and said, "And now you've left her."

"She is being cared for. By professionals. There's nothing I can personally do for her."

"Nothing?"

"No, besides sitting next to the body that she once inhabited and feeling empty."

She raised a hand to her throat. "And the children? How are they?"

"Not good. Roz is in denial about her mom never making a comeback. Sides with her grandfather, and Isaac is not accepting reality. He and I are at loggerheads. Mike is more realistic, but they're still reeling." I rubbed my face with both hands. "Honestly, I doubt if the mix of temperaments will ever equalize...until she's gone, truly gone. Even then, I think we'll all just drift away. The glue and the longing to rectify will dissipate, I fear. We will have exhausted our compassion because it will have all been drained away by the harshness of our anger."

"But you can't believe in such a bleak future."

"What did you say? *It is what it is*? I'm in the same fix."

"But we're still together, your father and I."

"For now. The day will come when you will need to put him someplace to be safe and cared for."

She shook her head. "No. I care for him and will...until the end."

I could only nod sympathetically. "I hope you can."

"And now you're going to Portland to see Floyd. What will you do there?"

I smiled. "Uncle Floyd has offered me a place to stay for a while. Maybe I'll do a bit of work for him." The brow of her sweet face wrinkled into a frown. "Look, Mom, I need a respite, time out. It's different for me. My partner is no longer where I can reach her. She isn't there, not like Dad who comes and goes. At least you get something. I get nothing."

"So is that all for Ashley?"

"No. Of course not. I'll maintain contact with the nursing home and her doctor. I will never give up trying to find who attacked us."

"But how can you do that?"

"There's a policeman, a detective working the case. In Latham. He knows I will never let up." I paused. "They gutted us. They took away everything. I will never quit. I will find the bastards. And they will pay. They will pay." I surprised myself by the huskiness of my voice and the potency that welled up within me.

She hesitated over my bitterness before lifting the album from her lap. "I've brought you the family photos. I thought maybe it would be something you'd enjoy seeing again."

I took it. She leaned over me and kissed my forehead. When she was gone, I opened the brown leather cover with the family initials tooled into it and leafed through the thick black paper pages with photographs attached by corner mounts. The early pictures were from the twenties and thirties. I scanned through them until I began to see our generation: my sister Corrine as a baby, Harrison and I on horseback, mom and dad square dancing at the grange, grade school and high school class photos, me with my first car, Harrison and Sybil posing before the junior/senior prom. Then grandchildren began to appear.

When I'd seen enough, I set the album aside and curled into a ball before falling into an uneven sleep. The photographs were in my head but only as artifacts, not as part of me.

-18-

I heard something. My watch on the nightstand indicated it was just after five o'clock the next morning. There were muffled voices and then the sound of footsteps on the stairs. When it was quiet again, I slipped out of the bedroom and used the only bathroom upstairs to brush my teeth and scrub my face; I dressed in the same clothes from the day before. The smell of cooking met me when I entered the kitchen carrying my duffel. Sybil and my mother were at the table eating eggs and griddle cakes and having coffee; my father was there, too. They all seemed to freeze in motion when I came in, perhaps wondering where things stood—the familial strain between Harrison and me. My father wasn't in on that, of course, and more or less looked at me as one would a weather vane that was immobile in a steady breeze. "Who's that?" he blurted and pointed his fork at me.

My mother reached out predictably and patted his shoulder. "It's Ned, Dear." He studied me, blinked several times, then lifted a wedge of pancake on a shaky hand and chewed on it; my presence had passed relevance.

"Morning," I said behind the best smile I could muster. "Thanks for letting me bunk with you. Much appreciated. I'll be heading out."

"But you need breakfast," Sybil said. She gestured to the plates of eggs and cakes.

I feigned a laugh. "Way early for me to eat. I'll catch something along the way later." I looked around. "Harrison already at it?"

They both nodded.

"Well, give him my best." I raised a hand and slipped away before any more was said, later regretting that I hadn't given my mother one more hug.

————————

Driving down the lane to the main road, I saw Harrison emerge from the big barn with another man I didn't recognize. He stood watching as I drove out and kept talking to whoever the fellow was. Neither of us waved. It was a beautiful morning: sunlight sparkled on the dew of the pasture, the cattle were already nibbling, the air was cool through my open window, the aroma was sensually earthy—and yet my brother and I did not share in the beauty of it at all.

It took some recollection, but in the light of a new day I recognized that big barn and other outbuildings I used to frequent as a kid and the potato fields where all the action for the harvest was taking place. From the lane, I saw a big self-propelled Ploeger potato harvester sitting at the ready. The machinery seemed newer and bigger than what we used back when, but I still understood what was going on. And a harvest truck was parked nearby; it looked like a Peterbilt 10-wheeler with a self-unloading trailer called a Spudnik. I'd participated in the family potato farming over and over; my memories were cold, but I'd been there. Many's the time I had held the freshly plowed silt loam soil of our farm in my hand, inhaled its earthiness, and let it run through my fingers. But those nostalgic days were long past and would stay that way.

By the time I drove into Baker City it was just after six o'clock, and the Inland Café out on Tenth Street was already open. The eatery looked the same, smelled the same as I remembered, and the same cast of early risers was eating food off the same menu. I took a seat at the back of the café where a dining counter faced the kitchen just like always. I could see the cook through the kitchen pass-through window, a big guy wearing a black tee shirt and baseball cap. I had an omelet, toast, and coffee, and was gassed up and back on I-84 in less than an hour. While the tank was being filled, my cell phone had rung; it was Sylvia Winters. Seeing her name, I almost ended the call. I should have.

"Sylvia." I had exited the Explorer and walked away from the gas pumps. I could hear her voice, but it was breaking up, bad connection. "Say again? I didn't get that."

"A moving van was at your house yesterday." Her voice warbled and became indistinct.

"What was that last?" I asked, holding a hand to my off ear.

"You weren't there."

"I'm selling the house, you know." When she asked what, I repeated what I'd said.

Suddenly her voice came in clearly as if she'd moved to a better signal. "Yes, but where are you staying?"

I hesitated. She asked again. "I'm on the road," I answered reluctantly.

"What? On the road to where?"

Damn, I didn't want to get into that with her. When I saw the gas attendant pull the hose nozzle from my vehicle, I ended the call. Bad connection. Must have been. I drove away from Baker City, ignoring Sylvia's attempts to reconnect, and traveled a stretch of highway I hadn't driven for a very long time, passing long-held landmarks of the journey, like the unincorporated town of Meacham at the summit of the Blue Mountains, which could be brutally cold and treacherous to drive in the winter. The same went for Cabbage Hill north of La Grande, also called Deadman Pass, known for its hairpin turns and six percent grades at an elevation of over 3,500 feet. I recalled the times my father drove over that stretch of highway in blinding snowstorms, sharing the road with eighteen-wheelers—I knew I was going to die. It was gratifying to drive such familiar ground again.

I hit Pendleton around nine thirty and pulled off for coffee and found the usual Starbucks in a strip center just off the highway. After a pit stop, I ordered an Americano and was back in the car when my cell rang again. I wasn't going to answer if it was Sylvia

Winters again. It wasn't. Gloria Denham sounded hyper when I answered.

"Ned, where are you?" she blurted. "Things are crazy here."

I set my cup of coffee in the armrest holder and inhaled slowly. "Gloria, what's the trouble?"

"It's your father-in-law."

I pressed the phone tighter against my ear. "Isaac. What about him?"

"Ned, he wants to buy the house."

I laughed with a big dose of insincerity. "Not surprised. Full offer?"

"No," she sort of coughed into the phone. "He's expecting a low-ball price..."

"Because Ashley's his daughter, right?"

"Yes. Absolutely. What should I do? He's really being pushy."

"Hell, I've only been out of town for a couple of days. You know what this is all about, don't you? He's certain that Ashley will recover, and he wants the house waiting for her."

"I thought as much from what he said...made references to it being her house and all." When I didn't respond, she asked, "What now?"

"Any other offers yet?"

"No, but it's only just come up on the multiple listing."

"So what do you think?"

"It's a great house," she said. "I'm sure you'll get some good offers. Not many of that quality on the market right now, though with the recession it'll be tougher. I think you should sit tight and wait him out. It's been fully detailed, ready to be shown. I'll set up an open house right away."

"Isaac may become aggressive. Don't let him push you around. I don't have to sell to him anyway, right?"

"No. You can reject his offer or even take the house off the market." She paused. "But just hang on, Ned. There'll be offers. I'll need to know how to get in touch with you. I have your cell number, but I'll need an address to send paperwork."

I retrieved a slip of paper stuck behind a rubber band wrapped around the sun visor; it had Uncle Floyd's address printed on it. She took it all down. I never for a moment thought that it was a mistake to give it to her. I was wrong.

"Thanks for all of this," I said to her. "Everything go okay with the movers packing up and clearing the house?"

"Yes, all's good."

"Ashley's things, they stored?"

"Uh-huh, have her inventory in separate storage."

"Be sure I get the bills for all of this."

"You can count on it." She waited a moment then asked, "She's not going to make a recovery...is she? Ashley. No chance?"

"No, no chance. I feel for Isaac, but she's gone. That's why I had to get out of town."

"I understand."

I hesitated to ask, but I had to. "How are you, Gloria?"

She hesitated as well. "I'm fine. Doing well, actually."

"I didn't mean business. Still getting married?"

Her answer wasn't immediate. "Strange you should ask. No, the answer is no. Things didn't work out after all."

"I'm sorry. Really. It seemed you'd found the right match. He's a Realtor too, right?"

"Yes. He is."

"I think of you," I said after a moment. I shouldn't have, but I did.

I could actually hear her silence, her processing. "That was then," she said finally.

She was right, but part of me wanted to start the car, drive back to Latham, and offer myself as a replacement. Instead I asked if there was anything I could do. She said no, promised to keep in touch regarding the sale of the house, and then we were disconnected. My coffee was cool by then. I drank it anyway. In less than an hour, I passed the small town of Boardman, just as I-84 claimed a full view of the wide swath of the Columbia River. It all looked familiar: the dry sweep of land called the Columbia Basin followed the river from Boardman to The Dalles, some of it cultivated as dry land farming for wheat. I wrote a school science report once about the basin and remembered my favorite line was that the natural upland grassland had the nickname of *scabland* due to its very shallow, stony soil. Some things you never forget.

A few miles farther on, a tugboat pushing a long barge downriver came into view. I pulled off the highway onto a wide shoulder just to watch that scene: the slow-motion gracefulness of the boat propelling the barge carrying two very long enclosed metal containers with big white letters S H A V E R boldly blocked out on their once-red skin, which had turned to an oxidized pink. I'd seen Shaver tugs on the river for years, and those of their competitor Tidewater Barges. It was pleasurable to watch the familiar, knowing that those containers making their way slowly downriver likely held tons of grain headed for Portland. I knew that. It was reassuring, the knowing.

Gradually, as I sat there watching and traffic large and small roared by, causing the car to quiver, I was mesmerized into recounting those voices, the ones that kept asking if Ashley was going to make it. As I watched the frothy wake of the tug churn out behind it and recede slowly, ever so slowly moving away, I began to feel as if the vessel mirrored my journey, and the barge carried within it my intentions and what I'd left behind. I stepped out of the Explorer just as a big rig thundered by, raising a cloud of dust. It was hotter now. The ever-present gorge wind whipped around me and attacked my hair.

The barge kept moving on, appearing smaller on the river. I slid down beside the car and leaned against it, sitting in the gravel of the shoulder. My mind tumbled through the circumstance of my being right there above the river, sitting on the roadside, considering who I'd been and especially the parts of me I'd never been able to share with Ashley, nor she with me. But in the aftermath of the attack, I had been able to disassociate from her. How could that have happened? And when did it happen, before or after the assault? Why couldn't I see her face clearly in my mind anymore? I kept telling those who asked that, yes, she was gone for good. I didn't have the courage to stay the course, unlike Isaac. What was the matter with me? Hadn't I told my mother that I would never quit, that whoever had ruined our lives would pay? Pay for what? For what had happened to me, was that it? Or what had happened to both of us, to our so-called marriage and whatever futures we might have had?

I didn't hear the car pull up behind the Explorer. So when the man's shadow fell across my view, I sat forward quickly and looked up, squinting into the brightness, which caused the person to appear as a dark silhouette. I scooted out and stood; the Oregon State Police officer stood about my height and wore a Smokey trooper hat, summer-weight short-sleeved blue shirt, and dark glasses. He studied me for a moment while I slapped the dust and grit from my butt.

"Morning," he said. His voice was steady but not authoritative. I nodded, wondering what I'd done to deserve his attention. "You okay?" he asked.

I nodded stupidly. "Fine," I said and pointed my head toward the river. "Just watching that tug boat." The trooper followed my gaze for a moment then turned back to me. "I've always loved seeing tugs pushing barges on the river," I added.

He took another look downriver. "It is a nice sight. Guess maybe I've gotten too used to seeing them out there."

"That can happen. Me, I haven't been by this way in some time, so it seems fresh again."

"Uh-huh. Where you headed?"

I looked at him, seeing my face reflected in his glasses. "Portland. Visiting an uncle there."

"Uh-huh. Just for the record, can you show me your driver's license, please?"

I did. He looked at it, compared my horrible picture to the person standing in front of him, noted I was from Idaho, said he had an aunt who lived in Pocatello, then handed the license back and wished me a good day. By the time the trooper had gone, the tug was a speck way off. I got back into the car and felt a compulsion to call the Garnet Nursing Center in Latham; I asked for Mrs. Carrington, the administrator. I'd only met her once, so when she came on the line I didn't recognize her voice. I introduced myself, to which she responded warmly as if she knew exactly who I was—she didn't. I briefly explained my plans, with limited detail, and told her that I would be checking in by phone from time to time on Ashley's behalf. She took it all with an occasional hum of understanding.

"Of course, Mr. Pine, you know that your wife's father comes by regularly."

"That may be, but I'm the one you need to contact if there is any change in Ashley's condition. You do understand that, don't you?"

There was a hesitation before she said, "Of course, but Mr. Tucker is right here in town and is most attentive—"

"Mrs. Carrington, that is beside the point. Certainly Isaac is fully committed to his only child, without question. But I am her husband, with full legal authority over any decisions regarding her care, whether I'm right there in Latham or not. You have our advance medical directive on file and my cell number, so I will expect to hear from you when needed."

"I understand," she said in a formal tone.

"So what is her status at this time?"

After a long pause, she said, "Yes, well as you know your wife, Mrs. Pine, is in a—"

"No change, right."

"I assume so," she answered. "I'd have to check with my staff, but the last I heard was...no change, right."

With nothing more to say, I ended the call and merged back

into the flow of vehicles eating up the miles along that lonely stretch of the Columbia Gorge. In less than a hundred miles I would be there. It was all so curious, the idea of me bunking with my oddball uncle; I was looking forward to it in a peculiar way, sharing time and space with someone who actually wanted me around.

-19-

Locating the St. Johns neighborhood in Portland was beyond my orienteering skills; I played around with my cell phone but couldn't get it to tell me how to find where I wanted to go. I called my uncle. He answered, forcefully declaring: *Floyd's Stuff, Still of Some Use.* I laughed before I could utter a word. He picked up on me immediately and roared, back asking where the hell was I? I told him, and he said *okay* three times, followed by *not far* twice. Shortly I was on North Lombard Street in the center of St. Johns. And there it was, a bright blue and yellow Floyd's Stuff sign affixed to the face of a two-story brick building that looked to have been built early in the last century.

I parked half a block away, stepped out of the Explorer, stretched, and looked around, taking in the environs I was about to inhabit. It was an old neighborhood with a long-lived temperament, carrying the feel of historic relevance coupled with the feel of a well-worn favored rug. No relation of Rodeo Drive of Beverly Hills, but it felt agreeable. The buildings burnished with decades of patina hosted an assortment of businesses, some appearing to have deep roots. There was a dive or two with mold-covered awnings and Oregon Lottery signs posted, while other businesses gave evidence of having shown up recently to *give it a try.* Maybe that was Floyd's status.

I let a car pass before crossing the street and entering the store. Amid the clutter of merchandise I saw a stocky, bald-headed man wearing jeans and a blue work shirt. He looked to be discussing the merits of a used toaster oven with a hefty woman whose expression told me she was unconvinced. It was my uncle Floyd all right. He opened and closed the door to the toaster oven and patted it as if verifying its worth. After a moment's hesitation, the woman shook her head and waddled away, pulling a wire grocery cart behind her on out the door.

I stepped over as he was repositioning the appliance. "No sale?" I said into his left ear.

He jumped and spun around. "Nedder!" He grabbed me and squeezed so hard I felt a rib threaten to give way. "Hey, let me look at you." He pushed me back at arm's length and grinned. "My god, this is a grand day, wouldn't you say?"

"I would," I answered, "unless you've changed your mind."

"Ha! Not on your life. No sir." Floyd looked around. "Where's your gear?"

I pointed. "Down the street. Half a block."

"Well, let's get you situated. Now drive down to the corner, turn right at the first corner, and circle back behind our building here. There's an alley. I'll meet you."

And there he was, swinging open a chain link fence gate and waving me into a storage yard. He had me park in a certain spot next to a trailer with a fiberglass rowboat on it. The yard was cluttered with two big Dumpsters, some battered push lawnmowers, a wheelbarrow, yard tools, and a couple of 55-gallon drums; amid all of that was an older Dodge camper van with an industrial-grade electric cord running from it and a Ranger pickup, once red, now a weary oxidized pink.

Floyd eyed the Explorer's load and grunted at the amount of belongings I'd brought. "Figured you'd store most of your stuff," he said.

"I did."

"Really? Well," he laughed, "push comes to shove, we can just sell your excess in the shop." When I raised my eyebrows, he added, "Just kidding." He jabbed me on the arm. "Grab what you'll need for now. We'll figure out the rest later."

He took me in a back door to the old building, and we clamored up a flight of stairs to the floor above the store. It was so different from the Whitewood Estates that I had to laugh, couldn't help myself.

"I know, I know," Floyd laughed with me. "Not the Ritz." He watched me looking around. "But it'll grow on you."

I walked over to a spread of three tall sash windows and looked out through the cloudy, unwashed panes down into the street; one was open halfway, allowing the warm outside air to vie with the sultry space. At that moment, when it came to me that I was comparing my privilege of never being hot on a warm day with the revised reality of getting by, a sense of calm took over my senses. Of course it felt strange—being there. None of it fit yet. And even in that briefest of moments I knew that place, that space, was not beneath me. In fact I wondered if I was good enough for it. It was stuffy and too warm, even with the two big pedestal fans whirling away, but I didn't care.

"You'll bunk over there," Floyd was saying, his arm gesturing. "I found that old trundle bed." My eyes widened when I saw a narrow bed in a far corner, and he added, "Sleeps better'n it looks. I tried it out last night."

The space was one big room. I'm no good at eyeballing distance, but it must have been sixty by sixty, something like that. "That'll be fine, Floyd. Any cot in a storm."

"And I'm over here on the other side," he waved an arm in the direction of an old double bed with a high ornate headboard and footboard. "There were actually apartments up here back in the day," he said. "Downstairs was once a furniture store, and the owner decided he needed a stockroom and ripped them all out, leaving this big open space. He left one bathroom intact and the remnants of a kitchen over there against the wall. We share." When I looked confused, he said, "Noah and me, we share."

"Noah?"

He knocked his forehead with a knuckle. "Didn't tell you about

Noah, did I?" I shook my head, wondering where this would lead. "He works for me, Noah does. We have this arrangement. He... did you notice that van in the yard? Well, that's Noah's bunk. Sleeps there. Showers and cooks up here. Works out well."

"I see."

"You'll meet him. He's covering the shop right now while I'm up here welcoming you to my B&B."

I walked over to the trundle bed and dropped my duffle on it. It was very low, covered with an ugly brown blanket; a thin pillowcase decorated with orange and black squares covered a flat pillow. There it was, my flop for the immediate future. As I stood looking down, Floyd came up and stood beside me. After a moment, he said, "Glad you're here." He put a hand on my shoulder.

"Me too, I think."

He chuckled. "I feel the same some of the time. So how are you, really?"

I turned and looked into his surprisingly blue eyes beneath dark eyebrows. "You mean..."

"Of course *I mean.*"

I smiled. "Hell, I don't know. One moment, I'm blown back in agony. The next, it's as if my grief has been commuted. I know that I should feel worse than I do."

He gripped my shoulder hard, painfully. "None of that. None of that. It was not of your doing. No sir." He pounded on my back. "Not your fault."

"Then again, here I am, seven hundred some odd miles from my wife's side. How's that stack up?"

He stood silent and looked at his shoes. "Time out," he said after a bit. "That's what this is, time out. You need some time for yourself. That's my feeling."

"You're the first one," I said.

"First one what?"

"Not to ask *how is she really?*"

"Hmm." He nodded. "Figured that's maybe what you're getting

away from. That question."

"Mostly that, yes. And the rest of it."

He nodded some more then said, "Let's go down to the shop, and I'll introduce you to Noah."

I reached for his arm. "Floyd, I need to warn you that there is the possibility of some nasty repercussions from all of this. Mainly from Ashley's father, Isaac Tucker."

Floyd squinted at me. "That right? How do you mean?"

"He despises my very existence, first off, and it goes out from there."

"So?"

"Once he finds out where I am, and he will, at the minimum you may get some nasty phone calls."

"Ha! Big deal. I get those every day. And that could just be over one chipped glass out of a set of six. What you're suggesting is nothing compared to that. Come on, meet Noah."

Noah Blue was big; I'd say at least six four with a linebacker's body. He was an African American whom I learned held a master's in mechanical engineering and couldn't give a flying leap for that discipline anymore and had never played a down of football. He was selling a skinny young man a stack of used CDs for a dollar each, less twenty-five percent just because it was Thursday. It was my first real look at Floyd's business. The place was jammed with racks of clothes, shelves of glassware, tables weighted down with tools, silverware and dishes, more shelves full of books, VCR tapes, DVDs, and way more: some small furniture, all kinds of figurines, lamps—you name it. I wandered around and took it in; it seemed burdensome, all that jumble previously owned by others. But at the same time freeing because none of it was my responsibility.

"Noah," Floyd called out when the customer had gone. "Want you to meet my most prized relation here."

The big man looked my way as he closed the cash register

drawer. "So you're the one," he responded on a toothy smile. His voice vibrated out of a deep well but with a tone of mellow friendliness. "I was wondering. Floyd, he assured me that he had one relative that he's on good terms with. Pure fantasy. But here you are. I'm Noah." He stuck out a big hand, and we gripped together.

"Ned."

"Thought it was Nedder."

"Only here." I studied Noah Blue, his close-cropped salt-and-pepper hair and his tightly trimmed goatee with the same graying coloration, accompanied by a broad nose and prominent ears. All in all, his was a muscular presence, but my impression was of a man of easy temperament, not an intimidating force. Standing next to my uncle. he made Floyd seem squat and diminutive.

"My hat's off to you," Noah said, smiling. "I understand you'll be sharing sleeping space with Floyd. That so?" I nodded. "Real courage, *real* courage." Floyd's face turned fuchsia. Noah held his hands up in front of his face. "Don't hit me now, Floyd. You know it's true."

"I snore," Floyd said.

"A mild term," Noah laughed. "Snoring is the reverberation of one's soft palate, not pleasant but tolerable in most cases. What you emit is the equal of rutting rhinos."

Floyd clapped his hands together. "Enough of that. Nedder and I will make it work, right?" I just grinned. "All right then, I'm closing early today in honor of my nephew's arrival. We'll crank up the bar-bee and throw on the marked-down New York strip steaks I bought at Safeway. Don't give me those suspicious looks. A little more aging is good."

While Floyd and Noah fussed about getting ready to cook the steaks and baked potatoes, I went out to the Explorer to get a few more belongings, and that was when my cell rang. Who now? I stepped away from the vehicle and looked at the screen: my son.

"Hey, Mike."

"Hi, Dad," he said. "How you doing?"

I paused. Damn, I'd totally forgotten to tell my kids what I was up to. "I'm good," I said while frowning at myself. "You?"

"I'm good, too," he answered. "Working at that summer job."

"What was it again? The job?"

He laughed. "Guess I never told you. Waiting tables. Place called Hawk's Inn. Good tips."

"Great. Having a good summer?"

"It's okay." He paused. "But I can't get Mom out of my head."

"I understand. It's a hard time."

"Uh...any change?"

"No, Son, sorry to say."

"Oh," he dropped a deep sigh. "Guess I'm not surprised, but I was thinking of driving down to see her...and you. You gonna be around?"

I clenched my left hand into a fist, damning myself. "No." I waited a beat. "Actually I'm visiting my uncle Floyd. In Portland."

"Portland. Really. Have I ever met him?"

"No, I don't think so."

"Strange, don't you think? Seems we have a bunch of relatives we've never seen, you know? Why is that?"

I took in a deep breath and let it out slowly. There was the question that had never been asked. "Well," I laughed lightly, "on this end it's because Floyd was a hippie. He was the real deal back in the sixties and thus became the family outcast. He has always been my favorite kin, maybe for that very reason."

"I'd like to meet him," Mike said with a mild degree of enthusiasm.

"Maybe you will."

"Yeah, that'd be good. So how long will you be there, in Portland?"

"Not sure, for a while, just got here." I hesitated. "There's something you need to know, Mike. I'm selling the house."

"What? Why?"

"I just...had to. It was crushing me without your mom there

with me. Too much baggage. I...I saw her and our life around every corner." Not really a lie, more of a justification. "Besides, that house never liked me. I was always a guest," I laughed.

He didn't react to my attempt at humor. "It was more Mom's place," he said, a fait accompli.

"Yes," I agreed. "You ought to know that your grandfather wants to buy it."

"Uh-oh. Bet that's not your choice."

"No."

"Let me guess. He's still convinced that Mom's going to recover, so he wants her house ready and waiting."

"Spot on."

"So why not sell it to him? What's the harm?"

I leaned up against a fender and watched as Noah Blue came out into the storage yard carrying a bag of charcoal briquettes. "Can't do it, Mike. Just can't. Need a clean cut."

"Your call. Hey look, I have to get ready for work."

"One more thing," I said in haste. "I'm selling my share of the CPA firm."

There was silence on the other end of the call. "So it's cut and run for you, right?"

His assessment hit my gut. He saw through me clearly. "That's one way of putting it."

"There another?"

"Survival," I answered. "Saving myself from going down for the count."

"Geez, Dad, it's that bad?"

I reached up and pinched my nose at the bridge. "It's not for you to carry the weight of my life. You have yours to live. Do it."

"I'm sorry for the cut and run slam."

"Sure, there's some truth to that. Do me a favor, will you?"

"What?"

"Call Roz, and fill her in on what I've told you about things, what's going on with me. Your sister and I have never been able to discuss things. There was always a divide. Can you do that for me?"

"I guess," he answered. "Won't be fun for me either, but I'll do it. But you know she'll be on you like stink on a skunk."

"I know, but she'll have at least absorbed it before coming after me. Another thing, your mother is in good hands at the care center. I will call in regularly to check on her status, and your grandfather goes to see her very often. Okay?"

"Okay. Bye, Dad."

-20-

Floyd's past-dated steaks were actually very good. Along with foil-wrapped potatoes baked on the charcoal grill, plus cold cans of PBR beer, it was a meal just right for three guys eating off a rickety card table on a gravel lot on a warm summer evening. It made me laugh inside, how at ease I was just being there. We discussed what medium rare *really meant* and whether that was what we ended up with or not. In the end, it was agreed that Floyd had hit the sweet spot on the meat: a rosy pink center with the outer tops and bottoms grilled to a dark brown with nice char marks. Noah's baked spuds came out of the wrapped foil steamy and eagerly absorbed globs of oleomargarine, topped with salt and pepper. It was the best meal I'd eaten in some time—no greens, of course.

That was the cover, meal talk. We each downed several beers scooped out of Floyd's ice chest and settled back in weathered Adirondack chairs that had seen better days. Eventually talk dried up after we had exhausted the depth and breadth of al fresco culinary dining. Darkness descended on three men digesting a good meal with a questionable lager, each of us probably mulling over what to say next with the new guy on site. I had questions, questions about Floyd's funky operation and how Noah Blue fit into it. But being a no-show relative for a couple of decades, topped off with a bizarre story of violence and relinquishment of my former life, didn't give me a lot of leverage to interrogate.

"Now what?" It was Noah Blue who asked the obvious.

I could still make out his features in the declining light. He was slouched in his chair across from me. The cluttered card table stood on splayed legs between us, a still-life study of bloody plates, crumpled foil, and a hockey team of drained aluminum cans.

"Guess we clean up," Floyd said.

Noah gave us an inner-chest chuckle. "Nah, not that." He pointed a finger at me. "Just wondering, who do we have here?"

"I told you," Floyd replied. "My long-lost nephew here for a visit."

"Visit." Noah looked over at the Explorer. "Travels heavy."

"He's here as long as he wants." Floyd stood up. "Now I'm gonna haul these greasy plates upstairs and call it good. Come on, Ned, let's get you squared away for your first night in the penthouse."

Noah and I caught each other's eyes, but nothing more was said. I gathered up a couple of plates and some silverware and followed Floyd up the back stairs. It was stuffy and airless up there except for the two struggling fans; one was complaining. Floyd washed up the dinnerware, and I dried. When he was stowing dishes in a makeshift cupboard, I asked him: "So, you didn't tell him about me?"

Floyd was over opening all three windows as far as they'd go. He propped one open with a sawed-off broomstick and shrugged. "Yeah. I told him—some."

"Like what?"

My stubby uncle smiled. "That you were coming. Like for a visit."

"Nothing else—about what happened?"

"Nope. I didn't. Figured that was your business. You want to tell Noah more, up to you."

"Thanks, Floyd, that was good of you."

He smiled, patted me on the arm in passing, and we got ready to bed down. The trundle bed was tolerable. I kicked the blanket off and lay on top of the sheets wearing only my shorts. For a time, I stared up into the dark, feeling strangely at ease but still out of place. I finally drifted off until some time later, having my slumber interrupted by an eruption of full-scale snoring. I listened; my eyelids fought it but finally opened wide as the muscular flap hanging from the roof of Floyd's mouth vibrated with the subtlety of a clogged sump pump. At first it was amusing; then it wasn't. I rolled off the bed and wandered over to the open windows and looked out onto Lombard Street, St. Johns' main drag. An occasional car went by and a city bus. Voices rose up from three men who came out of a bar across the street; they'd had plenty to drink and were feeling loudly sociable. Floyd continued his symphony. I slipped on my pants and shoes without socks and went downstairs and out into the storage yard.

The hum that came from being in a city was almost cacophonous compared to back home in the sterile quiet of Whitewood Estates. I stood in the darkness, modified by a nearby vapor pole light, and inhaled. The air had the tinge of cigar smoke. Then I saw the glow from an ignited stogie and made out Noah Blue reclining in one of the wooden chairs.

"What did I tell you?" he said.

I smiled, mostly to myself. "You warned me. On top of that, it's muggy as hell up there."

"I know. Same in my sardine can flop here."

"I can imagine."

"Grab a seat. Can I offer you a cigar? Not Cuban, from Nicaragua I think, but okay. They're called something, something Torpedo."

I crossed over, gravel crunching beneath my feet, and sat down. "Okay," I said after a moment. "Haven't smoked a cigar in years."

"This is my Friday night ritual: a cheap cigar sitting in this parking lot next to my crib while contemplating the way of the world and my place in it."

I took the cigar he held out and stripped the cellophane from it. "Contemplating," I returned. "Been doing a lot of that myself." I slid the cigar along under my nose and sniffed.

"Not bad for a buck ninety-eight." He reached over with a Bic lighter, flicked it, and set my cigar alight. When I had to clear my throat with the first puff, he laughed and said, "Like the proverbial bicycle, it'll come back to you."

I smiled, swallowed acrid saliva, and settled back in the chair, its surface rough against my naked back. We fell quiet. The smoke floating upward from our cigars was visible in the glow from the light pole. It had been near ninety in Portland that day, so it was warm even at that late hour but still better than upstairs with Floyd snoring.

"So why are you here, really?" Noah asked, entering my reverie. "'Course it's none of my business."

"No," I said. "But that's all right."

I took a pull on my cigar, didn't cough, then tapped off the ash and told him—most of it. It surfaced slowly. He listened in silence. I finished, dropped my cold cigar stub on the ground, and wondered how my tale had come across to a stranger.

Noah unwrapped another cigar and lit it. I said no when he offered me a second.

"And so here you are shacking up with your old Uncle Floyd. How's that feel?"

I laced fingers together in my lap. "His was the only offer I got," I laughed. "I needed space, and this is a good beginning. Still and all, I'm here, and she's there. No matter that she's gone to me forever, irretrievable, the what-ifs still hang over me. What if I'd done this or acted more quickly...and like that."

"My god, man, you can't do that to yourself. You'll go crazy."

"No matter. As long as she's breathing, I'm answerable, as I should be. And there are those who will forever and always judge me culpable."

"Heck, they must know you had no chance against a gang of thugs like that."

"No witnesses, only my version."

"Yeah but..."

"All you've heard is my side of the story." He fell silent, went back to his cigar; I could sense him looking my way in the gloom of the hour. "You'll see what I mean soon enough," I said. "My father-in-law will come after me when he finds out where I've gone to."

"You shittin' me?"

"Isaac, he's ferociously devoted to his daughter. She's the only link he has to his deceased wife. Isobel was her name—to Isobel. Like I said, he never wanted Ashley to marry the likes of me and detested my presence in her life from day one." I stood and circled around a couple of times then stood looking down at Noah. "He's threatened to kill me."

"What? Can't be."

"Who knows if he means it? But he thinks he does. That makes me swallow hard."

"But why? It can't be because…"

"I won't sell him our damn house." I sat back down. Nothing more was said between us until I spoke again. "What about you? Living out of a…out of this van with Calloused Hands Music painted on the nose of it."

"Ha! It belonged to a band called themselves the Calloused Hands. Got it cheap on Craigslist from an old lady whose grandson was in the band before it folded. I bought it because it has that fiberglass pop top and enough room for a bed my size."

"That tells me part of the story. What's the rest?" I asked.

"We're not all that different, you and I," he answered. "It's almost eerie, in a way. I had a good job as a senior mechanical design engineer for a global automotive electronics company in Chicago. Three grown kids, married over thirty years, thirty-two actually." His voice became husky. "She was a nurse, Agatha was. University of Chicago Medical Center. Pediatrics. She loved the children."

The sound of a Harley roaring by out on Lombard invaded the air; he stopped talking. I slipped off my right shoe and shook out a piece of gravel. As I slipped it back on he spoke again.

"She died. Three years ago. T-Boned by a CTA bus. Her fault. On her way home from work. Tired, I guess."

"Sorry," I said.

"Yeah," he breathed out. "Everybody was sorry. Sorry as hell. You know the drill."

"I do. And so now here we are hanging out in Floyd's back lot, you sleeping in that thing and me...well me trying to sleep up there. How'd you end up here?"

"Crashed and burned. Crashed and burned. Pathetic."

I waited some more. Whatever it was would come out of its own volition.

"First, I screwed that damn good job right down the drain. The kids, they knew I was hurting, so they gave me slack—in the beginning, they did. Tore my insides out. Agatha was everything. I caved in. I morphed into a worthless guttersnipe. Had to sell my house to stay afloat. Couple of years of that shit, and my children left me to my own demons."

"It was different for Ashley and me." I ran a hand through my shock of hair and held up.

When I didn't go on, Noah said, "Guess it's that way for most of us. Feeling like we're unique or something."

"Is it unique that we...that she never loved me?"

"That's way above my pay grade," he responded.

"That's the way it was, and I never learned how to break through to make her love me. And so I couldn't love her back. We existed."

Noah dropped his spent cigar and stepped down on it. "Can't imagine," he said.

"It just moved in on us like a low-grade infection, I guess. Yeah, that's what it was: a slow-moving communicable sickness killing us slowly from the inside out. I didn't fully get the rottenness of it until the attack." I felt rigidness in my chest. "Now that it's clear what we were doing to each other, it's too late." I looked in his direction. "That's why I'm here. Distance."

"The same. I'm here to get lost," he said on a quiet voice. "I succeeded. No one knows where I am, nor do they give a rip."

"We're a pair," I said standing up. "Do you feel it getting cooler?"

"Oregon's air conditioner, also called the Pacific Ocean. Marine air moves in over the coast range at night and can bring the temp down into the fifties. Nothing like Chicago's humidity. Manna from heaven."

"Very nice. Well, guess I'll give it another try upstairs."

"Hey, I got some earplugs I'll loan you."

Noah climbed into his van and rummaged around and came out with a set of foam orange earplugs. I asked for a peek inside and saw that he had expanded the bed to fill most of the rear of the van. The galley portion, small stove and sink, was piled with clothes; the toilet and shower were unused. The floor, courtesy of Floyd, was covered with a ratty red-and-blue Oriental rug.

"Cozy."

He merely laughed and held out a big hand. I gripped it as best I could. He said it had been good to go back over painful old ground with someone who'd been there.

My uncle was still emitting the grumblings of a mutilated iron lung. I stuffed the foam earplugs in, slipped back onto the trundle bed, pulled the sheet over me, and slept.

-21-

The next morning my cell phone began to serenade me. Floyd and Noah had just scrambled up a batch of eggs, joined up with coffee and toast, when the first call came in. It was my daughter, Roz. I suppose everyone's been ripped apart a time or two in their lives. Well, my morning wake-up call was just that. Rosalind gutted her father like a floundering trout; it was bloodless but only because I was out of reach. The accusations ran from abandonment of my spousal obligations to giving up on the likelihood that her mother would recover. She clearly sided with her grandfather and if given the opportunity would most assuredly pass me by if I lay dying in a ditch.

"I love you, Roz," I said when she took a breath. "And I wish—"

"Fuck you," she said. "Never you mind about mom. Grandpa and I will see to her."

The call ended on that note, abruptly, with no chance for me to say good-bye. I held the phone in my hand, watched the end-call screen turn black, and huffed a bit of sadness from my chest. When I turned, Noah was shoveling eggs onto three plates, and Floyd was holding up the coffee pot, looking at me.

"Seemed a little one-sided," he said.

I nodded. "My daughter...Rosalind. Didn't go well."

No one asked for details. We sat around a scarred oval table that had evidently been saved from the scrap heap by Floyd. It was just big enough to accommodate us. We each had the honor of sitting on a one-of-a-kind mix-or-match chair; mine was an old bentwood painted yellow and orange—a décor statement. The eggs were good, the coffee a little thin; the toast was white bread. I smeared some grape jelly on it, and it went down fine.

"When do you open the shop?" I asked.

"Anytime we want," Noah laughed. "What time is it now? Okay, going on ten o'clock.

Since some of us slept in after our late night, ten-thirty, eleven maybe?"

"I'm fine," Floyd said. "I can open."

"Sure, you're fine," Noah said. "You slept like a rock again while Ned here had to escape your nasal thunder until I loaned him some ear plugs."

Floyd's face reddened, and he gave me a guilty smile. "Sorry."

I'd opened my mouth to reply when my phone warbled again. I hesitated when I saw the caller ID: S Winters. I hit the kill button. I was in no mood for Sylvia. When I looked up, both men were staring at me.

"Busy morning," I said with a grin. "They're figuring out that I've left town."

"Tracking you down, huh?" Noah said. "You're more popular than me. No one has bothered bringing me to ground."

My phone lit up with a text message: Sylvia again. *I know where you are.* Coming from her, it smelled like a threat, probably was. I didn't respond. We finished breakfast without much conversation, mostly just the humming sounds of males consuming food. After an all-hands clearing of the table with each washing his own plate and utensils, Floyd and I headed downstairs to open Floyd's Stuff for another day. I wasn't expecting a line at the door, and I was right. When Floyd unlocked the front door with a brass key on a chain, all that came in was the noise of a busy street.

Floyd set up the cash register with change, scooted his rump onto the stool behind the sales counter, and raised his stubby arms. "We're live," he grinned.

"Okay. What can I do?"

He waved both hands at me. "Hey, I was only blowing smoke

about you working for me. That was just a ploy to get you out here. Give you space away from your demons."

"I understand. But really, give me something to do."

He pulled on his nose and gave me an impish smile. "Well, I did get in a shitpot load of dishes a few days back. An old lady died, and her kids were getting rid of anything they didn't like. So I got this complete set of classy dinnerware. Needs washing. Willing?"

"Will I get docked for breakage?"

"Damn right. Ding ya a dime for every broken plate, nickel per cup."

"What are you paying me, anyhow?"

"Danged if I know. What's minimum wage for working with less than fresh inventory?"

"Got me. In Idaho it's seven bucks and a quarter."

"Hell, that's more'n I can pay myself. This hired help thing is worrying."

"What do you pay Noah?"

"Got me. We haven't got that far yet."

"How long has he been here?"

"Couple of months. Guess I shoulda paid him something by now, huh?"

"Maybe. How did he end up here with you? Van out back and all?"

"We met across the street there, at the B&C Tavern. Kind of a sketchy place but good burgers, dozen beers on tap, pool tables, and you know. I saw Noah there two, three times, and we ended up drinking beer and having burgers right next to each other one night, sittin' elbow to elbow on barstools. We got to talkin' about this and that, and one morning when I opened up the shop, there he was standing at the door." Floyd lowered his head and laughed, eyes closed. "And he asked me if it was okay to move his van out back. I said, what? He answered: *Like we agreed to last night, you know, at the B&C.*"

"I gather you didn't recall making such a deal."

"Nope. But with my head pounding like it was, I figured that I'd agreed to something, so there he is."

"Seems like a good deal for him: free RV parking, shower and restroom, meals, and a place to hunker down while he readjusts his life. How about you?"

"Oh sure. He's smarter than ten of me and enjoyable to be around, pulls his share in the shop—so it works for me, too. And now I've got my own in-house CPA, right?"

I carefully washed the complete set of very nice Lennox China without any breakage and set out to explore St. Johns. Almost instantly, I had another text come in from Sylvia demanding that I respond. I didn't. In addition to her aggressive persistence, I fully expected to hear from Isaac Tucker, and not to wish me all the best in Portland.

Along Lombard Street, I entered the new space I might call home for an unknown measure of time. St. Johns readily tipped its hand as a place comfortable wearing its down-to-earth presence. It seemed to carry its blue-collar DNA and ethnic diversity securely; it was a neighborhood of acceptance. I could feel it. I saw no question in the faces I passed, only undeserved acknowledgement revealed by easy smiles. Having just come from the place I had called home but where I had not been openly reclaimed as the husband of that woman and where I felt no connection anymore, I felt at ease traipsing the blocks out from Floyd's place. At the main intersection of St. Johns' hub, I turned onto Philadelphia Avenue because I liked the sound of it but soon realized that I was headed straight toward a huge bridge. Dead ahead, I saw the Verde green gothic structure riding high above the Willamette River, looking very much a cousin to the Golden Gate Bridge. I could see two high towers with suspension cables slung between them. It was a magnificent view. Beneath the bridge, which appeared immense from down below, there was a park:

Cathedral Park. I took a set of wide cement stairs down into the park and located a picnic table in the shade out of the heat and sat down. It was peaceful, with a few people walking the concrete path that went down to the river's edge, others spreading blankets out on the grass, a man throwing a Frisbee to his black lab; it was mellow. Just as the dog was returning the red plastic disk to his master, my cell began to vibrate. Isaac Tucker was calling. I didn't answer. I waited until the call had gone to voice mail then took a listen.

Listen you asshole, he began, *I know you're out there in Portland with your uncle, or who the heck ever. As they say, you can run, but you can't hide. Better look over your shoulder, 'cause I'll be there when you least expect it. What you've got coming will not be denied.*

Gloria Denham—had to be. I called her. I opened too abruptly with, "My god, Gloria, did you put my whereabouts in the paper? Everyone I don't want anything to do with has been all over me."

She was remorseful. "Ned," there was a hitch in her voice. "I'm so sorry. I wasn't thinking. When that woman, Sylvia Winters, when she called all nicey nice, wanting to keep in touch with you, I just never thought about keeping your contact info private."

"Not your fault. I never asked you to."

"I won't tell anyone else. I promise."

I laughed. "That's okay, too late. My screw up. Any action on the house?"

"Some. But this darn housing crisis is a killer. Latham's like everywhere else, lots of foreclosures. The decline in prices could reach nine percent, Ned."

"Timing has never been my forte," I tried to laugh. "So, not many lookers then?"

"Not like I'd hoped."

"How about the price?"

"Well, we may have to revisit the asking price at some point.

But it's early. Let's give it a chance."

"Okay."

She waited a few beats then said, "And there's Isaac Tucker's offer. I know, not your favorite idea, but still—"

"No," I raised my voice. "I've been getting menacing calls from him."

"Menacing?" She sounded alarmed.

"Don't worry. He's just blowing hot gas. I'm not answering his calls, just listening to voice mail. Threatening to come out here and confront me."

"Really? Would he actually do that?"

"Hell, I don't know. Could just be listening to himself swell up. Regardless, his offer is not to be considered."

"All right," she said. "I have a couple moving here from Montana that I'll be showing around. The husband has been hired as Latham's new city manager. They'll be looking for a nice place. Yours is on the list."

"For Pete's sake, don't tell them about the break-in."

She hesitated. "It's common knowledge around here, Ned. They'll find out at some point. I'd rather tell them gently early on than for them to find out and wonder why I didn't tell them. Besides, it's not like someone was murdered there."

I flashed onto the comatose image of Ashley. "Not yet," I said.

She sucked in a breath and floundered around, trying to pull back from her misspoken moment. I assured her it was okay and then asked her to let me know if she got any bona fide offers on the house. We left it there.

I sat in the shade beneath the bridge for a while longer and let the mess of my life sift through my head. It remained as it was; chewing on it improved nothing. When a young family with two kids and a picnic basket came up, I got up and let them have the table. On the way back to Floyd's, I felt the urge for a good cup of coffee and wandered into Thelma's Coffee House a block and a half from the shop. It was a large room, filled with ragtag furniture, couches, old easy chairs, mixed and matched chairs and tables. In other words, it was comfortable.

That's when I saw her for the first time. She waited on me, took my order for an Americano, and asked if I wanted one or two shots of espresso. I held up two fingers. She smiled, revealing nice teeth, and nodded. She was nice to look at; I guessed around thirty-five or so. I noticed her amber eyes immediately; they seemed to grow brighter when she smiled. There was a thin, maybe three-inch, scar on her left cheek that ran at an angle from her ear toward her mouth. Her hair was brown, held up in a ponytail, and large gold hoops dangled from her ears. I hadn't evaluated a female that way in very long time, I mean other than noticing that someone was nice looking. I watched as she went about the business of compressing the espresso, running the steaming hot water from the machine, putting it all together smoothly, and setting it on the pickup counter. She seemed amused that I was watching her performance so closely and asked if I wanted anything else. I shook my head and moved away to doctor my drink with cream and sweetener, settled into an abused leather armchair, and enjoyed being anonymous in a city strange to me and a neighborhood that seemed to take me the way I came—taking no notice.

From my chair, I could watch the woman go about the business of being a barista. Once she caught me looking at her; our eyes met for a brief moment before I picked up a year-old copy of *Sports Illustrated* and thumbed through predictions of the past NFL season. I forgot who won the Super Bowl that year and didn't really care. When I peeked over the top of the magazine, she was gone. A skinny guy wearing his hat backward had taken her place. I put my cup in a bus tub and returned to Floyd's shop.

There, a worst-case scenario hit the fan.

Floyd was waiting on a woman who was buying a stack of assorted clothing. Noah wasn't about. I fiddled with a shelf of cups and drinking glasses, straightening them like I knew what I was doing, until Floyd was finished with his customer. He motioned me over to the counter and held out a business card. I took it and caught my breath: Sylvia Winters.

"She came in about an hour ago. You know her?"

"Unfortunately, yes."

Floyd tilted his head to one side and gave me a twisted little smile. "She wasn't real happy that you weren't here. Wanted me to go get you." He looked about. "I don't think she liked my shop much, kinda turned up her nose."

"She would."

"Asked if you really lived here. Shook her head when I said you did."

"What else did she say?"

"Said she's in town for a couple of days for some conference. Something about food, I think. That make sense?"

I nodded.

"Wants to see you."

"Why am I not surprised?"

"She wrote something on the back of that card."

I turned it over: Heathman Hotel, Room 400. *I'll expect you.* I groaned.

"Heathman, that's a pretty fancy place." Floyd studied me. "Card says she's president of that company. She own it?"

"She does," I responded. "She's a client of the CPA firm I just vacated."

He nodded in a befuddled sort of way. "Like I said, wants to see you. Pushy, you know? Expects you there tonight at seven. She was specific about the time. Said you haven't been answering your phone."

"Let's just say I'm being selective. About the calls I'm taking."

He smiled the smile that made him my favorite relative: impish and honest. "Does that mean more people might come in here unannounced, you know, ones whose calls you're not taking? Any more of those in my future?"

"Could be, I suppose. Sorry."

"Don't be. Sparks up my day having this sort of intrigue." He paused and looked over as a potential customer walked in. "Let me see what this guy wants. You going to go see her?" He pointed at the card in my hand.

I turned it over, read her name again. "Not sure."

"Think she'll be puckered if'n you don't." He grinned and approached the man who evidently wanted a cheap set of socket wrenches. "Oh," he added over his shoulder, "said she'll be taking you to dinner. Guess you won't be dining with me and Noah then?"

It was a negotiation between yea and nay: nay lost. I plundered the Explorer for some decent clothes and commandeered an abused steam iron from Floyd's small appliance inventory to freshen a pair of khakis and a dress shirt. The iron actually worked. I used the so-called dining table as an ironing board and after getting clear directions into the city made the drive against any common sense I might have proclaimed.

-22-

Portland's city center was alive with lights, cars, and people. I parked two blocks from the Heathman Hotel and pushed through a bronze and glass revolving door into a lobby of marble floors, lots of wood paneling, and splashes of large paintings on the walls. It wasn't Motel 6.

I found room 400 easily. The door swung open almost instantly after my light knuckle rap. And there she stood: her flashing white teeth, tangy perfume, and vivid red lips—all so familiar. Her hair was in its usual pulled-back style. She wore an expensive summer-weight suit in sort of an ecru, along with a necklace of small pearls and accompanying earrings. I felt counter-dressed in my new modish St. Johns' manner.

"Ned," she said looking me up and down. "Here you are."

"Yes, here I are."

"Come in, come in." She stepped back. When I closed the door, she leaned in and gave me a peck on the cheek. "Good to see you," she said with a tilt of her head. I merely nodded and she went on. "It's coincidental that our annual West Coast food distribution conference ended up in Portland this year. Usually it's in Seattle or San Francisco."

I agreed that it was a coincidence but couldn't think of anything else I wanted to say. Awkward. So I commented on how luxurious the room was. She glanced about and shrugged.

"I like to travel in comfort," she responded. "As long as I'm on the road for the company it's deserved." She studied me, and her eyes narrowed a bit. "I guess you know I stopped by your uncle's shop."

"He told me. That's how I got your invitation, if that's what you call it."

She ignored my gibe. "And you are actually living there?"

"For now. More of a guest, a working guest."

"Working guest? And what does a working guest do?"

I gave up a breathy laugh. "Well, today, my first day, I washed a complete set of fine china. Then I took a break and explored the neighborhood a bit. That's when you came by I guess."

"Where do you live?"

"Upstairs. Above the shop. I have a very comfortable trundle bed, though I have to put earplugs in because Floyd snores a bit."

"Really?"

"Oh, and there's Noah. He lives out back in a modified small RV. He works for Floyd, too."

She went over to the couch and settled down on soft cushions. "Tell me, Ned, what are you up to? You can't be serious about this. Shacking up in your uncle's junk shop."

I held up a finger. "Thrift shop. And his motto is *Still of some use*. I think he means himself as well as his merchandise. We had a very nice barbeque out back last night, steaks, baked potatoes, and beer, the works. Three guys enjoyed red meat and brews."

"So how long?" When I raised my eyebrows, she added, "How long are you going to play this silly game?"

"Not sure. As long as it works, I guess. Why?"

"Just wondering when you'll be coming back to Latham."

I sat in an armchair across from her and leaned forward on my knees. "Not sure I'll be going back to Latham. Not sure about that."

"You've got to be kidding. That's where your roots are," she said on a raised voice.

"Not really."

"What do you mean? Of course it is."

"If you mean Ashley, yes, she's still there, but as you know she will never recover. My kids are gone from Latham, I've severed

190

my business relationship, and soon I'll sell the house. There's nothing to draw me back."

The expression that formed on her face was one of bitterness. "Then you've forgotten."

"Forgotten what?" I asked, but I knew, and it chilled me.

"Forgotten what?" she repeated. "You know damn well. And you can't fight it. You know that." I looked across the space between us. My scalp tingled, but I said nothing. "How long?" she said, staring hard at me.

"How long what?" I asked.

She rose from the couch and stood with hands clenched at her sides. "Just how fucking long before you come to your senses and come home to *us*."

"Us?" My head was buzzing. "You mean return to the firm? I told you—"

"Damn you, no! To us."

I'd known for a long time that she had been infatuated with me; I'd known that ever since I'd had to take on her account for the firm. It had been a game, a little game of flirtation, one that I was able to manage, to keep at arms length without succumbing to something stupid—up until that one night when I lost focus and shared bed sheets with her.

"Sylvia, I'm not ready for that," I said. Dumb, but I had to defuse this moment.

She seemed to deflate and sagged back onto the couch. "But you yourself...you've said she will never recover. Ashley will never recover. You know that."

"Still I have the obligation. Don't you see? It will not be long. I'm sure of it," I added lying to her even as I knew Ashley could live very much longer.

After a long moment of silence, she looked at her watch and was reminded of her dinner reservation in the hotel restaurant. I endured a very fine meal of wild Pacific salmon and afterward managed to avert returning to her room. In parting, we embraced, and I went along with us sharing a kiss, reluctantly accepting her intensity.

Her conference was over the next day; she would be taking a late afternoon flight out of PDX, so there would be no time for us to see each other before she left. I feigned disappointment, and we parted, but not before she warned me that Isaac Tucker was one angry man and that I shouldn't take his ire lightly.

As I drove back to Floyd's, my mind was awash with the unnerving thought of Isaac flying to Portland carrying a shitload of anger and invading my life. I knew he was capable of it, but I sure as hell wasn't looking forward to a chest-to-chest face-off with him.

Back in St. Johns, I pulled into the alley and found Floyd and Noah sitting outside in the warm night air; they had consumed a few beers each, as evidenced by the cans scattered on the ground. I was greeted warmly, which I was beginning to enjoy. They asked about my extravagant night on the town and compared my gourmet salmon dinner to their chili out of the can with a great show of feigned umbrage. I passed on another of Noah's Nicaraguan cigars and went off to bed. By the time Floyd stumbled up the stairs, I had my earplugs in and barely noticed when his nightly serenade kicked in. Besides, my head was caught up in a nightmare; in it, I was being shoved back and forth among three people, from one to the other and back again. They were laughing hysterically: Isaac, Sylvia, and Ashley. Around three in the morning I sat up on the trundle bed clammy with sweat; Floyd's snoring had evidently broken the spell. After wandering in the dark to the john, I managed to get in two more hours of uninterrupted sleep but awoke with a headache and the realization that I had not escaped the milieu of disaffection in which I'd been embroiled for the past five months. Being miles away from Latham could not wall off what I wished to escape.

Floyd heard me getting dressed and sat up in his bed. He knuckled his eyes and looked across the room at me. "You okay?" he asked. "Heard you grunting or something in your sleep."

"That right? Sorry. Just having a dream, no biggie."

He swung his legs around and sat on the edge of his bed. "If you say so."

"Not to worry, Floyd. Merely a nighttime bogeyman."

He stood, wearing only his skivvies, and scratched himself. "You know, Nedder, the reason I invited you out here was so we could clean things up for you. Convince your gremlins to let loose of you, give you your life back. I know you can't forget all that's happened. I mean, hell, I know the drill." He wheezed out a short laugh. "Looka me, I been on the outside so long it's who I am: mister outside lookin' in. That's me." He raised his arms and stretched. "Yep, that's me."

I finished tying my shoes and went to heat up water for coffee. "Sorry, Floyd," I said. "Wasn't thinking."

"Not to worry, lad. I've built my own life miscue by miscue, and mostly I do okay with it. Family," he shrugged, "family, that's just something I ruminate about on dark winter nights. Where'd I go wrong? Did I go wrong?"

"And?"

"What do they say, that begs the question? Hey man, I went my own way. I did some crazy shit but enjoyed life all the same. Sure I woke up holding the short end of the stick a whole bunch of times, more'n I'd like to admit. Family? Mostly the clan didn't get the drift of my lifestyle—as they say."

"But at least you tried out many variations of life," I said.

He laughed, pulling on some well-worn jeans. "Many variations of life," he responded. "I like that. Course some of them variations was miles of bad road." He pulled on a blue tee shirt with the word *Hawaii* scrolled across his chest in rainbow colors.

The coffee maker began to gurgle. Floyd put out boxes of Cheerios and raisin bran, pulled a jug of milk from the fridge, and set out three cereal bowls. I found the spoons and put one beside each bowl. "Whatever, I thank you for inviting me to hang with you for a spell."

"Hell, it's one of my only chances to do the family thing, you know? Feels good."

I chuckled. "Seems as if we're giving each other the cure."

"There ya go," he said. "By the way, how'd your date go? You know, with that lady?"

I felt my brow crinkle. "No date," I said. "More of a command performance."

He shook Cheerios into a bowl. "That right? Never had one of those with a woman. Had a few who commanded me to disappear. What kind of performance did she command?" He grinned with a mouthful of cereal.

"Not the kind you're thinking of." The coffee was ready; I poured us each a cup. "Strictly an obligatory social visit with an acquaintance from back home."

He stirred the Cheerios floating in his bowl. "I'm forgetting you've been out of circulation for a long stretch. From what I saw, she was nice looking, dressed really swell, and was more'n eager to find you. We talking missed opportunity here?"

"Floyd, you are bad," I said, pointing a forefinger at him. "Fact is, that woman is on the short list of reasons why I took you up on your offer to get out of Dodge."

"And I thought my life was complicated." He lifted up his cereal bowl, drank the milk remaining in it, wiped his chin, and leaned back. "Okay. So learning the art of selling reusables isn't why you're really here. I'm crushed. What's that leave?"

"Not sure." I poured milk over a mound of raisin bran. "If you held a gun to my head, I still couldn't tell you for sure what I'll do next—after my stay in your resort here."

"All right then. You got me thinking here."

"Floyd, we don't have to analyze this to death."

"Come on now, Ned, not often I get to mess about in someone else's difficulties: for sure not family. Like I say, haven't been inside the family circle for...hell, forever." He raised a hand. "And now I got it."

194

"What?"

"The question. What about her...Ashley?" He had to think before saying her name.

"She's gone. I told you."

"That's it then?"

I shook my head. "Not really. I'm not giving up."

"Thought you said there's no cure."

"There isn't. I'm talking about finding who did it. The scum who attacked us." Floyd stared at me, curious. "They came into our space, Floyd, and terrorized us. They took it all—there's nothing left." I closed my right hand into a fist and pounded the tabletop; bowls and cups and spoons danced around.

Floyd waited a moment then asked, "How ya gonna do that? Find 'em?"

"The investigation is still open, still on the books. I keep in touch with a detective who has been on the case from the beginning."

"This detective, is he making any headway? What's it been, six months?"

"Just about five. Seems like a year."

Right then Noah Blue trundled up the stairs grumbling and called out for coffee. I cleaned up after myself and went outside into the back lot and pulled out my cell phone. Latham was in the Mountain Time Zone, making it going on nine o'clock there, so I started calling my list: first was the Garnet health center. There was no change in Ashley's condition. Next I left a message with Dr. Sneed, the neurologist, requesting an update on my wife's status. I saved Detective Morgan for last. I caught him taking an early break at the coffee shop across from the police station.

"Hey, Ned," he said energetically, "I've been meaning to call you."

"That right? My cell number's the same."

"I know, I know. We've been caught up in wave of car clouting. Lots of peeved taxpayers."

"What's up?"

"The security company? They called me last week. Looks like they might know where the guard is. You know, the one who was on duty the night of the attack?"

I felt the back of my neck tingle. "Might know? You think they're being straight or just playing you along?"

"There's always that possibility, but they have too much to lose."

"Don't tell me that the police in Latham have been dragging their feet on certain security calls?"

I could hear him suck in a breath. "Hey, hey, none of that talk now. You'll get my anatomy in a ringer if that gets out, but yes, and that's all I'll say."

"The security company, they tell you where they think this guard is?"

"No. It's just a heads-up that they may have something for us. Hey, I'll call you as soon as I know something for sure." I looked at the phone in my hand, shuddered, and took two deep breaths. Damn, what next?

I left a message with Gloria Denham asking about the house, then went back into the shop to pull my first shift at the cash register. It was all pretty basic: Floyd actually had us write down each sale by hand in a small ledger book. My first sale was a dozen Louis L'Amour westerns bound in leatherette covers. My dad used to read those cowboy novels, his favorites. At one point a teenage boy wandered in with three packages of sirloin steaks he wanted to sell. Thing was they were wrapped in Safeway plastic wrap packaging with price stickers still on them. Noah ran the kid out of the shop with a few colorful invectives. Floyd said he quickly learned that when something looked like it might have been stolen, it likely had been, and he always passed. But fresh shoplifted steaks, that was a first.

I was beginning to feel comfortable at Floyd's, living with the two men. I had only been there just short of three days, but the edge was beginning to come off of my unease.

That all began to change the very next day.

-23-

Breakfast duty that morning was mine. I rummaged around and found a package of Eggo waffles in the fridge freezer, brushed the ice crystals off, and toasted the whole box until they were kind of a golden brown. No one complained about the platter of limp waffles accompanied by a half-bottle of original recipe Log Cabin syrup. Breakfast with a touch of freezer breath, always popular.

Noah opened the shop while I took a ride with Floyd in his Ranger pickup out to a house on Tioga Avenue. It was a little bungalow, maybe built in the 1920s, fronted by a yard of dried-up grass and flourishing weeds. The white-haired lady who answered the door was stooped and wearing a face lined with grief. We were there to pick up a collection of her husband's work clothes. He had passed recently. While she watched quietly, we carried out the neatly folded and stacked overalls and work shirts, plus an assortment of boots. Floyd was pleased because men's work clothes were always in demand.

He noted my discomfort and made the case that someone in need of good work clothes at an affordable price would be the beneficiary of the man's death. Okay, I got it.

On the drive back to the shop, Dr. Sneed called me from Latham. There was nothing cheery or friendly in his tone. Due to my call, he had evidently been duty-bound to make a trip to the nursing home, look in on my comatose wife, confirm her status as the same—with some small decline. So he and I were sharing the obligation of monitoring a former human being for whom there was no possible recoupment. And yet he and I could never speak honestly of what we knew to be true: he for professional reasons and I to avoid recrimination. Harsh, I know, but true nonetheless.

After we'd unloaded the work clothes, Floyd told me to get out of the shop and take some time for myself. Guess he figured the dead man's clothes had put me off center. I took him up on it, and Noah went along with me to Thelma's Coffee House. She was there again. Noah kidded with her and ordered a latte. Our eyes met for an instant before I asked for another Americano.

Noah and I settled into adjoining beat-down black leather armchairs. He let out a big sigh before taking a hefty swallow of his latte. "Heard from one of my kids," he said matter-of-factly.

"That good?"

He grunted. "Hard to tell. My oldest daughter. She...well, there's just no warmth in her voice anymore, at least not for me."

I thought of Rosalind. "I can relate. My daughter, she's like that with me." I paused. "Your daughter, she have something special on her mind?"

Noah held his cup out in one hand and stared across the room. "Damn, why did she call?" He turned to look at me. "Now what does that say about my condition?"

"She delivering a message of some kind?"

He looked into his cup, took another swallow, then laughed out loud. "My aunt Edna died." We both laughed long and hard. "It was her voice, her tone of voice—that was all I heard. Dang."

"Were you close, you and your aunt Edna?"

"No." We laughed some more.

"At least she called, your daughter."

"There is that," he confirmed and chuckled some more.

The woman at the counter happened to look our way just then. I smiled, and she smiled back. "What did you say her name was, Noah? The gal at the counter?"

"I didn't," he answered. "But it's Terra."

"Seems nice."

"She is. I'm pretty sure her last name's Buck."

Terra Buck. I ran it through my brain.

"Something on your mind?"

"No," I said with emphasis, "just an observation."

"Sure," Noah baited. "I'm going for a refill. How about you?"

At the counter, I stood back as Noah shouldered up with a big toothy smile and ordered another latte. Then he reached back and pulled me up beside him. "Terra, I'd like to introduce you to my friend Ned here. He wants another of whatever he had. Ned, this is Terra."

I felt the fool. But she merely said hi, gave me her nice smile, and went about fixing our drinks while passing a word with a fellow barista—I'd truly made an impression. Noah just grinned and jabbed me on the shoulder. He ordered his latte to go and said he had to get back to the shop. After he'd gone, I settled into the armchair again, sipped my coffee, and rummaged through the pile of old magazines. I'd just read a piece about Steve Jobs in *Time* magazine and was finishing the cold dregs in my cup when there she was—standing over me.

"Hi," she said. "Ted, right?"

"Ned."

"Sorry. Done with your cup? I'm busing the tables."

I handed it to her. She moved away, gleaning dirty cups and plates from around the room. I stifled a laugh, recognizing how dormant my social skills were. I watched her for a moment before setting aside my fledgling sense of attraction and decided to do the familial thing and made a couple calls to my kin. After six rings, my mother answered at the farm; my brother and his wife were caught up full bore in the potato harvest. I got a report on my father's status and not much else; Dad was no better, no worse, she said. Yes, she'd tell Harrison and Sybil that I called to wish them a great harvest. No, nothing to report about herself. That was it.

My sister Corrine reacted to my call in the same vein as Noah's daughter: no warmth for her younger brother. After my simulated cheery greeting, I reported on things like where I was, Ashley's condition, and such, but excluded my downsizing activities. I could just imagine Corrine wanting to comment on the what-goes-around-comes-around aspects of my life. Instead, before she could squeeze that in, I asked about her family and her life instead.

"My life?" she snorted. "Life's life, right? Kids growing. We think Kyle's going to actually graduate from high school. Fingers crossed. Tommy's the best student, big on science—amazingly. Sally, what can I say? She's a giggler." After a moment, she added, "Glen and me, we're…what? We're getting up every day." She told me to say hello to Uncle Floyd, whom she barely remembered; after that we ran out of gas and said uninspiring good byes.

I sat in the chair, massaging the phone, and considered what had just occurred. Okay, I'd done the dutiful thing, but to what end? Locked up in my own head, I had the typical debate with myself: who was I, what value I did I bring to life—just like everyone did, I suppose. Mostly, we put on our different faces for different places and muddle or swagger our way through, wearing the appropriate demeanor for the moment. Right then with Ashley in my rearview mirror, and for sanity's sake, I felt the need to codify certain people linked to my life, to sort and file them according to those who thought ill of me and who in return were not my favorites. Shunt away the unpleasantness, file it, and allow space for the other side—I had a few of the others. I could work on it.

When I left Thelma's, the sidewalk tables were vacant in the August heat except for one person.

She looked up at me and smiled.

"Hello, Ned," she said.

I stood stark still and must have appeared at sea because she laughed.

"Terra," she said. "My name."

"Yes," I stammered. "It's…I wasn't expecting to see you."

"Especially after I called you Ted. That was my little joke."

I ran a hand over my stubborn hair and continued to study her face—not an unpleasant thing to do. "You're off work?" I stated the obvious.

Her smile played games. "I am."

"You worked here long?" I continued my lame interview.

"Long enough."

"Okay," I chuckled.

"Let's say longer than you've been in town. Would I be right?"

"You would."

"Thought so. And how long would that be?"

I smiled at her. "Less than a week."

"My, and you've already visited Thelma's twice."

"You have a good memory."

She sat up straighter, looked away then back. "It seemed our eyes met a couple of times."

I sat in a chair across the table from her. "I'll bet that happens often."

"Less than you'd think."

"Not sure I believe that."

"You should."

I nodded. People walked by on the sidewalk, traffic ebbed and flowed, while I wondered what to do next. Finally I think she tired of my silence and stood, saying she was going to head home. I swallowed my disappointment.

"Do you live nearby?" I fumbled the question.

She looked down into my face with a curious expression as if she'd been asked that more than once. "Yeah," she said after a moment longer, "a block over on Ivanhoe. My digs are an upstairs room in an old house there. Rent it from a widow lady. It's really muggy in this weather. How about you? Where do you live?"

I grinned. "My uncle owns Floyd's Stuff, you know, couple of blocks north." She nodded. "I live upstairs with him, above the shop. Muggy there too."

"Really? Isn't that where Noah lives, too?"

"Uh-huh, out back in his van. We're an odd crew."

"I'd say."

"Say, here's an idea," I ventured. "Instead of your hot room, why not take a walk into Cathedral Park? It'll be cooler, don't you think?"

"Good idea. Join me?"

I stood. "If you don't mind?"

Her eyes smiled at me. "What do you think?"

It was moderately cooler in the park. We strolled along beneath the towering presence of the steel suspension bridge and stood side by side out near the edge of the river. It was a quietly awkward moment. For a time we watched a few fishing boats drifting on water, lines out, and a kayaker who paddled by, before trading uncertain smiles and turning back into the park. When we came across the shady picnic table I'd used before, I motioned, and Terra nodded. We sat on opposite sides and leaned on our forearms. It was unsettling, the sensation of being attracted to a woman not my wife. I'd found other females generically appealing, but this, this was different. It was like spin the bottle, except the person across from me had been singled out on the very first spin. The imaginary bottle had stopped, and there she was.

"Nice down here," she said, breaking into my reverie.

I nodded and cleared my throat. "Yeah, it is—real nice."

"Where were you?" she asked. When I titled my head, she said, "Lost in thought, it seemed."

I smiled. "I'm out of practice."

She showed me her teeth in a coltish smile. "At what, chatting with a new acquaintance?"

I felt my face flush a little. I looked to the side as a skateboarder rumbled by on the sidewalk. Her eyes were on me when I turned back. "You got me," I admitted.

She shook her head a bit. "Nothing to get. Just kidding you."

I sat up and interlaced my hands on top of my head. "Okay,

new acquaintance, time to get acquainted. How about letting me in on who you are first? Start off by telling me about the scar."

She raised a hand to touch her cheek and studied my face. Was her expression one of curiosity or a bit of pique? A moment later, she took in a shallow breath and told me who she was, or at least what she'd done over the majority of the thirty-eight years she admitted to. The scar. A boyfriend on drugs attacked her with a kitchen knife when she lived in LA, a long time back when she was in her twenties.

She was born in Des Moines, Iowa, to a city planner father and a mother who had been a bookkeeper. Terra was an only child and a wild child by her parent's standards. They agreed to pay for her to attend Cal Sate University in LA to study film and media.

"They were happy just to get me out of town and on a possible track to adulthood. I lasted a year. Dropped out to live with the guy who gave me this, then in a witless moment married him. When the ninety-day trial period expired, I pulled the plug, and shortly after that I got my first job as a barista. That was longer ago than I like to admit." She laughed and squeezed her hands together. "Baristas, we're like shoe salesmen. You can do espresso anywhere…and I did. I've been here in Portland all of four months. Wanted out of LA. Had a friend from my short college tenure who'd moved up here. She offered me a cot for a spell, and here I am."

She paused, her face calm. "Now what's your story?"

That's when my cell phone brought me another call from hell. I looked at the caller screen: Isaac Tucker. After three rings, I looked across at Terra and shrugged. She waved a hand, encouraging me to take the call. I slid off the bench and walked a few steps away.

"Isaac."

"You still out there? In Portland, shacked up with your hippy uncle?"

"I am."

"Neglecting your wife and my daughter," he said loudly into my ear.

"No," I responded. "I asked Dr. Sneed for an assessment a few days ago. He reported back and confirmed that there has been no major change in Ashley's condition."

"You're still an asshole for running out on her."

"Anything else on your mind?"

After the blink of a pause, he said, "The house. I want it."

I turned. Terra Buck was still seated at the picnic table. She'd been watching me. I raised my left hand in a little gesture, and she waved back, smiling. I swallowed. My god, it had been so very long since I'd been on the receiving end of such a genuine smile.

I was brought back to Isaac when he shot out one word. "Well?"

"No," I responded. "That's been my answer to that demand. It still is."

"Listen up, you. I want Ashley's house, you hear?" I held the phone away from my ear to quell the sandpaper of his fury. When I didn't succumb to his taunt, he came at me with, "You know the housing market has gone to hell. They're practically giving houses away. Foreclosures everywhere. You won't get squat for that house. Best you take my offer."

I walked out a ways and looked toward the river. "It's just been put on the market. We're looking at offers," I fudged and wondered if Gloria Denham had gotten any interest from the new city manager and his wife.

"Ha! In your dreams. I know this town inside out, don't forget, and right now flipping burgers is a step up from selling houses. Times are tough."

"So I've heard."

"That right? Is that fact getting through your thick skull?"

My heart was making itself felt. A young woman passed by, pushing a stroller but carrying the child that should have been in it. I watched her for a long moment and inhaled. I'd had enough.

"Isaac, listen to me. I am never going to sell you that house, so get over it. And what's more, I suggest you concentrate on keeping your construction business afloat and get off my back. I'm seeing to Ashley's care. While she will never recover, I still intend to fulfill my responsibility to her as long as she lives. Now, old man, hear this: leave me alone, and don't call again."

"Listen, you prick," he fumed into my ear. "I know where you are. I can make your life miserable, so keep looking over your shoulder." Then he was gone.

-24-

I palmed the phone, jammed it into a pocket, and turned back; she was still watching me. I walked back slowly. "You still want my story?"

"Yes. Of course." I saw empathy in her eyes of the kind everyone desires but infrequently receives.

I pulled my phone out again and held it up. "That was it." She looked at the phone but didn't ask, just raised her eyes to mine. "It is why I am here, in Portland. That phone call."

She leaned forward. "It seemed difficult."

"It was." Our eyes remained on each other. "I'm not sure how to do this." Her eyebrows rose. "I mean, how to tell you...or if I should."

"Up to you."

I sagged back down onto the bench seat and swung my legs around. My smile was cheerless; I knew that. "But then I know all about you."

"Not everything, but a lot. Doesn't matter—tell me or not." She reached out. I gave her a hand, and she held it. "It's okay, Ned."

Damn, that feeling. I looked at our hands together, and it crossed my mind that it had been so very long since my body had felt the pulse brought on by the touch of another. I circled my thumb on the back of her hand.

"Sorry," she said, "my barista's hands are so dry. Goes with the job."

"I like your hands." We laughed for a moment, and then I began. I told her...well, most of it, and all the most important parts.

Afterward, after a minute or so, after she had studied me a bit, she tilted her head back and said, "And that was him on the phone...Isaiah. That was him, just then?"

"Isaac. Yes, that was him."

"What now?"

"Like?"

"Her. Ashley. What can you do?"

I shook my head slowly. "Nothing. Not a thing."

"I'm sorry."

"No. That's all right." I got up from the bench, paced out and back and looked down into her expectant face. "It's been hard," I said. "But I finally had to admit that she isn't coming back. Ever."

"How awful."

"You know," I said, "it has been terrible. It has. But for some reason, from the moment the doctors told me that my wife was gone and would never be back, something happened in my head. They took my hope away. All of it. They did that. They had no choice. Still they did it." I laid a fist into my palm and rolled it around. "I had to find a way to set myself apart from the inevitable. So I did."

I smiled at her quizzical expression. "How did you do that?" she asked.

"I don't really know. Thinking back on it, I guess when the neurologists gave me the verdict, the medical certainty, I was able to separate myself from her, from us really. I had to put space between the ugly event and what's left of my life."

"How did you do that?" She repeated.

"What?"

"Separate yourself from your wife?"

"I just did. She was there—the next moment she was gone." I came around to her side of the table where there was more shade, sat down, and wiped a hand across my damp forehead. She turned to look at me, questioning. "Look," I said, "I left out a big thing when I told you my biography."

"You don't owe me any explanations. So far we're just coffee acquaintances."

"Okay. Maybe I need to protect my ego or my borderline reputation, if there is such a thing."

"Up to you." The lilt was gone from her voice.

I ran a forefinger along the groove between the tabletop planks. "The thing...the big thing is that Ashley and I, we were always a work in progress. Right from the beginning. I doubt that she would have missed me any more than I miss her, if things had been reversed."

"That so? You don't miss her?"

"Yeah, maybe like you and your one-time husband. You miss him?"

She swung her legs out from beneath the table and stood. "I should be getting on home."

"Too much self-examination and revelation between strangers?"

She offered me a thin smile. "Could be. Not sure."

I walked along beside her uphill to Ivanhoe Street, where she stopped in front of an old two-story house with dark green clapboard siding. She pointed to an upstairs window; that was her room, she told me. She walked away; I stood on the sidewalk like a bumbling adolescent and watched until she'd entered the house before I made my way back to Floyd's. The shop was quiet except for two throaty box fans fighting the heat. Noah was at the counter thumbing through an old *National Geographic*, and Floyd seemed busy rearranging—just rearranging—an ongoing state of affairs.

The days trundled by. I grew into the routine of the shop, bunking with the two men, sharing housekeeping, and not expecting much out of each day. It was mostly a comforting existence. During that time, I didn't go back to Thelma's Coffee House, instead began patronizing a nearby Starbucks. When Noah asked why the switch, I tossed him off with an untruth about liking their coffee better. So he joined me there and asked me no more about it. That is not to say that I didn't feel a pull to go into Thelma's to see if she was there, not to engage her, just to see her. But I didn't do that.

During those weeks, I never heard from nor made contact with any of the people related to me, nor from Isaac Tucker, nor my Realtor, and certainly no word from Detective Morgan about the attackers. And I felt no compunction to contact anyone; what would have been the point? If the house had an offer, I'd hear from Gloria, same from C. T. Morgan about the investigation. No need to flex my stress points.

So it was a surprise when on a Friday night in late August I received a call from my brother. Being another warm day, the three of us were sitting out in the storage yard after sharing a sack of cheeseburgers and fries from the nearby Burgerville. We had iced down a twelve-pack of PBR and were feeling just fine. It had been a busy day at the shop.

We were relaxing in the glow of the vapor light pole when my cell came to life. I fumbled the phone out of my back pocket and saw H PINE lit up on the screen. I accepted the call and rose from the Adirondack chair, a cold beer in my other hand. I cleared my throat and said Hamilton's name.

"Hello, Ned," he replied.

"This is a surprise," I said. I mouthed *My Brother* to Noah and Floyd. They nodded and went back to their food. "Nice to hear your voice. How'd the harvest go?"

There was a pause before he said, "Okay…it was okay…pretty good actually."

With that more or less complete sentence, I heard it. He was drunk. His voice was the kind of mushy soft you hear when someone is inebriated. I could tell he was fumbling to get his tongue to cooperate. I didn't think I'd ever witnessed Hamilton intoxicated.

"How are you?" he finally got out. "You doin' okay?"

"I'm fine, Hamilton. Enjoying the good life with Floyd."

I heard him snort. "I'll…I'll just bet."

"You okay?" I asked.

I think he blew his nose; that's what it sounded like anyway. "Yeah, mostly okay."

"Mostly?"

He was quiet for a moment before he began to cry. I said his name twice, but he continued to weep. All I could do was wait. Finally, he sniffed and said, "I'm sorry. Sorry."

"What is it, Hamilton? Has something happened?"

He gurgled a laugh. "Life. Life happened…still is…happening."

"I'm in that club, too."

He thought that over, I guess. "That's right, you are. Aren't you?"

"Hamilton…"

"Dad," he said. An ice pick stabbed my chest; had our father died? "I can't reach him anymore. The son-of-a-bitch…he's…slipping away, Ned. We're losing him bit by bit."

"Is it worse than when I was there?"

After a loud grunt, he said, "Of course he's worse, you dumb shit. You fucking no-show absentee son-of-a-bitch. That's why I'm calling you."

I forced myself to stay calm; it wasn't easy. I wanted to rip my brother a new one myself.

"Are you calling to tell me that dad is dying?"

"My god, of course he's dying. We're all dying."

"So why…"

"Because I can't reach him now. In fact…in fact," he slurred, "he's gone. He's breathing, but there's no one home. In his mind… there's no one there. You get that, Ned? Do you fucking get that?" I couldn't remember a time when my big brother had spewed out such profanity.

I glanced over. Floyd and Noah were paying me no mind. "Listen, Hamilton. I understand what you mean—better than you know, actually. I'm in the same place. Do *you* fucking get that?"

"Wha…what you talking about?" I let him wander. "Oh, okay, I get it. Yeah, okay, maybe you do get it."

"I'm sorry," I said. "What do you want? Why did you call?"

He grunted into my ear. "I hated his guts at times, you know. Wanted to beat the holy crap out of him…more'n once, let me tell you. Now what?"

"Let him go, Hamilton. Just let him go. That's what I had to do with Ashley. Let her go."

"I can't…I can't…"

After a long moment, I realized he was gone, probably fallen asleep in his stupor. It was sad, but there was nothing to be done. I hadn't even had the chance to ask about my mother. How was she doing?

After the call, I returned to the remnants of a cold burger and flat beer. When asked, I merely said it had been my brother and lied to Floyd that Hamilton had said hello. Floyd nodded, smiling, and I felt okay about it.

———

A week later, right before Labor Day, Gloria Denham called. The new city manager and his wife had passed on buying my house. Gloria advised me to hold the price as it was, in spite of the recession; she was confident that there would be a full-price buyer out there. She hadn't heard from Isaac for some time, thought maybe he'd given up on his quest to get the house. I chose to not deflate her optimism, but I knew he would never give up.

That Friday, Floyd and Noah took off in the pickup out to Scappoose to pick up a batch of hand power tools Floyd had bid on from a cabinet shop that was going out of business. That left me to run the shop. With school set to reopen right after Labor Day, we had a number of customers in looking for good used school clothes. The selection was pretty okay. There was a big demand for jeans, the more worn the better. And there were mothers with limited budgets looking for any clothes that were in good shape and low in price. I felt bad for some of the kids who were embarrassed to be trying on used, hand-me-down clothes.

I was just completing a sale of two nice cable-knit sweaters when Terra Buck entered the shop. She caught my eye then wandered around the store while I rang up the order. When we were alone, she came up to the register. We both smiled self-consciously.

"There's word in the hood that you've abandoned Thelma's for that other place," she said. "That true?"

"Could be." I raised a hand of greeting to a tall man in a Panama hat who entered the shop. He waved and went directly to the book section, his regular haunt.

"It's also being spread about that you took another good customer with you."

"He went of his own accord."

"Sure he did."

"How are you?" I asked.

"Been missing your face at Thelma's."

I laughed. "Heck, I was only in there a couple of times."

"No Matter. I might get a bounty if I can lure you back to Thelma's. Any chance?"

I folded my arms. "You know, I figured that I'd done enough damage to my reputation. Seemed best to give it some space. My life right now is a mess of contradictions and ugly circumstances. Remember?"

She looked down into the counter's glass display case where we kept the best jewelry and watches. "I remember someone who shared the bare truth of their life with me. Honest and painful—but genuine."

"Part of it did not set well, as I recall."

She pointed at a necklace. I brought it out. "I thought on that," she said while draping the gold chain over her hand. "Then I thought about some coarse stuff in my life that I didn't bring out into the open that day."

I recalled a few disturbing episodes I still had in the time-lock vault. "No one knows everything about anyone, do they?"

"I suppose not."

I chuckled. "Not sure any person could hold their head up if all of their inner thoughts and secretive actions were shown on a big screen."

"My, we're waxing philosophical today, aren't we?" She held out the necklace. "I'll take it. How much?"

"Says fifteen bucks on the tag, but everything is twenty-five percent off today. How about ten bucks?"

"That's more than twenty-five percent."

"I'm manager of the day, and I say ten bucks."

She unzipped her small shoulder purse and fingered out a five and five ones in a wad and handed the money to me. My lips had parted with some words forming when the book buyer ambled up and dropped a stack of hardbound mysteries on the counter. By the time I'd taken his dollar per book, she'd waved and was gone.

On Monday, Floyd declared the shop closed for Labor Day. As displaced persons, all three, we managed to squander our time by sleeping in, rousing late and going for pizza, then taking in a movie at St. John's Cinema, a just okay action flick called *The Expendables* starring Sylvester Stallone. After that we each had a couple of beers at the B&C Tavern then fell into our various beds and were enveloped by the sleep of the pure at heart. I was getting very used to an unstructured life with no schedules, client meetings, deadlines, or general expectations.

Still, I was compelled from within my newfound apathy to fret about my kids and desire better relations with my sister and my big brother, whom I finally called back to learn if he was okay after his late-night rant and meltdown. As one time before, I caught him waiting up for Sybil to get home from choir practice. We traded some trivial farm chat, tied to his obligatory question about my status with Floyd, before I asked if he was okay. Here's the startling thing to me: he had no recollection of having called me that night. Absolutely none. And he didn't acknowledge his collapse about Dad. Denied it, in fact. Groused that I must have been drinking. It took all the restraint I could muster to withhold an impulse to ask about his drinking. I'd never seen him drink to excess; it would have been against his moral plumb line. He could never admit to having been intoxicated, never, or to sobbing to me about our father.

Well, that did it for me. I was able to cut away some of the obligatory marionette lines.

No longer, I reasoned, need I be a puppeteer responsible for monitoring the umbilical connection between those with whom I shared DNA. Did I care? Of course, but caring is a two-way boulevard. It wasn't as if I'd been a stalwart go-to person anyway, so maybe I had earned the disconnect. I bid Hamilton good bye knowing that he would meet Sybil at the door, give her a peck on the cheek, and go off to bed before rising at five o'clock to tackle another day on the farm. Bless him, I guess.

It was time to move on.

-25-

Okay, so I went back to Thelma's, with Noah as my cover. It was Tuesday, the day after Labor Day. While Noah and I placed our coffee orders, Terra and I gave each other silly grins. Noah laughed loudly and punched me on the shoulder; he knew what was up.

That enchanted moment wouldn't last, I found out.

At the end of her shift, I met Terra out in front of Thelma's. We both grinned again and, as agreed, set off for another walk into Cathedral Park. We walked and talked and laughed and enjoyed the sunny but not overly warm day. I guess we had set aside the unsettling parts from each of our lives, at least for that moment. I wasn't in denial about those coarse episodes in her life; I didn't care about that. And I assumed that she had considered that I had a comatose wife and was accepting of what I'd told her about how I was handling that—for now. She was a lovely person, and I wasn't about to give up this time of mutual attraction. Of course Ashley was ever present. The image of her inert body had taken up residence in my brain; the recalculation of how we had once been together was lodged in my psyche. But regardless of my first bouts of chronic grief and guilt, I'd become more desirous of wanting a life beyond what had been. Fairly or unfairly, Terra had walked through the crosshairs of my disconnect at a vulnerable moment.

We were on the stairs heading down into the park when it happened. He suddenly appeared, well down the wide flight of concrete steps, standing spraddle-legged and looking up. Isaac Tucker.

"Who's this?" he bellowed. "Your wife lying in a hospital bed, and here you are cavorting with another woman?"

"Isaac," I said, shocked. "What are you doing here?"

He came up a few steps, his hands closed in fists by his sides. "I told you," he said. "I told you to look over your shoulder. That I'd be there one day. Well, here I am."

I let go of Terra's hand and brushed her behind me. Even a dozen steps below me, Isaac looked twice my size. At nearly seventy, he was still an imposing figure; I wasn't sure if I could handle him if he got physical. I set my feet and swallowed against the bowlful of apprehension that was rolling about in my gut.

"Okay, here you are," I echoed. "Now what?" I forced some conviction into my voice, way more than I was feeling. "Gonna kill me?"

He took another step up. "I should. Told you I would, didn't I?"

I nodded. Terra's hand pressed against my back.

Isaac looked past me at her. "Who is this, your harlot?"

"Watch your mouth." I reached back and touched her arm. "A friend," I said.

His lips drew back, revealing his age-yellowed teeth. "I'll just bet. Well friend," he said snidely, "you don't hold a candle to my Ashley. You couldn't stand in her shadow."

I felt her body stiffen, but she didn't respond. I was glad for that. When Isaac inched up another step, I reached an arm around to her, perhaps the most protective act I'd ever taken. My heroic stands had been few and not notable.

"Stay right there," I said. "We can talk from where we are. So again, why are you here?" I knew, but I wanted him to say it so I could stick it in his ear one more time.

He came up one more step; I raised a palm, and he stayed where he was. "You know very well why I'm here."

"My answer is the same."

"I want it."

"No, and again no. That house is mine to dispose of however I wish, and it will never be to you." I raised a forefinger. "Never."

There was a long moment of silence when a group of grade school-aged kids ran past us up the stairs. He watched them, and when they'd passed, he jammed his hands into the pockets of his Levi's and stared up at me once more. His silver gray hair was cut in the old crew cut style. With that brush of hair and his square-shouldered stature, he reminded me of some retired military officer. I had no idea if he had ever been in the military; we'd never gotten to know one another that well—by choice.

"That is her house, you prick. I want it waiting for her when she is back to normal."

I shook my head. "Isaac, you keep replaying that line. How many times have I heard you deny reality?" I felt Terra pat my back as a caution. I shrugged and spoke out stupidly. "I spoke with Dr. Sneed recently."

"That right? What'd that quack have to say?"

I inhaled. "Nothing's changed. In fact, he said there had been some decline. Decline, Isaac, no recovery. As much as I'd love for her to, Ashley will never recover."

I'd barely gotten those last words out of my mouth before he charged up the steps between us and tackled me around the legs. Together we slammed onto the concrete steps and began to roll downhill, bouncing from step to step. The sharp edges of the stairs were ripping into my shoulders; my head bounced at least once on one of the cement stair risers before we rolled off onto the grass. I was stunned; my eyes couldn't quite focus, and the ability to defend myself was acutely diminished. I took a couple of blows to my head and face from Isaac, who had managed to survive the fall better than I had. He was astraddle of me and in an uncontrolled rage. His weight and strength were such that I was nearly helpless to guard against his blows. I could hear Terra yelling something as I deflected his pummeling with a windmill of my arms and elbows.

It was Noah I heard above the din. His voice rose over me, roaring something to Isaac about knocking it off, and then he was dragging my father-in-law away from me. I lay there gasping and reached up to touch the part of my scalp that was throbbing and bleeding. Terra was on her knees next to me saying something, but my ears were ringing such that I couldn't make it out. I smiled meekly; that was all I felt like doing.

When I was finally able to sit up, my Uncle Floyd was sitting on the grassy slope beside me. He was holding out a big red farmer-style handkerchief. I took it gladly and held it against my head wound, which only seemed to throb more when I pressed against it. Terra had her hand on my shoulder, not moving or patting, just there. A small crowd had formed as a result of the brouhaha. I didn't look at them, just felt their presence and heard their murmuring and a few laughs. When I took the handkerchief away from my head and looked about, I saw Noah kneeling beside Isaac, who was on his back. Noah had a big hand on Isaac's chest, pressing him down, restraining him.

I rolled to one side, got up on a knee, and pushed myself up into a wobbly standing position. Floyd stood beside me and put an arm around me to keep me steady. I turned to Terra and smiled. "Nice day, huh?" I said to her. She grinned and shook her head.

Noah rose and stood back while keeping an eye on my father-in-law. "Should we call the cops?"

Isaac and I caught sight of each other; he was red-faced with indignation and breathing hard. I shook my head. "No."

"But he assaulted you." Noah looked down into the face of Isaac.

The man was humiliated. Maybe he'd never been physically bested. I had been pummeled and mortified many times as a kid. Isaac, maybe never. "Let him be," I said.

Noah looked into my face, disbelieving. Then he stepped away from the prone figure. Isaac lay still for several minutes before rolling over and rising to his feet. He looked over at me while he brushed grass and grit from his shirt and pants. After spitting something out of his mouth, he looked around at those observing him, squared his shoulders, and began the climb up the stairs out of the park. I didn't know where he went from there, but I didn't see him in St. Johns later.

People drifted away, chatting about what they had witnessed. The four of us stood on the steps quietly until I started to laugh. It was one of those times when things aren't funny but they are. I could barely breathe after a couple of explosive bursts. In fact, I had to lean over and gasp, but I could not stop laughing. Soon, everybody was laughing.

Noah was wiping tears from his eyes when he said, "It was my fault, you know."

"What?" I said, swallowing my laughter.

"Him finding you, my fault."

"Not really now, Noah," Floyd interceded. When he saw my confusion, he added, "I was upstairs using the john when he came in, your father-in-law. Now I know the score you have with him, but I wasn't present at the time, so Noah, he—"

"Hey, I know all that stuff, about your grudge match with the man," Noah said. "You told me out in the yard that night, when we were smoking cigars. Remember?" I nodded. He raised his big arms and dropped them. "But damnation, that was plumb outa my skull when he wandered in. Seemed like a nice guy just looking for someone, a friend...or whatever. So anyway I told him... where I thought you might be. Figured you and Terra, hell, I knew you and she would hook up after her shift was over. Knew that..."

Floyd jumped in, "So when Noah told me about helping some guy find you and what he looked like, damn, it came down on me like a sledgehammer."

Noah barked a laugh. "Man, Floyd, he took off like someone berserk. And I...I left the store to itself and followed as best I could, but Floyd left me in the dust."

"The adrenaline was a pumping, I tell you," Floyd said.

"I'm sorry, man," Noah pled. "How's your head?"

"We're taking care of it right now," Terra said. "My place is close. I have bandages, so we're going there. Right now!" she repeated when we all stood there immobile.

Floyd told me to keep his handkerchief, and he and Noah watched Terra march me off. I told the men that I'd see them in a while. But I didn't. Terra's upstairs room in the old house was large and mostly tidy: a double bed, an old rocker, a chifforobe, dresser with a mirror above it, a small dropleaf table and a chair, a toaster oven and a hot plate. There was only one bathroom in the house, she told me; she shared the use of it with her elderly landlady and was also allowed discretionary use of the kitchen.

She had me sit in the table chair and brought out a small cardboard box, which held a mix and match of Band-Aids, antiseptic ointments, bandages, cotton balls, and a pair of small scissors. She stripped open a foil packet with an alcohol swab in it, cleaned the wound on my head, and stuck an adhesive bandage over it. After assuring that it held firmly, she tossed the packaging remnants in the trash, sat across from me in the rocker, and studied her handiwork.

She hadn't spoken while she patched me up; in fact she hadn't said but a few words since Isaac pummeled me. Now we looked at one another. "How's that feel?" she asked after a bit. I nodded and said I felt okay. Then we sat some more and looked at one another. Finally, I laughed and touched the bandage.

"What?" she said.

"Nothing. I was just thinking what I had to go through to be invited into your bedroom."

A toothy smile and those flashing amber eyes came at me. "You think that's what this is?"

"It's not?"

"Just the infirmary, buster, just the first aid."

"I don't get the sympathy vote then?" I said. "Didn't that dust-up confirm the truthfulness of my tale of woe?"

She rocked the chair. "It did that, all right. But you didn't have to prove yourself. I already believed you."

I smiled, but the call from Sylvia Winters ran through my head; it had come late on Labor Day. She'd been drinking, I could tell. *When was I coming home? When was I going to live up to our future,* as she slurred it. She threw around phrases like *our predestination, the chemistry between us that cannot be denied, this was meant to be, it is kismet,* and so on. When I didn't respond in kind, she became afire within her intoxication and demanded to know when I would return to Latham. I said not for a while and bid her goodnight. I did not pick up her repeated calls or respond to the dozen texts she unloaded on me.

I hadn't mentioned Sylvia in the telling of my life to Terra, nor Gloria Denham. Sure, it had been an intentional sin of omission. How could I justify my abominable behavior as my wife lay incapacitated? I bunched up my indiscretions, beginning with my Gloria Denham affair, that perhaps being the lesser of my evils, the one I had justified by Ashley's remoteness to me. But Sylvia had been a sinkhole of my most deplorable moment—and remained so. What then did my attraction to yet another woman make of me?

"But you shouldn't have," I said, "believed me. Not utterly so."

Terra stopped the slow rocking, her head tilted forward, and she gripped the arms of the chair. "Is that so? Do you mean that you withheld some very private information from me? That on our very first occasion to speak, you didn't regurgitate every black spot of your life to a complete stranger?"

"Yes but…"

"How dare you. I am truly offended."

"Very funny," I responded. "And yet…"

"And yet what? Do you think for a moment that I spewed out the entirety of everything in my life that I'm not proud of to a guy whose been in town five minutes and is living above a secondhand store?"

I shrugged. "Okay, I get it."

She tilted the rocker forward and looked hard at me. "First, you're in this room to get a bandage, nothing more. Okay, we noticed each other and sort of liked what we saw. So far we've had two walks in the park. The first time we kind of got acquainted, spilled a few beans to one another. Then we took a short breather. Next time, one of your demons came out of the shadows and ruined our walk. Hey, could just as easily have been my ex-husband waving a knife."

"Yeah, but it wasn't."

She sat back, waited a beat, then said, "Ned, I don't know where this is going—between you and me." She spoke softly. "Don't know if there's any there, there. Maybe there is. Maybe not. But I kinda think so. Be nice if there was."

"I'd like that."

She nodded. "Okay, I say we start from right here. That stuff over our shoulder, in the rearview mirror, doesn't count. Well, of course it counts in our lives, but not in whatever we make of this... this, what? Too early to say relationship. How about friendship?"

"Okay," I nodded. "But if this goes someplace, one day I'll need to tell you some things."

She waved a hand. "Enough of that. Time for a beer. I'll be right back. Take it easy."

With Terra's body heat absent from the room, silence took over. My head throbbed a bit. I held Floyd's red handkerchief against the dressing and looked about her space. I viewed the things she cared enough about to hang on the walls, display on a table, or scatter on the floor. What the hell was I doing there? This woman, this new person, had emerged from a dark cup of coffee. And from that simple moment, I'd felt drawn to her, drawn to the notion of possibility. But right then such a possibility rested naively amid the swirl of what had transformed my life on St. Patrick's Day, 2010. I had been caught up in a whirlwind, a twister that had picked up my life, *our lives*, and thrown them up into a maelstrom from which we could not extricate ourselves. Ashley...well, she never would. That left me flailing about like a kite in a hailstorm.

Terra breezed back into her room brandishing two long-neck bottles of Budweiser. "Here you go," she said, a smile on her face, and held out a bottle. "Cold and therapeutic. Here's to you." She clinked her bottle against mine. I twisted the cap off, and we raised our drinks.

I swallowed and looked at the bottle. "Hits the spot."

She came over to my chair and looked at the bandage on my head. "How you feeling?"

I nodded. "Okay, a little throb, but okay." After taking another swallow, I said, "Terra, my life is fucked up."

"Join the club."

"No, I'm living in a fog, no good for myself, let alone anyone else." When she tilted her head and looked at me quizzically, I said, "I can't do this to you. I can't. Not fair."

She pursed her lips and responded, "Nor I to you. How's that for reciprocity?"

Her laugh was endearing but let me off the hook too easily. "Terra. You deserve better."

"Says who? Maybe you do, too…I'm no prize. Besides, do what? A walk and a half doesn't constitute a pledge of devotion, does it?"

I could only smile. I rose from the chair, endured a minor throb of my head, shoved Floyd's handkerchief into my pocket, and downed the rest of the beer. "I'd better go. Thanks for the first aid…and the beer."

The doorknob was in my hand when she said, "So that's it? You use my emergency room and walk away?"

"I'm serious. I'd just mess up your life."

"Can't we be okay with our mutual deficiencies for now? You know…enjoy the moment? No obligation. Agree to a get out of jail free card?"

"Look, there's more dark stuff hanging fire for me. Don't get caught up in it. Let's just shake hands and call it good."

She crossed over and came right up to me. "Maybe we can do more than shake hands." She leaned in and kissed me on the cheek.

"I thought this was just an infirmary visit. Isn't that what you said?"

"A girl can change her mind."

-26-

Her body was graceful. She showed herself to me without hesitation and with no chagrin over the gentle tummy lines or the small tattoo cluster of poppies on her right hip. Her shoulders were square, hosting a scattering of freckles. After disrobing, she looked at me and held her arms out to her sides—indicating my turn. I was not as open and at ease with showing my own nakedness. As I undid my belt buckle and unzipped my pants, I was already regretting that she would see my small potbelly and my less than toned body. I'd let myself go.

She smiled at the self-consciousness written on my flushed face. Ashley and I had been so inept the first time we'd had sex in her little house in Latham, it had been as if we'd dutifully followed the numbered steps in the manufacturer's handbook. It never improved, our desire for one another. Our sexual encounters were executed by decree; that's how we produced our offspring.

I followed Terra, slipped between the sheets of her bed, and pulled the cover up, relieved to cloak my body. We shared the flattened pillows in the bed and smiled at each other. It came to me that this woman actually wanted to be with me right then. It wasn't a formula as it had felt in the past.

"Hello." She brushed strands of her hair aside and reached out to touch my face.

"Hi." I took her hand, held it, and kissed her fingers. "You're sure?"

She slid closer and came in to kiss me on the lips. "I'm sure. You?"

I breathed a chuckle. "I think we can forego further interrogation. May I hold you?"

She nodded eagerly and moved closer. I reached an arm out and drew her to me. My hand felt the contours of her body: the smoothness of her skin, the dip and rise of her hip, the depression of her spine, the softness of her bottom, the gentle pressure of her breasts against me. She willingly yielded to my exploration and reached out to investigate who I was. Once there, she found my utter willingness to be right where we were. I could not recall how long ago it had been since Ashley and I had made love, and it wasn't on my mind at that moment—that recollection and consideration came later. But on that date, the day my father-in-law assaulted me, I discovered what I never had before, the sharing of myself with another who in return gave herself to me with great willingness. It was wonderment. As the afternoon melded into evening, we came together with no reservations more than once and in the end lay spent, rewarded, and contented. We embraced long and hard at her door, and I slipped away quietly, avoiding Mrs. Shanahan, the landlady whose rules included no men in the house after dark.

————————

Floyd and Noah were sitting out in the yard digesting their fallback standard bowls of canned chili and beer. When I came out of the warm evening darkness, they fell on me: where the hell had I been, how was my head, and had there been any more contact with Isaac? First, I asked if I could have some chili, which I consumed while they continued to pepper me with questions. I kept nodding until I'd finished eating; then I answered in this order: my head was pretty good, no I had not heard any more from Isaac, and lastly I'd spent the afternoon with Terra in her room after she'd patched up my head. On that note the silence was deafening, after which Noah erupted in a tuba-blast of laughter and called me a son-of-a-gun; that got Floyd to laughing too.

We cleaned up carelessly, leaving our chili bowls in the sink, beer cans in recycling, and went to bed. It was humid upstairs, but I slept hard anyway in spite of Floyd's snoring.

The call I that I had been anticipating for many months came the following day.

———

I was waiting for Noah to finish an interminably long shower the next morning when my cell began its annoying ring. My heart gave a turn when I retrieved it from the swirl of my unmade bed-clothes and saw the initials: C. T.

"C. T.," I said as I plopped down on the bed and pulled a ratty bath towel off my shoulder.

"Hey, Ned." The detective's voice sounded the same, maybe a little higher pitched, or was I hearing what I wanted to hear? "Is this a good time?"

"Good as any. Got news?"

I could hear him inhale. "Well…," he strung the word out. "Yes, I do have some news."

I held my breath until my lungs complained. "What?"

"They found the guy." He paused. I waited. "The security company, A-Ball, they've located the guard who was on duty that night…of the attack."

"Are you shitting me?"

His laugh was one of self-awarded amnesty. "No, I'm not shitting you."

"So what's that mean? What's next?" I gripped the phone. "Do you have him, the guy?"

"No. Not yet. After he took it on the lam, he came to ground in St. Louis."

"St. Louis? You have to extradite him or anything?"

"As far as we know for now, he didn't officially commit a crime. He broke company policy and violated the contract with the homeowners' association, but that's it for right now."

"How can you get to him, to ask what he knows? You know, interrogate him."

"Working on that."

"What's that mean?" I said again. "Damn!"

"Now hold your water, Ned. I'm pushing on A-Ball Security to get into the act. This guy, the one who let the attackers in, he's working security again in St. Louis. That's the good news."

"Really?"

"You bet. If we start an inquiry with his current employer, that new job will likely be toast. And if A-Ball makes contact with the security company there, same outcome. A-Ball is a pretty big name in security. That should give us some leverage. My guess is the guy'll want to keep his job. Hopefully that will make him compliant."

"Where's that leave us?"

"Look, as soon as A-Ball puts the fear of god in him, I'm going to St. Louis to have a face to face with this character. Doubt if I could get him to come here."

"I'm going with you."

Morgan hesitated. "No can do, Ned. No can do. It'll go better if it's just me in a closed room with him." He laughed. "Hell, if he knew one of the victims was within range and might want to kill him, he'd vanish and end up in Africa or someplace. We'd never learn what he knows. You'd like to see him fess up, right?"

"I'd like to see him face down in a big pond."

"See? No ticket to St. Lou for you."

"You leaving right away?"

"Gotta wait until we see what A-Ball can do. But they are motivated to move on this, and they can put the screws to this character better than we can. A trip back there will stretch the department's limited travel budget, but since it's still an active case that got a lot of press, the chief gave me the green light. I'll let you know what I find out as soon as I do."

Before we disconnected, I told Morgan about my altercation with Isaac Tucker in Portland. He was disturbed but agreed with me to let it lie. The answer was no, he hadn't told Isaac the news yet about locating the long-lost security guard. At my urging, he agreed to leave it that way for the time being. I took a hot shower, scrambled some eggs, ate them with toast and coffee, then went for a long walk to let C. T. Morgan's news sink it. Floyd listened to my telling of the possible breakthrough, gave me a big hug, and told me to get lost.

When Terra had a break at Thelma's, I was waiting. We took our coffees outside and sat at one of the tables. We held hands for a few minutes and did the silly-smile routine before I shared the news with her. She was immediately sober and squeezed my hand.

"So now you wait?"

"Yes. I wait."

"Then what? What if the guy, the guard, doesn't know anything?"

"Oh, he knows. That's why he blew town."

"What do you think he knows?"

I took a deep swallow of coffee and looked into her questioning eyes. "That attack...and I've felt this in my gut from the beginning...that attack wasn't random, and it wasn't even a robbery."

"Nothing was taken?"

"A bag of silverware. It was nothing, a ruse to give the impression of robbery."

She examined my face; I wasn't smiling, didn't feel like smiling right then. She started to say something, pulled back, then went ahead. "So you think it was planned?"

"Yes. I don't know why, but we were targeted, I'm sure of it. They need to get that security guard in a room and grill the holy living hell out of him until he caves in."

"What if he doesn't?"

I looked down at the tabletop and shook my head. "It can't end that way. They...whoever they are...ripped apart our lives. My wife will eventually die from their act of violence. I cannot let that stand."

"Of course," she said.

I knew immediately that I'd sliced away a piece of our newly discovered attraction and put a dead-to-the-world presence between us. When I attempted to rectify my blunder, she merely smiled and squeezed my hand.

"You must do this," she said.

"Terra, I didn't mean..."

"I know you didn't, but still it's there, isn't it? You do what you must, and if it matters, maybe we'll come back to this."

We hugged, and she went back to work. At first light on Thursday, I gassed up the Explorer and drove back to Latham.

-27-

That night I bunked on the Idaho border in Ontario, Oregon, at a Motel 6 and hit Latham's city limits on Friday about mid-morning. I felt a wave if déjà vu. It had been just over a month since I'd packed up and left town, but it felt like I'd been away for a year. I drove the streets, saw familiar sights, knew how to navigate my way around—still, it felt odd. When I had stopped for breakfast in Twin Falls at Mel's Café, I made a call to Gloria Denham; we agreed to meet at Rudy's Diner for coffee. She was sitting in a booth studying some papers when I slid in across from her. We generated no-harm no-foul smiles and with calculated caution acknowledged that we were glad to see each other. I guess I looked at her too long or too intently because she suddenly looked away, then back at the papers in front of her. I could tell that she had taken my assessment the wrong way; I was merely recalling what had once been, but perhaps she read more into it than that. The thought of telling her about Terra flitted by, but no, how foolish that would have been. I didn't know if there would even be a Terra waiting for me when I had run the table on the mess of my life.

My coffee arrived. "So, any serious lookers?" I asked as I sweetened my drink.

The papers were shuffled too abstractly for any serious business to be among them. "The city manager, he dropped out, as you know," she said. I nodded; she paused for moment, still examining said papers. "There've been a handful of lookers, bargain hunters mainly."

"You hold any open houses?"

"Couple." She smiled. "Had to check the front door to see if I'd forgotten to leave it unlocked."

"So nothing then?" I said, trying to catch her eye.

She finally looked up. "No." She sighed. "Nothing really."

"No low-ball offers?"

"Nope, not even those."

"Pretty bad, then."

"Bad all over. Foreclosures. Mortgages under water."

"What's it going to take?"

She looked at me. "Sell to Isaac…if you want to sell the house quickly."

My smile was cynical in response. "Did you know that he came to Portland for that very purpose, to force me to sell to him?"

"No. Really?"

"He did. Tried to beat it out of me, in fact. If someone hadn't stopped him, he might have done it, too."

Her eyes widened so that I had to chuckle. "You're not serious?" she said.

"I am serious. So if he couldn't get me to sell by beating on me, I'm sure not going to roll over now that I'm back in town."

"What do you want me to do, then?" she asked.

"Keep plugging," I shrugged. "It's only been a month. I can hang on for a good while longer. If at some point it pinches too much, we'll talk about the price or maybe renting it. Any action in renting?"

"Some. More than selling, that's for sure." She smiled at someone she knew who walked by then turned her attention back to me. "Why are you here? You didn't come all this way for this miserable report on your property."

"You're right, I didn't." I gripped my hands together on the tabletop. "You know, the case is still open…on the attack." She nodded minimally. "There may be progress in the investigation. Not sure, but maybe."

She stared at me intently. What could she say? What was there to say? After a long silence, I pledged her to secrecy to avoid any disruption of the investigation. She bobbed her head in agreement. It crossed my mind right then that she hadn't asked about Ashley, not even after I brought up the monstrous act. That was all right; it gets tiresome, plowing such dismal ground. We gave each other a perfunctory hug, and she agreed to keep in touch on the house. When I said I thought I'd stay at the house, she reminded me that the place was mostly empty; there was some show furniture but no bed. I drove out to Whitewood Estates anyway, pulled into the driveway, past the For Sale sign, looked at the place, and felt nothing. Gloria was right, not much in the house, mainly chairs and tables in the living and dining rooms. I decided I could make do sleeping on the couch and hauled in some clothes and toiletries.

The house didn't feel any more like home than when we'd lived in it. However, forget the damn house, my mind was more focused on whatever C. T. Morgan was uncovering in Missouri. I had promised myself to cool my jets until he was back in town, but I couldn't live up to that. I wandered out onto the backyard patio, stood in the mid-seventies sun, noted that the lawn needed mowing, and methodically punched in his cell number; he answered after five rings. Still in St. Louis, he told me, scheduled to catch an early Delta flight out on Monday morning. When I asked about the security guard, if he'd learned anything, he hesitated before saying, yes, he had. But when pressed about what he'd learned, if anything, he told me to hang tough, that he'd fill me in on Tuesday. We agreed to meet at the police station around nine o'clock that day.

After the call, I went back inside and wandered about the hollowed-out house, room to room; in the kitchen I stood still and looked at the backdoor. The flashback was like a grainy replay of an old movie. In slow motion: the wood splintered again, the lugged boots exploded forth again, and the scream, Ashley's scream, reverberated again. Those images and the shriek came over me in a dreamlike wave. As the memory faded, I sank to the floor, wiped perspiration from my forehead. I don't know how long I rested there on my knees because I blanked out. Maybe half an hour, maybe five minutes, I do not know. However long, I finally roused, sucked in several breaths, and struggled to my feet. *Ashley.* I had to visit her, for my own sanity if nothing else. I drove out to the Garnet nursing center, parked in the visitors' lot, and sat in the car, looking at the flat-roofed elongated building. Visitors and staff members entered and left; no one gave me a second look.

It was heading on toward dusk when I finally decided to go in. The woman at the reception desk looked up. I signed the roster of people who had come and gone; she checked my name and was about to say something when I walked away. She came after me to say that Ashley had been moved to a different room, that I would have to turn left instead of right, which I did. The place smelled of the same mixture of oldness, sickness, and astringents. The sound of residents calling out, groaning, and speaking to whomever passed, hung in the air. At room 12-E I paused, took in a breath, and stepped through the open door.

There she was, the same prone, immobile figure, covered in the same light blanket, and the same lights from the monitor signaled that she was alive. As before, a small lamp on the nightstand cast soft ambient light. I stood just inside the doorway before willing myself to approach the bed. What had Dr. Sneed said, that she had suffered *some small decline*? It had only been a month or so since I had seen her last, a mere month, but I wasn't expecting what I saw.

I stood beside the bed, hands at my side, and took in the facial features I knew so well. Except the countenance I saw was not what it had been even four weeks ago. Mostly, her features had withdrawn: her cheeks were slightly shrunken, her skin had a sallow pasty cast to it, and her body seemed diminished beneath the pastel blue blanket. Her hair had been cut severely short. I was still frozen in place when I heard someone enter the room.

"Mr. Pine." It was a woman's voice. When I didn't turn, she said, "I'm Margaret Carrington." She stepped up beside me. I could sense she was looking at me and wanting to engage. I kept my eyes focused on Ashley. "It is good to finally meet you," she added.

When I did turn to her, I saw a woman about four inches shorter than I was, maybe in her fifties, with short salt-and-pepper hair nicely styled. Half-frame glasses hung on a lanyard around her neck, and she was dressed in a white blouse and gray skirt. A name badge was pinned to her blouse; it merely said *Mrs. Carrington*. She was slender, not skinny. She had a pleasant, if nondescript, face.

I held out my hand. "Ned Pine."

She returned my grip firmly. "Yes. Are you back in town now?"

I looked back at my wife. "For the time being."

"As you can see, we moved your wife to a new room."

"Why?"

She hesitated. "Your father-in-law wanted her moved. He thinks the light is better in this wing of the building."

I turned to face her. "He said that? The light is better?"

She looked at the floor and clasped her hands at her waist. "Yes. I guess his daughter...your wife enjoyed rooms with lots of light."

"That's true. She did, back when it mattered." Her lips tightened, and she nodded. "More for him than her, I suppose."

"Perhaps," she responded. "Is there anything I can do for you, Mr. Pine?"

I shook my head. "No. She has regressed slightly in the last month."

"Oh, do you think so?"

"Yes, and so does Dr. Sneed. It's obvious having been away from her for many weeks." I looked directly into her eyes. "I know that Isaac would never accept that observation. I'm sure you know that. And I know that as the administrator, you have to walk a fine line between what is reality and what some people want to believe. Do you get my meaning?"

She drew her shoulders back. "I do."

"Do you agree?"

Her eyes narrowed, and she studied me before answering. "Mr. Pine, I know the difference between hope for a desired outcome and the understanding of a logical outcome. In my position, as you may surmise, I hold the hands of the hoped-for adherents but leave medical realities to the physicians. Do you understand my position?"

"I do." I looked at Ashley. "And I'm sure Isaac will enjoy the light. Best open the blinds before he comes." I nodded toward the closed slatted blinds. She smiled.

Just then I heard the sound of a small compressor, and beneath Ashley the mattress began to rise very slowly on one side. Her body started to rotate upward. It was eerie seeing her moving. When I stared, Mrs. Carrington explained that it was the new lateral rotation mattress. It was meant to help prevent issues that can develop from immobility like bedsores and pulmonary complications. I nodded like I understood and wished it would stop.

She stood beside me for a bit then excused herself, and I was alone again with Ashley. When the rotation was over, I pulled a side chair up to the bed, took hold of a lifeless hand, and as a matter of rote, said *Hello Ashley*. Her skin felt like that of an aged apple. I lifted each finger in turn. There was no response. None was expected. Before I left, I leaned over the vestige of my wife and kissed her on the forehead, not from love but to confirm the past.

Departing that place, a holding pen for those in severe decline, most of whom would never be free of those corridors, left my gut feeling as if it were lined with lead. The last sound I heard on the way out was that of a frail female voice calling out: *mama, mama, mama.*

I was jolted awake Sunday morning by a lightening bolt of pain that skewered my back. I slid off the couch and lay on my back until the spasm subsided. Rolling back and forth seemed to help, but when I crab-crawled onto my knees and tried to stand up, a sharp-edged ache came up with me.

To work off the pain, I sauntered aimlessly about the place in my underwear and then took a very brief cold shower. I toweled my goose bumps, dressed in the same clothes, and headed out for breakfast. As I drove off, I saw my old neighbor, Guy Stewart, walking his little dog like always. He stood in his driveway and gawked at me. I didn't wave; it would only have confused him.

Rudy's Diner was open for Sunday brunch. I chose the buffet, loaded my plate with too much food, and picked out a booth toward the back of the big room. Before I'd really gotten up to speed, a voice called out my name, and there was my former CPA partner, Jack Jackson. He and his wife Violet were smiling at me, each holding a plate of food and dressed in church clothes. At my invitation, they sat across from me, and we all shared buttery smiles.

"Thought you were in Portland," Jack said. "Last I heard anyway."

"Have been. Just back for a bit."

Violet fussed with placing a napkin in her lap and said, "Any news about your wife?"

Jack looked uncomfortable, patted his wife's arm, and changed the subject. "How do you find Portland?"

"I like it," I said. "Been living sort of an unconventional life with my uncle out there."

Jack filled a fork with hash browns. "Unconventional? That sounds intriguing, doesn't it?" He smiled at his wife. She nodded and looked at me expectantly.

I told them about living above a secondhand store, taking my turn at being a retail clerk, and enjoying the uniqueness of being part of the north Portland blue-collar community of St. Johns.

Jack wiped the residue of food from his mouth and murmured, "Interesting. So why are you back…to check on things?"

"I saw Ashley yesterday," I responded. "Nothing has changed, nor will it change, at least not for the better."

They both wore sober faces at those words. "I saw your father-in-law recently," Jack said smiling. "Isaac Tucker. He seems to expect a positive outcome."

"Yes, he is being optimistic. But the medical experts have assured me, and Isaac, that Ashley will never recover. Her coma is permanent and irreversible."

"But Isaac…"

"I know, Jack, I know. He's wrong, and he loathes me because I know what I know, and that is that medical science says no."

Jack and Violet looked at me with the sad eyes of basset hounds. "If that's the case, why are you back?" Jack asked.

"Two reasons. Trying to sell our house…and yes, I know Isaac wants it, but not going to happen." More sad expressions. "But mostly I'm here to follow up on the investigation."

"Investigation?" Violet said hesitantly. "You mean?"

"Uh-huh. We may have found someone who knows how it happened."

The gentle couple stared at me as if I was an alien being. "By we, you mean the police?" Jack said.

"Yes. I'll know more by Tuesday."

"Tuesday?" Jack looked at his wife.

I knew the conversation was going nowhere, but I couldn't stop myself. "A detective on the force here has been following up on a recent lead. He's been in St. Louis tracking things down."

"St. Louis?" Jack and Violet said simultaneously.

"Long story." I looked down at my plate of congealing eggs, cold sausage and limp toast. "I'm feeling very optimistic about catching the bastards."

Jack had ceased eating. He looked at me. "Then what? Will they be arrested? I mean can anything be proven?"

"It's likely. Yes, very likely. But it doesn't matter. They will get theirs no matter what."

Jack lowered the fork he had been holding put and set it on his plate. "What do you mean?"

"They ruined our lives," I said. "They did that."

"Yes, but what…" he fumbled for the words.

"Jack." I dropped an open hand on the table; dishes jumped. Violet drew back. "Jack," I lowered my voice. "I will get me an aluminum bat if that's what it will take to make things right. That's what I mean."

They left their plates of unfinished food on the table and were gone within moments of offering me peace and comfort. I watched as their backsides moved toward the exit, stabbed a link sausage, and stuck it into my mouth. I sort of blessed their hearts for being good souls and toyed with the undeniable fact that I was leaving too many people in the wake of my anger, people I'd left shocked, dismayed, weirded out, and certainly disappointed. Over the years, I had from time to time thought on those in my life who had faded away, whether family, friends, or mere acquaintances, and engaged in what was a self-critical assessment—not often, but on occasion. I say not often because I found it to be a disappointing exercise, one that confirmed my basest flaw of too easily sliding into the sin of omission. That discovery, the one I suppressed even when I drew it out into the full light, was my ability to stow away my loss of contact with others, certainly of my blood, but also others with whom I'd experienced unpleasantness. It was so much easier to move on to other, less complicated relationships and jettison the ones that would require confession, forgiveness, and reconciliation. Those would be too damn hard.

The next day, I went to my old office, now just called Jackson & Vogel CPAs, sought out Jack Jackson, and apologized for my behavior. He accepted my regrets with a sober face. It was obvious that he was harboring doubts, perhaps regarding my sanity. I urged him to give my apologies to his wife, and he agreed to do so. We shook hands, and he went back to the papers on his desk. I had lost the man's warm regard for me and probably his trust.

On the way out, I encountered Sylvia Winters.

-28-

Sylvia and I stood face to face in the reception area. We didn't speak for a very long moment. I spoke first. "Sylvia." That was it. As usual, she was stylishly dressed: beige pants suit, open-toed wedge shoes, hair pulled back, gold chain necklace with a jade ornament. It made my teeth ache.

She cast a quick glance at the young receptionist. "Ned, just what the hell are you doing here—in Latham, I mean?" She whispered the pointed question.

"Personal business. You still a client here?"

"What personal business?" she demanded without answering my question. "And you were going to let me know when?"

I took her by the arm and escorted her to the outer hall. "I wasn't," I answered once clear of listening ears.

"You weren't?" She raised her voice.

"No, just a quick trip, no time for scheduling time with folks."

"Folks? You're calling me just *folks*?"

I paused until two men coming out of the elevator were out of range. "Look, Sylvia, this isn't going anywhere. You really need to accept that."

"This? What's this, Ned? Because if you're referring to our future, it is way more than a *This*."

"No," I said. "No, it is not. We had that mistaken moment, but—"

"Mistaken moment? You bastard. It is way past time for you to accept the inevitability of our future. It *is* going to happen. You know that."

There was a drinking fountain right there. I stuck my head down and sucked in icy water, swallowed, and wiped the wetness from my mouth. "If you're thinking that we have some sort of joint destiny, you're wrong."

Her face became so inflamed that I almost laughed, but I didn't. She stepped right up to me. I could feel her breath against my face. "You have led me on, you son-of-a-bitch. Right from the start, you've led me on. Now you think you can..."

I raised a forefinger; she batted it away. "Sylvia, I did no such thing, and you damn well know it. You must stop this...this deception. What you wanted to happen was in your head, not mine."

"Liar!" She slapped my face so hard my ears rang. "You liar."

I grabbed her arm as she hauled back to hit me again. "Stop this." I pushed her arm down and went to the stairwell entrance instead of waiting for an elevator. As I opened the door to the stairs, she yelled, "You find some young pussy out there in Port-Land? Is that it?"

I started down the stairs, and as the fire door slammed shut, I wondered if she actually knew about Terra; had Isaac said something to her? After striding to the Explorer in the parking lot, I drove off before she could follow me down. It wasn't long before she started calling my cell: over and over and over. Then the text messages: *I'm sorry dear one, we can fix this; Call me, I love you; Call me, damn you.* I finally shut the phone down. That evening, after another meal out, I stopped at the Whitewood Estates security booth and instructed the guard on duty to not let anyone in claiming to be visiting my address or using my name. I slept on the floor that night.

I awoke Tuesday morning with a stiff back, but at least it wasn't excruciating. No one rang the bell or banged on the door during the night, so either Sylvia had been turned back at the gate or hadn't tried to get in. After another cold shower and ice-water shave, I donned the same clothes for the third day, but with clean underwear, and was waiting at the police station when C. T. Morgan wandered in a little before ten o'clock looking the worse for wear. He stopped at the reception counter and spoke to the sergeant on duty. They laughed about something until the officer pointed in my direction; I could hear him say my name.

Morgan turned, looked at me for a moment; his head dropped momentarily before he walked over to me. "Ned."

"Detective. Good to see you. You look beat."

He rubbed a hand across his chin and grunted a low-level laugh. "How can ya tell? The flight was delayed out of Salt Lake. Didn't get home until the wee hours this morning. So yeah, feeling like pig slop."

I stood and looked into his red-rimmed eyes. "But you found out something."

He took in a deep breath, looked down at his shoes, and exhaled slow like. "Could be."

"Could be? That sounds weak."

"Look, give me some time to report in to the boss and get myself organized, okay? Then we'll talk. Give me twenty minutes."

I was watching a couple of patrolmen march in a handcuffed man who seemed under the influence when Morgan emerged and motioned me to follow him. We ended up in a small interview room with a table and a couple of chairs, where we sat across from one another, leaned on our forearms, and looked into each other's eyes. Morgan didn't have any papers, no notepad, nothing.

"Okay," he said finally and leaned back. "I saw the guy. Name's Benny Ball. Rolls off the tongue, doesn't it." He smiled. "Anyway, mid-thirties, not married, no family in the Latham area, basically a loner. A-Ball's file on him is skimpy."

"Does he know who did it?" I blurted.

He raised his right hand. "Hang with me a bit. I'll get to all there is to know."

"He must know. That's why he ran, right?"

"Ned, relax." When I settled back, he went on. "He was panicky, afraid he was going to lose his job. Had to assure him that neither A-Ball nor our department was going after him and wouldn't be contacting his employer. That got us down to the crux of the matter: what did he really know about the attack? It gets murky."

"Murky?"

"Yeah. You see, he isn't really sure who was behind the attack. He was just paid to look the other way. Let the attackers drive in."

"Horseshit. What did he think when that scum showed up, that it was some sort of sightseeing tour around the neighborhood?"

Morgan smiled. "Oh, he knew something illegitimate was up, but for him the money was too good to pass up."

"So who recruited him and paid him?"

Morgan shook his head. "Told me he never knew. It was all handled with anonymous phone calls. He got the money at a drop after the attack, said he picked it up on the way out of town. Just like in the movies."

"We've got nothing then?"

"For now, you're right. Nothing to act on—at the moment. Fattens the file. That means we can keep the case active."

I snorted. "Sure, looks like progress but isn't."

"Could look at it that way. I don't."

I was on my third pint of Idaho Pale Ale at the Lodgepole, drowning my pissed-off attitude, when my cell phone began to vibrate in my pants pocket. I determined it could only be someone I didn't want to talk to, so I ignored it. After about six or seven more attempts by whomever it was, I pulled out my phone, intending to give the caller a rude send-off. *Unknown caller*. Great, just great.

I hit accept call and said, "Look here, whoever this is, quit calling. Got it?"

Was it hesitation, or had they disconnected? "Uh, is this Mr. Pine? Ned Pine?"

A voice I didn't know. "Yeah, who's this?"

"You don't know me. My name is Benny Ball."

A chill hit my shoulder blades. I sat up straight and stared out across the pub packed with the after-work crowd. I was tongue-tied.

"You still there? Mr. Pine?"

"Yeah...I'm here," I faltered. "And I know who you are. How'd you get this number?"

He waited a beat before saying, "I had it from before. You know, from the A-Ball list. From that Whitewood list of people who lives there?"

"I met with Detective Morgan today. That ring a bell?"

"Oh," he said. I could barely hear him over the din.

"So, Benny, why the call?" His hesitation was so long I thought the call had been dropped. "Benny?"

"Yeah...uh, it's about that thing that happened."

"Thing?"

"Yeah, that there attack on you people. You know."

"I do. I was there and know what part you played in it. My wife is still in a coma. Do you know that?"

"Yeah, I heard about that. Too bad. Really."

My head was clearing some from the adrenaline rush I was feeling. "Forget that too bad shit. Why are you calling me?"

"'Cause...well 'cause I know some stuff."

"Stuff? What stuff?"

"About what happened. Maybe stuff you'd like want to know. You know, information like."

I held my breath; was this really happening? "Okay. Is this information you didn't tell Detective Morgan?"

He waited before admitting, "Yeah. I was gonna, you know, but then I didn't"

"Why?"

"Like I said, I figured maybe you'd like to know it." There was a pause before he added, "And maybe it'd be worth something to you."

"Worth something. Like how much."

"I dunno, thinking maybe a thousand dollars."

I forced myself to laugh at him. "A thousand dollars. Now what would you know that would be worth that kind of money?"

"Well, that's the thing. I can't tell ya'll unless I have the money. But it's worth it, believe me."

"Believe you? Why the hell would I trust the son-of-a-bitch who brought all of this down on my wife and me? Why?"

"'Cause I figured you want to get at them peoples, the ones that done it."

I stuck a finger in my ear opposite the phone to muffle the din. "Okay, I'm listening. You have to give me something. Something. A hint that you have information worth that kind of money."

He sounded flustered. "Gee, I dunno. Maybe you're trying to trick me."

"I could be, but I'm not." When he didn't know what to say next, I said, "Tell me this: do you really know who was behind the attack?"

"You mean for real?"

"That's right, for certain. Do you?"

"Well, uh, not sure, but I think maybe. I mean I have some names."

I felt another chill with that admission. "Names? Of real people?"

He hesitated again. "Yeah, I think they're real people. I mean, I never met 'em or nothin'."

"How many names?"

"Two, two names." He perked up. "I ain't sure what they done, what part of it all that they did. But I was told by this guy who knows that they's the ones who done it."

A waiter came up and pointed at my empty glass. I shook my head, and he went away. I inhaled and asked Benny Ball how to get this done, get his information. He was all set, told me to wire him the money using Western Union. Western Union? I hadn't used them in years. But Benny knew the drill. I was to go to the

Walgreens on Main Street; they were a Western Union agency. But I would have to wait until the next day because I would need a cashier's check to make the transfer. Western Union wouldn't take a personal check, and I didn't have that kind of ready cash either. As soon as he had the money, he'd call me and give the two names and whatever else he knew regarding them. I had to go along with him, but I warned Benny that I knew where he was, and if what he was offering didn't prove out, I'd turn him over to the police and call his employer. He got the message and promised it was all good, what he had to tell me.

I was so agitated that I had to get out of the pub and do something. I drove around the center of town circling and circling, processing what had just happened, before I broke away and headed out of town for about five miles and ended up at Latham Woods Park. It was a popular gathering place with a wading pond, covered picnic tables, lots of wildlife and wildflowers, and a loop trail. It was quiet, not many people out. I walked the trail from the parking lot; after about an hour I ended back where I'd started, somewhat mellowed and accepting of the fact that I had to wait until the next day to learn what Benny Ball really knew. It was going on dusk when I finished my walk. I sat on a bench overlooking the pond and watched the sun set with a vibrant blend of pink and orange. The heat of the day had turned to warm with a nice breeze; it was a lovely evening, I guess, but my mind and mood were elsewhere, caught up in the bizarre circumstance of maybe finding out who did what and why.

-29-

When I returned to the house, *he* was there: Isaac. His white pickup was at the curb out front, and he was in it, waiting. Of course, he still had access privileges to Whitewood. I parked in the driveway, turned off the engine, and wondered how much crazier the day could possibly be. After a nowhere meeting with Detective Morgan and the freaky phone call from the runaway security guard, would I now be assaulted by my father-in-law in my own front yard, making the day preposterously perfect? Not sure how much time elapsed with me sitting behind the wheel, my hands at ten and two, before I heard a knuckle rap on the side window. His face was framed in the glass; he held up a hand and signaled for me to get out. I gave myself a visceral grunt and opened the door.

With the door halfway open, I sat sideways on the seat, feet dangling out, my hand on the armrest, and looked into the man's implacable face. "What now, Isaac?" I asked on a sigh.

"We need to talk," he answered and actually stepped back.

"About what?" I stepped out and closed the car door. "You wanting a rematch? By the way, how did you know I was in town?"

"Sylvia."

"Of course, you two are thick as thieves. Guess she told you we had a nice chat yesterday."

"She mentioned it." He stood calmly, clad in a tee shirt with his company's logo on it, hiking shorts, and sandals.

I pushed past him and in the passing said, "So we need to talk?"

He gave more ground. "I'd *like* us to talk. That better?"

"Some." I looked up into his face, saw nothing decipherable. "Let's go around back." He followed me to the rear of the house where the patio still had its furniture, a staging touch Gloria Denham had wanted. I dropped onto one of the chaise lounges and stretched my legs out. "Have a seat."

"I'd rather stand," he responded.

I could make out his features pretty well since the outdoor lighting was lit; still on the timer, I surmised. "Okay. What sort of tirade are you wanting to lay on me this time?"

He looked down and nodded. "I deserve that."

I chuckled. "Now that's a first. Act as nice as you want, Isaac. Still not selling you this place."

"I know." He folded his arms across his chest. After a moment, he pulled one of the patio table chairs over and sat down facing me. He leaned over and clasped his hands between his knees. Something was eating at him.

"What is it?" I ventured. "What do you want?"

He sat that way, hands intertwined, head down. "Nothing. That's not it."

His demeanor intrigued me. "Then what is it?"

I'd never seen the man at a loss for what to say next, or seeming not in control of himself. He rose and walked to the edge of the patio and looked at the house to the immediate south; it was alight with people in it I didn't even know. If Isaac had asked whom the neighbors were, I couldn't have told him. I knew more people personally during my short time in St. Johns than I knew in my own neighborhood.

He came back after a minute or so and looked down at me as I lay sprawled on the lounge chair. "I...I drove over here fully aware of what I intended to say and...I can't."

I scooted forward and sat up. "Is it something...has something happened to Ashley?"

"No, no, not that. But it is...in a way it is." He grunted and scoured his face with both hands.

And there it was, the opening for something I'd always wanted to know. "May I ask *you* something?" His expression was one of *Yes please, ask me something, anything.* But I needed him to agree. "Okay?"

He nodded, relieved it seemed. "What is it?"

"Who are you really, Isaac? That's my question."

If I'd hit him with a two-by-four he could not have looked more baffled. "Who am I?"

"Yes." I felt a sense of release. After all those years of knowing him only as the man who despised me for marrying his only daughter, I could finally ask him to divulge himself. "I've never known you. I don't know you. Except for confrontation."

He stepped back and sagged onto the chair. "And there you have it," he said.

"What's that mean?"

"That's my façade." He laughed lightly. "A stubborn know-it-all façade. In all my years of constructing shopping malls and the like, there have been many façades. Some of my best work, I might add."

"What am I to make of that?" I asked. "It's all okay because it wasn't really you? Do you know that on every occasion when I was in your presence it was always hell? I had to strap on my emotional body armor every bloody time I saw you. It was wretched."

He stared at me, put a weathered hand over his mouth, and closed his eyes. I had never witnessed actual emotion from the man, except warmth for his daughter and anger toward me, of course. His actions right then were alien to me. When he wandered over onto the backyard grass and dropped down onto his knees, I was hard-pressed to believe what I was seeing. I witnessed his back heaving and heard his gasps of remorse, or what I assumed to be remorse.

What could I do? What did I want to do: go to him or let him stew in his own juices? I waited; I was watching a stranger. When he finally seemed to gain control, I stood up, waiting for him to turn on me, return to his old ways, and excoriate me. Instead he leaned back on his haunches and remained that way for several minutes, unmoving. When he rose and came toward me, I squared my shoulders and took a step back, ready to take him on.

"I don't know if I can tell you who I am *really*, as you put it." The calmness on his face was surprising. "But I did come here with something to tell you. May we sit at this table here?"

I nodded and joined him at the round, glass-topped patio table. We sat across from each other. The temperature had dropped as the evening bore in; I felt a chill, but I was not going to interrupt what was happening just because of that. Just then the timer cut the patio lights off causing Isaac to hesitate.

"Ned," he said, finally. That was a shock also because through all the years he had never said my name. When addressing me, he always used *you*; with Ashley it was *your husband*, and with others I was *my daughter's husband*. He must have seen my eyes widen because he smiled and said, "Yes, I know your name."

"Nice to know," I said.

"I can imagine. Sorry."

"That's okay. I always knew who I was."

He nodded. "I'm not here to argue about buying this house or to disagree about Ashley's prognosis. But, yes, this is about her... about Ashley. And you." He paused before going on. "I'm not sure if you and the doctors are right that Ashley will never recover, but that may be the case. I've been troubled since the break-in, when you were both attacked. No, not troubled, that isn't it." He inhaled. "Look, Ned, I've been considering what I'm here to say for a while now, and I promised myself that I would be candid and aboveboard."

"What is it, Isaac?"

"Please hear me out."

"I'm just at sea here. If you're trying to set me up with this new language just so you can nail me with something, just spit it out."

He chuckled in the dark, his silhouette visible from the light

251

cast by light from nearby streetlamps. "Trust is the hardest of human traits to earn, as I've learned in business, and I've never given you reason to trust me, have I?"

"You could say that."

"Uh-huh. Okay, so I can't ask you to trust me out of the blue then. But will you at least hear me out?"

"I'll do that, yes."

"Good. All right then." He hesitated. "Since you and Ashley were married, I have intentionally undermined you."

"Isaac, this isn't new information. I've known from the beginning that you disliked me. Hell, you loathed me. I knew that. I endured that for your daughter and our kids, your grandchildren."

"And I grudgingly admired you for your strength of character, if you will."

"And now, when Ashley is gone and my kids and my kin have doubts about me, now you say this? Well gee, I feel so warm and fuzzy inside to know this at this late date. Thank you so damn much."

"You're not going to make this easy for me, are you?"

"Get on with it."

He fell silent; I held myself in check. Finally he went on. "It was one of those moments in a parent's life when you don't agree with a child's decision. It was about her getting married. I had plans, you see. I even knew who she was certain to marry."

"Really?" It wasn't simply that he hadn't liked me—I hadn't even been relevant.

"Oh yes, I knew exactly who she would marry. I'd groomed him and thought I was building him up in her mind." He paused. "I was sure of myself. And I did all of that so she would have a good life, a successful life."

"The life you wanted her to have—for you."

"Of course. But then she brought home the runt of the litter, you. All my best-laid plans were washed away."

"Who was he?"

He chuckled. "No need going there. No need, except to say that in the end he proved to be less than you, much less. I tried to rationalize that if he'd married Ashley, he would have proven out. That she would have been the difference. It was Isobel, Ashley's mother, who set me straight. She took me to the woodshed once she sniffed out my, what she rightly called my manipulation. Ripped me good, she did. Of course that was before you came into the picture. Once she passed on, my Isobel, once she was gone, I went back to my *manipulation*."

I hummed a sigh. "It must have been a crusher when Ashley showed with up a bean counter who stood many inches shorter than you and wasn't the man you were."

I could make out that he was massaging his hands. "That's right," he said, his voice barely audible. "I was pissed from the beginning about you coming in and wrecking my big plans. You bollixed things up good."

"I'm no one exceptional, but I was the one Ashley chose. And you fucked up any chance we had for a good marriage. Remember telling me that I would never earn your respect, never?"

"You want to hit me?" he said. "Lay a big one on me, like to do that? I've got it coming."

An urge came. I reached out and grabbed his right forearm and squeezed; his arm was muscular and leathery. "Oh yeah, I do. Or I did. What's the use now?"

He pulled his hand loose. "I lied to you," he said, not reacting to my aggression. "And others."

"What do you mean?"

"That's why I'm here. What I came to admit…to confess." The smudge of darkness shrouded us from each other; I didn't speak, just let him come to me. And he did. "I…I didn't want her to love you. I didn't want you to love her. So I invented, in my own head, I invented the division you lived with all those years." I heard a fist drop onto the table. "I did manipulate, just like Isobel accused me of. What do you remember of your marriage?"

"What do you mean?"

"Was it all you had hoped for?"

I didn't know how to answer that. "It was what it was, not perfect but not imperfect either. No, I guess it wasn't all I'd thought of as marriage. We...we were a lot like ships sailing side by side. I guess you could call it an orchestrated life. So no, our marriage was not all I'd hoped for. How could it have been?"

"My god, man," his silhouette said. "How did you do it? Live like that year after year?"

"I don't know, come to think of it. Guess I became numb to it." I stopped for several breaths. "I was weak—that's all there is to it. No courage, or I would have stood up for myself and walked away. I knew she didn't love me, not really. She may have cared for me in some sense, tolerated me, but because of the kids. It was a strategy, not love. Did I love her? I don't know. That what you want to hear, Isaac?"

"No."

"What, then? Why are you here? Why now?"

I could see his jaw bulge from biting down. "You had me...at the bridge."

"What?"

"That big man, he took me down. In Portland." He took in a deep breath. "But you told him to let me go."

"So? What of it?"

He folded his arms and looked at me. "It meant something. It did. It brought me up sharply. Made me think." He waited a beat. "You see, my Isobel...she was my north star. My conscience."

"You miss her."

"Yes. I do. And there under the bridge it was as if she came to me. Like she used to."

Oddly strange talk from Isaac. "Really? And...is there a message?"

"Damn it, to...to tell you that Ashley did love you."

I laughed. It was a crazy man laugh. "Now that's a hoot. I lived with her, you know. I was in the room—it was like living with an automaton that was programmed to function as my wife. Did a pretty good job of it, too, except for the compassion part."

"My god, you can't talk like that," Isaac said, his voice straining. "It's not true, it's not true! She did."

"What are you doing? This is insane. It's over, my life with her. Besides, you can't come in at the last moment when she's gone and proclaim that all the declarations you've made far and wide, the ones vowing that she only endured life with me, are now not true."

"Ned, please," he said on a whisper. "That was me, all on me. I need you to know that Ashley loved you, totally loved you. Many times she asked me to help her tell you. As smart and tough as she was, she was paralyzed when it came to letting you know how she felt. She couldn't do it...and that made me glad. Oh, how I enjoyed watching you live that mundane life all the while knowing what you didn't, that my daughter had no way to confirm her feelings for you. And there you were, twisting in the wind."

As what he was saying sank in, the lost capacity to feel actual rage invaded me; it filled my chest with heat. When he finished his last word, I stood, grabbed the edge of the table, and heaved it up and into him. I yelled something indecipherable and shoved as hard as I could. Isaac fended off the nearly airborne hunk of furniture and pushed back. The table crashed down, shattering the glass top into minute bits and pieces that sparkled in the subdued light.

We stood, each of us, looking down at the debris. Nothing was said.

———

We circled about, our feet crunching through the carpet of broken glass, and walked back around the house to where his pickup sat at the curb; we'd said nothing until then. The vapor streetlight at the nearest corner provided enough illumination for us to be seen each by the other. It was claustrophobically quiet. All adjacent houses were dark; not even a dog barked. Isaac put a hand on the post of the For Sale sign and smiled at me. What should we do now, I wondered. Perhaps he did, too, because he extended a big hand. I took it, and we held onto each other for longer than one usually would.

"Well," he said and left the word hanging.

"Yeah, well," I said back; we both smiled. "Maybe we can move past this."

"Who knows? You're still angry though…aren't you?"

I shrugged. "Sure. But you and I have Ashley to think of—together."

He stared down the street for a long moment. "Tell me," he said then, "that woman I saw you with, in Portland, who was she?"

"Her name is Terra. Met her at the coffee house I go to."

"You attracted to her?"

I stalled. "I think so. Haven't known her long, but we get along well."

"That's only fair, I'd say. You deserve better." He faced me. "In my heart I ache for Ashley to come back to us, but in my gut I know now that she won't. All we can do is wait."

I didn't tell him about Benny Ball; I would later, once I tried to run the table on who had ruined our lives.

-30-

I watched until Isaac's pickup had disappeared into the dark, and I entered the empty house. Cleaning up the broken glass on the patio could wait until the next day. I took a leak in the bathroom and prepared to sleep on the floor again. I'd rummaged around in the Explorer earlier and found my old Coleman sleeping bag. Once nestled into it, I had the urge to call Terra. It was an hour earlier in Portland, so why not? Still, it was after eleven. I took the chance anyway. She answered after only two rings.

"This really you?" she said. Damn, I enjoyed the sound of her voice.

"It's me. You're up late. Waiting for my call?"

"Aren't you the arrogant one."

"Just hoping. Lovely to hear your voice."

"Thank you. Same back at you. How are things in Idaho? How's Ashley...your wife?"

"The same. We're just bound to wait things out."

"We?"

Without rolling out all of what was said between Isaac and me, I told her that we had managed to claim some common ground. She found that amazing after having seen the man pound on me beneath the St. Johns Bridge. We traded accounts of day-to-day before lowering our voices and exploring the part that started with *we*. We would most assuredly see each other once I returned to Portland; it was an agreement of some appetite. I enjoyed the feel of it. She did not ask more about my irretrievable wife, nor of my feelings for her. I suspected that we would have to go there at some point, the two of us exploring our other aforementioned lives, but not then.

Even knowing that Ashley had cared for me more than was ever evidenced, those years had passed, and it was likely that if she'd lived we would have never breached that divide anyway. I was unable to suddenly reverse course and paste over a marriage that had been so totally lacking in the elements of a devoted partnership; there was no coming up on the other side now claiming all was good. From what Isaac had revealed, self-recrimination had visited me for my share of a wrecked marriage, but it wouldn't stick. Not now.

Terra yawned; I could hear it. "I've got the early shift tomorrow. Better get some sack time."

"Wish I was there to share that sack."

"Now, now, don't be naughty—unless you can back it up."

Before she hung up, I told her of my meeting with the detective and about Benny Ball. She didn't like the sound of that; she admonished me not to play detective. I mumbled something short of acquiescence. When she asked what it would mean if I found out who was behind the assault, I had no answer, not really. All I could muster was *I guess we'll see.* That exchange hung in the electronic space between us and faded slowly until we whispered our goodnights.

The next morning I cleaned up the mess from the patio table, set things upright, and called Gloria Denham to see if she could get someone to replace the glass top. She would try but said it would be cheaper to just buy another table.

I had received several more texts from Sylvia Winters overnight, trying to make nice. I deleted them. At least, she wouldn't be able to gain access through the guard station now.

I drove out of Whitewood Estates a little before ten o'clock that next morning, waved to the passive guard and drove straight to my bank. Had I been a first time bank robber, I couldn't have felt any more like a criminal than when I drew out the one thousand dollars and stood by as the teller cut me cashier's check. I strode by the security guard, guilt plastered on my face, and headed for Walgreens. It was a Western Union agency, just like Benny Ball said. They processed the money transfer, and I rushed to the parking lot and waited in the Explorer for the call. It came twenty-three minutes later. True to his word, Benny spilled everything he knew. I scribbled it all down on a scrap of paper. I was so nervous I could hardly make the ballpoint pen work. After the call, I looked at what I'd written, read it over, and again, my respiration exacerbated by what was there; the shock hit me physically as if I'd been punched in the solar plexus.

I don't know how long I sat there in the Walgreens lot. A long while. In spite of my dismay, I digested Benny Ball's rambling account and strung it all together until it began to make sense; like pieces of a puzzle, things came into focus. Merely sitting there, in the vehicle, my body reacted physically. It was as if I had run a race: I perspired, my chest tightened, I felt the need to inhale often.

What next? Detective Morgan. Should I tell him what I'd learned? What would he do? I drove to the Lodgepole and ordered a Rueben sandwich, then couldn't eat it. So I ordered an ale and waited. C. T. Morgan wandered in and found me hunched over an uneaten the Rueben and my beer glass still nearly full. He slid into a chair and we stared at one another.

"So?" he said. I'd left a vague message on his phone. "You got a call from Benny Ball?"

I sipped warm ale and said simply, "I did."

He propped himself up on the arms of his chair and looked at me with a suspicious air. "Now why'd he do that?"

"Why you think?" I said and squirmed in my chair.

"I'm not into twenty questions, Ned. Spit it out you. You called me."

I forced myself to take a other swallow and set the glass on the coaster, and said, "This is something else, and I'm nervous as hell."

Morgan leaned forward and patted the tabletop. "Okay." He was getting that maybe I was onto something. "Let's just take it slow then."

"That'd be good." A waiter came up; Morgan waved him off. "He called me after you and I met in your office."

"What'd he want?"

"Said he had information for me. Things he'd held back from you, I guess."

"The bastard. He say why? Wait, let me guess. He wanted money."

I nodded. "That's right. Kept the good stuff to sell."

"How much?"

"Thousand."

Morgan shook his head and grunted. "You do it? Sure you did—that's why I'm here."

"Wired the money this morning. Benny called as soon as he had it in hand and told me what he didn't tell you, I guess."

Morgan slouched back in his chair and shook his head slowly side to side. "Call for a drum roll here? Good stuff?"

"Maybe, I think…well, it's sobering."

"So you know who the culprits are? Crew and all?"

"Benny, he had two names. He gave me two names."

He leaned in. "You gonna spill it, or do I have to draw it out of you inch by inch?"

"I don't know," I said. "No, really, I don't know if I should or not."

"What the hell does that mean?"

"Tell me," I began, "what does it take to convict someone of a crime?"

He studied me for a long moment "Why don't you just tell me what you found out and let me take it from there?"

"What's it take?" I pressed.

"Okay, you want to play it this way? Takes evidence,

preponderance of evidence to begin with. Lowest bar for burden of proof."

"What about conspiracy to commit a crime?"

"You playing lawyer? Conspiracy. That's harder. There has to be an agreement to commit, and proof of agreement is harder."

"So you're saying that unless the animals who attacked us can be found and tied up with who planned it all, no conviction?"

"What's going on, Ned? Yes, it can take time and effort to tie everything into a package that will survive the courts."

I nodded. "Figured."

"Come on, what've you got? The two names, you recognize 'em?"

I held my breath for a moment. "One I do. One I don't."

"Benny, he know who they are?"

"Said he didn't, except he knew one was local and the other was from out of town. Two of the guys who attacked us were from out of town, I guess. Only have the one out-of-town name though. "

"Two names, three perps then. Let's go get 'em."

I played with my ring finger, the depression in the skin where I'd worn a wedding ring all those years. The dimple was less but still there. "I need some time to think all this through."

"What's to think through? The sooner we have what you know the quicker we get back on the case and kick some butt."

"You're probably right. Tomorrow or the next day, I'll give all to you then. Okay?"

"I have a choice? Jesus, Ned, you can't do this to me, withholding information. I want to solve this thing as much as you."

Our eyes met, and he knew. "No," I said. "There's no way you want this more than I do."

"You're right. Sorry. But I want it bad."

"Soon. I'll give it to you soon. It'll keep."

He followed me out to the parking lot. We stood with our hands in our pockets, both of us considering, just considering. "Look, Ned," he said finally, "don't go doing any of your own police work now and end up in jail yourself. I'm telling you, it'll be crazy if you do."

"Time, that's all I want. Some time. I'll be in touch soon, very soon."

———————

I didn't need time; I knew what I would do once I heard the agonizing legal process outlined by Detective Morgan. Not that I had an exact plan in mind, I just knew I couldn't wait to set things right. That afternoon, I visited Ashley again, saw nothing encouraging in her condition but spoke to her quietly about what I had learned from Benny Ball. Before I left, I did notice that the light was indeed better in that room. I'd have to concur with Isaac sometime.

Around six o'clock I made the call.

-31-

Sunset came in a tad before seven-thirty that day. Dusk would hold off total darkness for another hour or so. It was quite lovely at Latham Woods Park, with the remaining light playing gently on the surface of the wading pond. I parked in the farthest lot near where the walking trail struck off, and there were no other cars. I was anxious, questioning what I was about to do, checking my watch every minute or so and waiting.

Then, as dusk was giving way and darkness was descending, I saw the silver BMW roll into the parking lot, pause, then come in my direction; its headlights caught me looking. The car pulled up silently next to the Explorer. I stepped out and walked around to the driver's side window, which was smoothly descending as I came up. We looked at one another and exchanged smiles; mine was not honest.

"Hello, Ned. What a nice surprise and a lovely place to meet."

"I thought we would appreciate the privacy." My forced calmness covered the tingling I felt in my hands and the sudden tightness that invaded my chest. I placed a hand on the roof of the car.

The driver's door opened. "I like that, privacy. Very thoughtful." I moved aside when she slid out and stood. "So you've finally sorted things out? Resolved matters so we can claim what is rightfully ours?"

My tongue had gotten thick. I ran it over my lips. "Yes, I have sorted things out. You're right about that."

"Good." She stepped closer; her perfume floated in, the same tangy aroma. When she put a hand on my chest, I felt an inward flinch. "I'm glad that you've been able to make peace with yourself."

I retreated just a bit and said, "There's been a development in the case."

She looked quizzical for an instant, then her expression froze. "The case? Do you mean about what happened to you?"

"The attack, Sylvia, That's the word—attack. And yes, that's what I mean."

She just looked at me. Her hair was down; she was dressed casually but nicely. I could sense that she'd come expecting something, something more akin to an accomplishment than what I had in mind. "Development." She repeated my word. "Like what, something about your wife? Is she recovering?"

I bit down. "Of course not."

Her face softened. "I thought not, but you never know."

"Oh, but you know that well, so very well. You've known that she's irretrievable and permanently so—for some time you've known that."

"Ned," she said on a voice of disquiet, "what development then? Do you mean us?"

"Us." I almost choked getting the word out. "There's never been an us."

"Why of course there has, you silly. From the first time we met, you knew. It's only been a matter of time until…until we were certain."

I shuddered. God damn her. "Certain? You mean certain that Ashley would never recover, that she would die one day without ever consciously being my wife again. Isn't that what you mean?"

She seemed in shock. Her face was slack. It was getting darker and harder to see each other clearly. "My god," she said. I could just make out the hand she raised to her mouth. "What are you doing? Do you want me to say it? Is that it? Force me to what, confess our intentions?"

Right then a parking lot lamppost lit up in the descending darkness, and I saw her face in full as a mask of dismay. "Our intentions?" I raised my voice. "No, your intentions."

"Ned, don't do this." She came to me and tried to embrace me.

I pushed her back and gripped her shoulders. "The *development*," I said, "is that we have new information about the perpetration of the crime." She had nothing to say. "The police finally located the Whitewood Estates guard who was on duty that night. That's right. And the police have interviewed him in St. Louis where he'd gone."

"That can't be." She stepped back from me and sagged onto the fender of her car.

"Not only that, Sylvia." I moved in on her. "Not only that, you bitch, I've spoken with him myself. His name is Benny Ball, if you want to know. Benny told me what he hadn't told the Latham police because he wanted money, so I paid him. I paid him to reveal what he knew.

"So when I called you, what did you think? That I would at long last conjoin with you and we'd ride off into the sunset to celebrate a new life? That's what you believed, right?" I smiled. "The look on your face is priceless, and I am enjoying it. Because you know what Benny Ball told me, don't you? He gave me names. Names he'd been told were those behind Ashley and me being beaten. And you know those names—yours being one of them. Odd, I was less harmed than my wife. At the time I thought that was just chance or destiny."

All the life had gone out of her face. Her eyes were wide and staring. "But it was all a plan, wasn't it? Ashley was supposed to die, wasn't she? Injure me, kill her, and when I recovered you would claim me as the spoils of war or something. You'd groomed me, or so you thought. Like ripe fruit, I'd fall into your arms. I have no idea why you chose me, nor do I want to know. It just freaks me out." She looked away, immovable and in shock.

"Look at me. Sylvia, look at me." She finally turned her face so we could see each other.

"You are evil. You took everything we were and all we ever

would be—you destroyed our lives for some warped, hideous personal intention. I despise you for that. Do you hear me? I abhor you."

She stood up, erect and stone faced, from where she'd leaned on the car fender. "I hear you. So now what? You can't prove anything."

"That's all you can say? I can't prove anything?"

"What else is there? Now it's survival, my survival, don't you see?"

"You are despicable." I raised a forefinger and aimed it at her face. "I will tell all Benny Ball told me to Detective Morgan, and he will begin the process of ferreting out the truth."

A smile overtook her face. It was the smile of one possessed.

"Smile if you want, but soon your name and face will be on the front pages of newspapers across the state. The lead story on local television will shred your reputation. It will go like this, *Sylvia Winters, well-known local business woman, was indicted—*"

"No!" Her voice rose in a throaty snarl, and she was on me, clawing and kicking. I was staggered; she caught me by surprise. She managed to shove me with enough force that I stumbled back and fell to the ground. She kicked at me and stomped a high-heeled shoe, catching me in the throat. I heaved a gasp, clutched my neck, and struggled to get back up.

When I leaned against the Explorer to gain my equilibrium, she spun around, yanked the car door open, and climbed in. Almost instantly, the BMW's engine erupted with a surge. I could only watch while she backed away, tires spinning, and sped off in a hail of grit. Her taillights grew bright when she braked at the road leading to an exit. Still dizzy, I blinked, and a burst of adrenaline fueled my rage. I pounded both fists on the hood of the Explorer. It couldn't end there; I had to bring her down.

I was staring after her, my anger building, when a pickup rolled up; a heavyset man in a baseball cap leaned out of the vehicle's window. He told me that the park closed at dusk and

I needed to leave the premises. The wording on the door of the truck said City of Latham Park & Recreation Dept. When the fellow repeated his ruling, I nodded, withdrew, and got into the Explorer. He waited until I drove off and followed me out. Once I'd passed the entry gate, the pickup stopped, and I could see the man get out and swing the long metal gate arm to its closed position. At the main road, I stopped, looked right then left. Which way had she gone? Left was back into town; to the right was a commercial business park a couple of miles out. Beyond that, nothing but woods out Arrow Rock Road; beyond that, farmland.

I debated with myself. Whatever direction I chose, it would be a wild-ass guess. I was in a frenzy by then—I had to find her. With my chest heaving and hyperventilating, I yanked the wheel to the right and headed west, guessing that she'd gone to the Teton Acres Business Park where Winters Fine Foods had its offices and processing plant. I pushed the Explorer until I was going over eighty miles an hour, listing around bends in the road; then I saw the big monument sign for Teton Acres. I took the entry road at full speed, experienced some loss of traction, but kept the vehicle on the pavement. A security gate was partway open; she must have opened with a key card or something but raced off before she got it fully closed. I veered around the gate arm and drove in. I knew exactly where to go.

When I slowed to weave my way around and through the rows of buildings, the Explorer took a thunderous hit from behind. It was Sylvia. She had rammed me with the BMW; I could hear the roar of the car's engine as she kept shoving my vehicle until it was driven into a loading bay. As my SUV smashed through a roll-up warehouse door, I vaguely remember a boldly lettered No Admittance sign just before bursting into a warehouse full of insulation. The Explorer came to rest against a stack of pink fiberglass; several rolls came down onto the hood and reminded me of the cotton candy I loved as a kid.

It was suddenly quiet, except for my engine running. Sylvia had gone; she'd put me out of action and taken off. Before I could communicate with my saner side, I had the Explorer in reverse, roared back out of the warehouse, and left rolls of insulation cascading off and careening about as if in total surprise. I made the choice well before I hit the main road and hung right onto Arrow Rock Road. The Explorer took to the accelerator with aplomb, and we began eating up the road. A mile later we hit the curves for which the road was known, the A-Rock Bends as the five-mile stretch had been labeled for decades. My eyes were nearly bug-eyed as I searched for any sign of the taillights from her car. I had to slow due to the curves but maintained all the speed the road would take.

I saw the flashing taillights before the vehicle they were attached to, a flatbed farm truck. My headlights lit up a tall man in overalls waving a flashlight. I slid to a stop and jumped out.

"What is it?" I yelled.

"Car." He yelled back. "Went over into the ravine. Went by me like I was stopped. Bat outa hell, I tell ya."

We both ran to where the guardrail had been breached and looked down. It was Sylvia's car. Its headlights were still lit up, so we could just make out that it was on its side.

"These dang Bends, you just can't drive that fast on 'em," the man said, shaking his head.

I knew exactly where we were. The same spot where my former client and friend Ralph Stokes had gone over and died. It was 100 feet down there. There was no way from up there to tell if she survived, alive but injured. I assumed she was gone.

"You call 911?" I asked the farmer.

"No, don't have one of them cellular things."

"Okay, never mind." I dialed 911, and then we waited.

By the time the fire department and the sheriff's office responded, a small crowd had gathered, further obstructing the road. One of the deputies began sending people on their way and managing the new traffic coming by. I parked the Explorer off the road and waited. The fire department rescue crew rappelled down into the ravine, confirmed that a deceased female was in the car, and hauled her up the cliff in a litter basket. Her dark hair was wild and matted; her bludgeoned face was beyond recognition. I stood back as they zipped her into a body bag and put her into the ambulance that had arrived on the scene. It was eerie.

The sheriff's deputy in charge finally got around to interviewing the farmer and me. He confirmed that the farmer, Clyde Schmidt, had witnessed the accident and that I was the one who called 911; then he took down our names and numbers and thanked us. Over and done.

"How'd it happen, Ned?" C. T. Morgan stood at my elbow when he spoke.

I jumped. "Damn," I responded. "Where'd you come from?"

"Station picked up the accident on the scanner. When your name came up, the desk sergeant called me. I had to wonder what the hell you were doing out on this piece of road in the middle of the night."

"Out for a drive."

"Obviously. But why?"

"Do you mind? This has been unnerving."

"Who is…was she?"

"They said her name was Winters, Sylvia Winters."

"Really? Of Winters Foods?"

"Maybe, I don't know," I lied.

"Sure you do."

"What?"

"Small town, Ned. Used to be one of your clients, right?"

"Okay, so yeah."

"Why the deception?"

I turned to look at him. His face was severe in the still-flashing emergency lights. We studied one another while I considered. "I had that talk with Benny Ball."

"Is that right? Get your thousand worth?"

I nodded.

He looked after the ambulance as it pulled away. "That why you're out here?"

Just then, Clyde Schmidt, the farmer, came up to shake hands and commiserate a bit about our mutual misadventure. He said a couple of man alives before he got into his truck and drove off.

"So he was first on the scene?" Morgan asked.

"That's right. He saw the car go over."

"But you were close behind. Why's that? And don't tell me you were out for a warm summer's evening drive." He waved to one of the deputies he seemed to know. "So Benny Ball, he tie Sylvia Winters into the case?" When I looked at him, he smiled and added, "That what you got for your thousand?"

I stood quietly. One of the firefighters was telling the deputy in charge that a local towing company would be out in the morning to pull the car out of the ravine. I thought about answering Morgan's leading question but didn't.

"She was behind it all?"

Before I could answer, the lead deputy came up to speak to Morgan. "Some deal," he said. "You know that woman wasn't wearing her seat belt? Head through the windshield. Too big of a hurry to put on your belt, who can be in that big a rush?"

"Go figure," Morgan said while glancing my way.

When the deputy went on his way, I said, "She was."

"And you knew her well," Morgan said, "I mean more than as a client."

"Fatal attraction," I said.

He gave me a curious look; then it came to him. "Holy shit, you mean...you mean like in that movie?"

"The same."

The last of the emergency vehicles pulled out, and we were left standing alongside the road in the dark. Morgan dragged a shoe through the roadside gravel. He chuckled. "Man. And now there's no there, there. The case that never got underway can't ever be closed."

"Seems like."

"Tell me, you were on her tail, right? Before she went over."

"It was a nice night for a drive."

-32-

I went to the historic Rifle Bar downtown, a watering hole since 1910; it stayed open until 1:00 a.m. I just had time to decompress over a boilermaker, usually not my favorite drink. But that night a gulp of whiskey followed by a brew was what I needed. I sat at the bar and relived the events of the past five or so hours; it didn't help. It was over, but it wasn't, not yet.

The drive home was slow and deliberate. I took a long piss, drank a full glass of water, stripped down to my shorts, and crawled into the Coleman sleeping bag. Strangely, there were no dreams, no hallucinations, no night sweats—I slept like my brain had been erased. I awoke when a sliver of sun found its way in through a living room skylight and flickered across my eyelids. Not sure how long I lay there, my head pulsating, before I decided what I wanted to do and scooted out of the bag.

The big breakfast at Rudy's Diner was what I needed; I was ravenous. I grabbed a paper out of the rack on the way in, but there was nothing about the wreck out Arrow Rock yet; the paper had already gone to bed by the time Sylvia Winters had taken flight. After the three-egg omelet, I called Isaac Tucker. We agreed to meet—in twenty minutes. Then I called Terra. An anonymous electronic voice recited her *I'm unavailable* blurb. I left a short message telling her I was all right but something had happened; I would call her later.

Isaac was already in Ashley's room when I arrived. It was an awkward reunion between us. And an awkward place to be, but it had to be there. We shook hands and stood beside her bed; I assumed each in our own minds remembered the person only vaguely represented by the shrouded figure on the bed.

Isaac turned to me. "This," he said, his head nodding downward, "this is beyond heartache. I am numb. She's not there, is she? You've known that from the beginning. I fought it."

"I guess we each took it in as best we could."

"That's bullshit. Hell, I knew the day after the attack that she wouldn't make it. Knew it. But it's like I told you, I wanted her to make a comeback so I could set things straight between you. Needed her to recover so I could confess."

"Never mind, Isaac, history now. We'll kill ourselves trying to make it right. Time to move on. Take care of her, but move on." I gripped his arm closest to me.

He pulled loose. "So why are we here if not to rub my nose in it?"

"Sit down. I need to tell you something."

"Like what?" His usual aggressiveness was in evidence, but he did take a seat.

I told him. He listened like a person in a trance, his expression one of stupefaction. When I'd recounted the whole story, from beginning to end, he continued to stare at me. Then he looked at his daughter, or what merely represented her. We sat there in the vacuum, sharing the nothingness of a life that had been.

"I knew something wasn't right with her, Sylvia." He grimaced. "But then I set her on that course. I shared my fabrication with her, about Ashley and you."

"I know. I think she very much enjoyed telling me your view of our marriage." He scrunched up his face and cursed silently to himself. "That and building on her game plan by lamenting that Ashley *was no longer in the now*—that was to give me permission to be with her. Free me from guilt."

We sat there a while longer, saying nothing. One of the nurses came into the room, smiled at us benignly, gave a cursory once-over of Ashley, and left on silent feet. At that point we both rose and kissed Ashley's forehead in turn. We shook hands once more in the parking lot and said our good-byes.

In the Explorer, I checked my phone; I had a message from Detective Morgan. He wanted to meet. My stomach rolled. What could he want? I returned his call, and we agreed to meet at the coffee shop across from the police station. He was waiting, sipping a cup of coffee and nibbling on a scone. I declined getting a cup, even his treat.

"Rough night," he said. I nodded. "Noticed your SUV when you drove up. Someone gave you crunch job on the rear end." I nodded again. "Her?" I nodded once more. "Not very talkative today."

"You said you had something to discuss," I replied.

"I do. Sure you don't want a cup or some of this scone I shouldn't be eating?"

"I'm good."

"Okay, here's the recap. They pulled the car up this morning. Sheriff's office impounded it at Red's Towing lot until the insurance people have looked it over. I chatted up the deputy that was out there last night. We have no jurisdiction. It's a county matter. I just said I was curious—how they were going to write it up and all."

"And?"

"Accident. Driver error. Like the one they had a month or so back, same location."

"Ralph Stokes," I said.

"Right."

"I knew him. One of our clients."

"Really. So two of your former clients have met their end out on the A-Rock Bends. Interesting."

"That it?"

"Yeah, you're in the clear. Lucky that farmer was there first and saw her go over. Otherwise, might have been enough suspicion to wonder about you and Mrs. Winters. Take for instance the parks and rec guy who saw two cars out at Latham Woods Park last night just as he was closing the gates: a big BMW and an SUV he had to escort out. Came forward when he heard about the crash. And then there was a hell of a mess out at the business park. Someone drove a vehicle through the bay door of Kramer Insulation. Scattered pink fiberglass all over the place. Left some paint scrapings, too."

"She rammed me. You saw it, the damage."

"I did. All comes together. The bitch ruined your lives, and now she's paid for it. Fair trade."

"I guess."

"And you didn't lay a hand on her. Just prodded. Looks like she ran from her own destiny and paid the price. What's next for you, going back to Portland?"

"Probably."

"I think it would be a good idea, you know. Sold your house yet?"

"No."

"Tough market."

I shoved my chair back and stood up. "I'd better be going. Thanks for everything." I held out my hand; he rose and took it. "Keep up your golf game."

He laughed, and that was it.

Epilogue

And so it ended, almost. That next Saturday morning, Gloria Denham called, and it wasn't about the patio table. She'd sold the house. The day before, while I'd been out tying down loose ends, she'd shown the place to the new general manager of Verdant Equipment Company. When she started listing the things that would need to be done for the sale to move forward, I told her to do whatever it took and left it in her hands. I did a jig in the kitchen, saluted the once-ruined kitchen door, and began ticking off the next steps in my so-called life.

In the days that followed, I signed paperwork on the house so the sale could move forward, traded in the damaged Explorer at Buddy Truscott Ford, and got a good year-end deal on an Eddie Bauer model. Truscott had been a client.

The funeral for Sylvia Winters was held a week after she died. By that time the news media had splashed the story of her tragic demise across the front pages in bold type, and it was broadcast as the lead story for several days. Of course there were questions of what might happen to Winters Fine Foods with her death. I hadn't known that she and Reggie had children; we never talked about them anyway. There were two of them, a daughter and a son, he being the oldest. Neither had chosen to take part in the food business and lived elsewhere. They returned home to manage what turned out to be a huge memorial service held at the namesake Winters Performing Arts Center. I did not attend. I learned that the son was urged to take over the company and did so, moving his family from Seattle and giving up a successful law practice in the wake of his mother's death. I read that the daughter returned to San Francisco; I assumed happily so.

Terra and I talked often. For me it was a necessity—hearing her voice and wanting to be with her was a reason to waken each day. I gradually gave her the entire story of the previous six months, including the perverse actions of Sylvia and her violent death. She took it all in, absorbing the eeriness and asserting disbelief. That opened the door for us to share more of the unvarnished details of our past lives, and in the process we began building on the implied trust and authenticity of our natures. Neither of us had been with someone who had shown us steadfastness over time; thus we both assumed that what we had experienced before was inescapable. In our conversations, the ones that peeled back our life histories, we would often pause and whisper: *Isn't this something?*

I drove into Portland on September 30, a Thursday, and showed up unannounced at Floyd's place. He and Noah welcomed me back by staging another one of our back-lot barbecues; that meant steaks from Safeway's distressed sale meat case, PBR beer, baked spuds, no greens, and Noah's Torpedo cigars. It had been in the mid-eighties that day, but by the time we cut into our red meat it was dusk, and the temp had dropped into the sixties.

They let me eat and chat about the drive over and my new SUV, but as soon as we each lit a cigar, the inquisition was on. I gave them the whole megillah. They listened as if I'd been on death row, threw in *I'll be damned several times*, and sat quiet in the darkness when I stopped. I dropped the stub of my spent cigar into the sand bucket Floyd had insisted on if we smoked, told them they were swell, just not swell enough, and left for Thelma's Coffee House.

Being a Thursday, I knew she would be on the late shift—and there she was. Damn, she was something to see. I stood back out of the light just to watch her do nothing special, except when she did it, whatever it was, it was a treat to my eyes. It was maybe ten minutes or so before she caught sight of me grinning like a goof. She stopped like she'd been unplugged and looked right past the young woman trying to order something; finally the customer turned to see where Terra was focused. After a moment, she put two and two together and moved over to the other barista behind the counter seemingly unmoved by our eye-to-eye celebration.

She said something to her coworker, who nodded, and slipped out from behind the counter, marched over to me, and tugged on my arm until I followed her outside. Once free of the cacophony of the hissing espresso machine, she grabbed me in a big hug; I reciprocated most willingly. Then we laughed and hugged again. The sensation of holding her face in the palms of my hands was beyond my past experience. Her eyes softened, and when I kissed her she was there, truly there.

I waited around until she and her colleague closed up and walked her home in the cool but enveloping evening air. Mrs. Shanahan, her landlady, was an early-to-bed person, so our entry went unnoticed. Her room looked lived in: bed unmade, clothes hanging over a chair, remnants of a meal—I loved it. Even more, she didn't make any excuses because she wanted me as much as I wanted her. Amazing. We embraced again, holding each other and grinning smiles that couldn't be tamed. With no need for invitations, we slowly disrobed. Again I thrilled seeing her strong, lithe body, touching her and knowing that she enjoyed touching me. Even her barista dry hands were sensual. She laughed when together we pulled back the covers of her rumpled bedclothes to provide access to the tousled sheets and scattered pillows. Neither of us were concerned with décor.

It was…well, if we go back, you will understand when I tell you that it was astonishing, that night with Terra. While I had been with Ashley in that way, I had never felt any joy from her mere desire to procreate. Unkind if you will, surely so, but damn it all—it was so breathtaking to be one with a person who truly wanted me. Sadly, Ashley, no matter what she felt for me, was never able to express it. That meant we all ended up never sharing our true selves with one another: not she, not me, not her father, and of course we also handicapped our offspring.

Perhaps the unsettling aftermath of our lives allowed Terra and me an exemption. We were not absolved of our scar tissue or our flaws; we just accepted them, understood them, and found ourselves together among the ruins.

I settled in, worked at the thrift shop, spent more and more time with Terra, wherein we discussed our future, whatever it might be. We had no clue. We didn't care for the moment. I knew I wasn't going to be on Floyd's staff for much longer, but nothing beyond that was becoming clear. Noah Blue made a trip back to Chicago to see his kids but was back sooner than expected. The sale of my house in Latham went through; nice to get that off of my ledger. And so it went, day to day. Nothing jumped up and grabbed me until the day Terra told me the couple that owned Thelma's wanted to sell. They were older; due to the wife's declining health, they intended move to California to be close to kids and grandkids.

So yeah, we kicked it around and decided two things: first, we were going to spend the rest of our time with each other, and second, why not make coffee together. We made an offer, which was accepted. After the sale was complete, the couple packed up and moved to Sacramento in less than sixty days. And there we were. Thank god Terra knew the coffee business.

On that next New Year's Day, my brother called to tell me that Dad had passed away on New Year's Eve, quietly and with no pain. We had one of those somber, tearful conversations siblings share when they lose a parent. Floyd went with me when I drove to Baker City for the funeral. We stood solemnly with the family at a graveside service; the farming community had turned out in numbers equal to turnout for a local square dance. We returned to St. Johns immediately after we had faced dozens of ranchers, shaken their calloused hands, and shared sympathetic smiles with their wives. To our family, I'm sure Floyd and I exemplified the odd couple, but nothing was said of our relationship.

Ten days later, I received a call from Isaac Tucker. Ashley had succumbed on January 10, ironically on what would have been our twenty-fourth anniversary. I returned to Latham to tend to the last affairs of her life and to take part in a quiet memorial service. My children both came to honor their mother. We hugged and cried, I suppose as much for our struggles to remain connected as for her death, which we'd all known would happen. There was a sense of calm among us now that she was no longer living in a suspended state and was hopefully at peace. I chose to not tell my kids what was going on in my life; once the harsh freshness of losing their mother had passed, I would do that. Isaac and I actually hugged that day and agreed to stay in touch. Even C. T. Morgan slipped into a back pew for Ashley's service and came up afterward to say hello and share another handshake. Another moment of closure for the tragic event, as he put it.

When I returned to Portland and our enterprise, Terra and I decided that we should move in together. We had no doubts about who we were and no concerns about showing how much we cared for each other. On the day Terra and I had settled into an apartment of our own, Floyd and Noah gave us a little party and I said goodbye to the cacophony of Floyd's snoring.

On the last day of March, just over a year from the attack, Terra and I completed our first two months as entrepreneurs. I'd returned from a run to Safeway for more half-and-half and found her in an intense conversation with a man about her age: long hair, nose ring, Grateful Dead tee shirt, and an indecipherable tattoo on his right arm. I put the two half-gallons of cream in the fridge and walked over to them.

As I came up, Terra turned and tossed me a curious smile. I must have looked confused because she looked at the fellow then back at me and said, "This is Chip. My ex-husband."

"Is that right? This is who you've spoken about?" The scar was at once more distinct.

"Uh-huh." She gave me one of those *don't do anything stupid looks*. "He's just passing through on his way to Seattle." She saved the day with that line.

"Is that right?"

This Chip sort of squinted at me. "Yeah. And who are you?"

"I am Ned Pine."

———

Acknowledgements

I am indebted to Bob and Sonja Alamia, former owners of "What A Deal" Thrift Store in the St. Johns neighborhood of Portland, Oregon, for serving as my tutors on the art of selling things still of some use. They befriended me and welcomed me every time I once again entered their store with more questions.

Many thanks to Dr. Jeremy Ciporen, neurosurgeon affiliated with Oregon Health Sciences University. Dr. Ciporen's tutorial on head injury, brain trauma, coma, and related matters, provided me with the framework I needed to take on traumatic head injury as an integral part of this novel. Any technical missteps are my own.

Denny Hassler of The Man's Shop in St. Johns for his many insights into the soul of the neighborhood; and to the rich character of St. Johns and the people there who allow all to enter with no credentials required. I wandered the streets, entered coffee shops, barbershops, retail stores, and of course visited the marvelous St. Johns Bridge and Cathedral Park beneath its span. I always felt at home.

I Am Ned Pine would never have come to life were it not for the incredible skills of my editor Karen Brattain and the artistry of Dennis Stovall for designing a physical presence Ned can be proud of. Both Karen and Dennis have given hope that something worthy resides within.

Much appreciation to photographer Marshall Snyder for his wonderful photo of the St. Johns Bridge, which adorns the cover of this book.

And to my wife, Betsy, for her endurance and loving encouragement as my first reader.

—George Byron Wright

George Byron Wright is the author of six previous novels: *Baker City 1948, Tillamook 1952, Roseburg 1959, Driving to Vernonia, Newport Blues: A Salesman's Lament,* and *In the Wake of Our Misdeed.* He lives with his wife Betsy in Portland, Oregon.